For J. R. R. Tolkien, who wrote,
"It's a dangerous business, going
out your front door."

And for Peter Jackson, who said,
"The most honest form of filmmaking
is to make a film for yourself."

And for my brothers, Evan and Conor,
who say, "Keep writing, Stinker Face."

PRAISE FOR *BREAKING SKY*

"An action-packed thrill ride that smashes through all kinds of barriers at a Mach Five pace."

—Carrie Jones, *New York Times* bestselling author of the Need series

"A nonstop thrill ride...will keep you reading at the speed of sound. *Breaking Sky* is one of the most exciting reads of the year."

—Thomas E. Sniegoski, *New York Times* bestselling author of the Fallen series

"Had me in its grip from takeoff to landing. Chase is a kick-butt female and the swoon-worthy flyboys kept me up way past my bedtime."

—Joy N. Hensley, author of *Rites of Passage*

★ "Replete with fighter-pilot jargon, plausible science-fiction elements, and nerd-friendly literary allusions, this taut, well-crafted novel should have broad appeal, for fans of everything from Roth's *Divergent* to Wein's *Code Name Verity*."

—*The Bulletin for the Center of Children's Books*, Starred Review

★ "Strong characterizations, action, adventure, and emotion combine to produce a sci-fi novel that is more than just the sum of its parts."

—*School Library Journal*, Starred Review

"Smart, exciting, confident—and quite possibly the next Big Thing."

—*Kirkus Reviews*

PRAISE FOR *YOU WERE HERE*

"Wrenchingly beautiful in its honest and achingly accurate portrayal of grief and how it breaks us—and the way unconditional friendship puts us back together."

—Jo Knowles, award-winning author of
See You at Harry's and *Read Between the Lines*

"Through razor-sharp wit, no-holds-barred momentum, and heart-wrenching twists, Cori McCarthy dares you to climb through the broken, abandoned wreckage of the past, stand on the edge of the world, and face something even scarier: the truth."

—K. A. Barson, author of *45 Pounds (More or Less)* and *Charlotte Cuts It Out*

"McCarthy deftly intertwines the character's stories, filling them with authentic pain and heartache as well as soaring moments of grace and humor."

—Maggie Lehrman, author of
The Cost of All Things

"A skillful blend of storytelling, emotion, and adrenaline-fueled daring."

—*Publishers Weekly*

"Readers who appreciate stories of searching for personal truths will be happy to join this meaningful quest for identity and independence."

—*Booklist*

NOW A MAJOR
MOTION PICTURE

ALSO BY CORI McCARTHY

Breaking Sky

You Were Here

Now a MAJOR MOTION PICTURE

CORI McCARTHY

sourcebooks
fire

Published by Sourcebooks Fire, an imprint of Sourcebooks, Inc.
P.O. Box 4410, Naperville, Illinois 60567-4410
(630) 961-3900
Fax: (630) 961-2168
sourcebooks.com

Library of Congress Cataloging-in-Publication Data
Names: McCarthy, Cori, author.
Title: Now a major motion picture / Cori McCarthy.
Description: Naperville, Illinois : Sourcebooks Fire, [2018] | Summary: In Ireland with her brother during the filming of a movie based on her grandmother's wildly popular Elementia trilogy, Iris, seventeen, decides to shut down production and end the annoying craze.
Identifiers: LCCN 2017030612 | (pbk. : alk. paper)
Subjects: | CYAC: Motion pictures--Production and direction--Fiction. | Actors and actresses--Fiction. | Dating (Social customs)--Fiction. | Fans (Persons)--Fiction. | Brothers and sisters--Fiction. | Ireland--Fiction.
Classification: LCC PZ7.M47841233 Now 2018 | DDC [Fic]--dc23 LC record available at https://lccn.loc.gov/2017030612

Source of Production: Marquis Book Printing, Montreal, Quebec, Canada
Date of Production: February 2018
Run Number: 5011138

Printed and bound in Canada.
MBP 10 9 8 7 6 5 4 3 2 1

Film: Elementia

Director: Cate Collins

On Location: Day 1

Aran Islands, Ireland

Filming Notes:

CLIFF'S EDGE scene. SEVYN'S STUNT DOUBLE and MAEDINA on deck.

No dialogue will be recorded. Aerial photography and a sea-level crew component. Safety first, people!

Etc. Notes:

M. E. Thorne's grandchildren arrive at Shannon Airport via Aer Lingus Flight 280 at noon. Volunteer to pick them up?

Dinner at Tí Joe Watty's following the day's wrap.

I DON'T WANT TO ALARM ANYONE, BUT THERE'S AN ELF AT BAGGAGE CLAIM

THE GUY WAS probably a painter. Possibly a drummer.

College age and wearing all black, he'd been the unique focus of my thousand-hour red-eye. My inflight boyfriend. It was a torrid, imaginary romance. We'd gone on at least a dozen dates and told adorable anecdotes to our future children about how their parents met a few miles in the air.

Now we were no longer separated by two Aer Lingus seats. We were shoulder to shoulder, dazedly watching the baggage belt spin. *Just say hi. Ask him something.*

I hugged the neck of my guitar case. "Do you know the time?"

He checked a large, silver watch. "Half twelve."

"What?" I blurted. The bags began to emerge, and I was suddenly under new pressure to break the ice before we parted ways. After all, an entire transatlantic daydream depended on it. "Is that six? Eleven thirty? I'm so jet-lagged it could be either."

"Twelve thirty." His Irish accent made his words feel like lyrics to a decent song.

"Yeah, that doesn't make sense. Half of twelve is six." I smiled.

"Americans," he muttered with a snicker.

And he continued snickering as he reached for a suitcase, leaving me with the unparalleled awkwardness of being embarrassed by and disappointed in a complete stranger. I'd mentally dumped him four exotic ways—my favorite involving a baseball stadium video screen—by the time my little brother came running back from the bathroom.

"Iris!" Ryder yelled. "I peed for like two whole minutes. I should've timed it!"

The baggage claim crowd parted for him—people tend to do that when someone's yelling about their urine. Now I really felt like a gross American. *Thanks, Ireland. We're off to a great start.*

"Eleven days," I murmured. "Only eleven days."

Ryder showed no sign of jet lag. He wrestled a foam fantasy axe out of his backpack, spilling weapons everywhere. He then engaged imaginary opponents in fierce battle while the people from our flight continued to back away. My ex-in-flight boyfriend even gave him a dirty look—before giving me a dirtier look.

"I'm not his mom, you know," I said as I collected Ryder's weapons off the floor.

A well-meaning Irish granny stepped up. "Is this your first time in Ireland?" she asked Ryder, placing a steadying hand on his shoulder. My brother nodded and squirmed. I checked my desire to tell her that, in America, we don't touch kids we don't know, but I didn't want to call more attention to our swiftly amassing cultural differences. "Are you going to see the Giant's Causeway? Or the Cliffs of Moher?"

"No," Ryder said, breaking free from her hold. "We get to meet famous people and help out on set and probably even get bit roles."

"No bit roles, Ry. You know that," I said.

McGranny looked to me for an explanation. I zipped up Ryder's backpack and said it fast. "He means the adaptation for *Elementia*. They're filming here for the next two weeks. We've been invited to..." What were we supposed to do? "Watch, I guess."

"Our grandma wrote that book!" Ryder said so loud we now had an even larger audience. Everyone who'd been groggily waiting to claim their luggage had tuned in.

"Excuse me?" My ex-love was back in the picture, not snickering this time. "Did you say your grandmother was the author M. E. Thorne?" The spark in his eyes seemed desperate to rekindle our imaginary flame.

Get out of your own head, Iris.

"Yeah," I managed.

"Have I got something to show you." He started to take off his shirt.

"Oh, for the love of…" I whispered, staring down at my red Chucks.

"Look!" Ryder proclaimed. "Iris, look! He's got the map of Elementia on his ribs!"

I had to peek. It was an awfully big map. Alas, my curiosity was rewarded by a rich paleness smattered in black chest hair.

He put his shirt back down and smiled, but I kept hearing the way he'd grumbled *Americans*. "So are you excited about the film adaptation?" he asked. "Are you having a hand in its development? How do you feel about them changing the ages of the characters?"

I braided my hair back and said nothing, reminded once again of my life's golden rule. People usually treated me one of two ways. One: like I was M. E. Thorne's granddaughter, gifted with an otherworldly glow. Two: no one. I'd give anything for a third option.

"This is all you talk about, isn't it?" he continued. "You've probably been reading your grandma's books since you were a kid. I discovered them a few years back. Then again, I bet you can't say anything because of the movies. Top-secret insider information, right?"

I chewed on my response. The gristle of this fantasy talk would not go down. Everyone assumed I'd be over the moon about the adaptation, but it meant the story's fandom would triple. Quadruple. Soon everyone would revise their interest in me, just like this guy.

"Ryder, see if that's our bag," I said, moving us to the other side of the carousel. When I had my back to everyone from our flight, I squeezed my eyes, a little scream coming up from deep inside.

"You okay, Iris?" Ryder put a hand on my shoulder. I opened my eyes. Not his hand—it was his foam dwarf axe. At least his little-kid expression was earnest.

"I'm fine." I rested my forehead on the top of my guitar case. I knew better than to check out when I was on Ryder duty, but I couldn't help it. One moment later, my brother was lunging for his luggage, and the next, he was on the carousel, disappearing through the plastic hanging strips and into the bowels of Shannon Airport. "Hey!" I yelled. "Ryder!" Fear slapped me awake, and I almost crawled through the plastic strips after him. "Hey!"

"Need some help, then?"

I turned toward a new Irish voice and almost fell over. "Oh no."

The boy had elf ears. Honest to God, pointy and flexed into his hairline elf ears.

"Oh no?" he returned, his eyebrows sky-high.

"What're you… What *are* you?"

"I'm an elf," he said as casually as if he were telling me he was an art major. "I'm here to give you a lift." He held up a printed sign that read THORNE.

"Put that down. These people are already too curious." I grabbed the paper and balled it. "And if you're here to help, solve that equation." I pointed to the baggage exit. "One brother went in. No brothers are coming back out. He's probably on the runway by now."

"Ye of little faith," Elf Ears said, crossing his arms. "He'll pop back through in a moment." He leaned over conspiratorially. "It's a circle, you know."

I couldn't believe that a stranger with artificial ears was "ye of little faith"-ing me. "What if security catches him? In the United States, the TSA confiscates firstborns for this kind of thing."

On cue, Ryder came back through the plastic strips, sitting on my duffel and wearing my sunglasses he'd pillaged from the outer pocket. He knew he was in trouble, and yet he grinned. Then he saw the guy beside me, and his mouth dropped open. Ryder jumped down and ran over, leaving me to fetch both of our bags from the carousel.

By the time I'd returned, Ryder's face was a full moon of excitement. "Iris. This is Nolan. *Nolan*."

Nolan held out his hand as though we hadn't previously met, i.e., argued. "It's Eamon. Eamon O'Brien."

I dropped Ryder's bag to shake Eamon's hand. "What a name. Did you spring from the roots of Ireland itself?"

I had to hand it to him—he didn't flinch.

"And you're Iris Thorne. Nothing to slag there, right?"

Ryder pulled on my shirt, revealing way too much of my bra, while hissing, "It's Nolan."

I grabbed his hand and yanked up my neckline. "Stop it or I'll snap your dwarf axe over my knee." I plucked my sunglasses off Ryder's face and put them on in time to catch quite possibly the dirtiest look an elf has ever given a human. "Oh, come on. I don't really break his toys. And how come there are three of us, but I'm carrying all the bags?"

"It's not a toy," Ryder snipped. "It's a costume replica."

Eamon continued to glare, proving his eyes weren't blue but a crystal color that felt digitally enhanced. No wonder he'd been cast as the famous elf in Grandma Mae's books. Nolan—Eamon—whatever his name was threw the strap of my huge duffel over his shoulder and tried to take my guitar.

"Don't even think about it," Ryder said for me. "She's married to that thing."

"Is that legal in America these days? Do you share health care?"

I stuck out my tongue, and Eamon grinned wildly, which encouraged me to put my tongue away and wonder how he'd reduced me to Ryder's maturity level in a matter of minutes.

We passed under the green banner of NOTHING TO DECLARE, and I tried some light conversation. "So, if you're one of the actors, why are you doing airport pickups?"

"I volunteered. I'm a huge fan."

Good Lord.

"Hey, I read about you," Ryder said. "This is your very first movie!"

I couldn't help myself. "Then how'd you get the role?"

"That's a fine story. I love *Elementia*. It's in my blood. I first read it with my mam when I was, oh, about this high." He held his hand to Ryder's head, making my brother beam. "When they announced the movie and open casting, Mam and I decided to dream big. We made an audition video in a wooded bit on Saint Stephen's Green."

"Elijah Wood did that to become Frodo," Ryder said.

"Right, right." He knocked Ryder's shoulder, best friends already. "I thought, if it worked for Elijah, why can't it work with me?"

"Because Elijah Wood had an established film career before he did that," I muttered.

"What was that?" Eamon asked.

"Nothing." I knew where this story was going. Without a doubt, it would conclude with "then I met the grandchildren of M. E. Thorne and it was the most magical thing to ever happen to me."

Eamon continued. "Lo and behold, I'm cast as Nolan. And today I'm getting fit for my ears when Cate Collins, wonder director, needs someone to pick up M. E. Thorne's grandchildren. I volunteered, quick as light." Eamon shifted the bag on his shoulder and glanced at me. "This is when I meet a tiny, axe-wielding hero and his mountain troll of a guardian."

My guitar case slipped out of my hand, banging hollowly on the ground. "What the..."

Ryder's smile was wider than both of the hands he used to cover it.

"Pardon that." Eamon winked at me—the sassiest thing I'd ever seen a guy manage. "I'm prone to descriptive exaggeration, me springing outta the roots of Ireland and all."

I blushed, an odd mixture of offended and ashamed.

"Iris Thorne!" an unfamiliar voice yelled from behind.

I turned, my pulse turning into a drum. Just like there were two ways people treated me, there were two kinds of Elementia fans: the ones who loved the trilogy—and the ones who'd reconstructed their lives for it. The latter group called themselves *Thornians*. They wrote letters to my family. They knew my birthday.

And one of them tried to abduct Ryder when he was six.

I was sort of relieved to see it was my ex-in-flight boyfriend, the newly redubbed Mr. Nerdy Torso Tattoo, jogging over. "How do you know my name?" I asked, my voice breaking a little as I put out an arm to keep him from getting too close to Ryder.

"Your brother was yelling it. I didn't even know M. E. Thorne had young grandkids."

I relaxed slightly. "I'm not that young."

"I'm crossing my fingers you're eighteen." The guy leaned close with flirtatious wickedness, reminding me of what had drawn my attention to him during the flight. Lanky gorgeousness. The glasses. Blue eyes. Dark, tight swirls of hair. He rested a long-fingered hand on the top of my guitar case. Definitely musician's fingers. Also, it was suddenly quite obvious that I'd been wrong; he was *well* beyond college age.

Earth to Iris. Walk away, Iris.

"I'm…seventeen." I stepped back, oddly relieved to bump into Eamon. "Have to go."

The guy pulled out his wallet and handed me a business card. "Shoot me a message around your birthday. I'll take you out, and we can talk about the movie, or the books, if you prefer."

Neither, thank you. "I live in LA."

"I'll make the trip." He smiled at the person he thought was me. He walked away. And I hated M. E. Thorne more than usual, which, to be honest, was already a lot.

We walked toward the parking lot, and I kept my head down.

"You work fast, Lady Iris," Eamon said, low enough that Ryder couldn't hear.

"No way," I muttered back. "That guy has the hots for my dead grandma." He glanced at me, concerned. "I'm fine," I added, hoping I looked annoyed—bold and unflappable— but from the way his expression fell, I think maybe my sad was showing.

WHAT DO YOU MEAN "WE'RE GETTING ON A BOAT?"

EAMON STUFFED MY duffel into the hatchback trunk of the smallest vehicle I've ever seen. Its color was rust red, by which I mean that the rust was eating all the red. It also only had two doors.

"We're not going to fit in there." I glanced around the parking lot filled with cars exactly like the one before me. The big, shiny SUVs I was used to were nowhere to be seen.

"Sure you are." Eamon propped the front seat forward so Ryder could scurry into the back. He shoved Ryder's bag in too, smooshing my brother against the far side.

Ryder's delight was palpable. "Hey! These seats are buckets!"

"Did my dad tell you to pick me up in this?" I asked.

Eamon stopped shoving to peer at me. "What would I have to do with your da?"

Good question. I glanced at my watch, exhaustedly disori-
ented. It was 4:46 a.m. back in LA. In a few hours, the sun
would wake up, brilliant and hot. In Ireland, the clouds were
cement. Thick and gray. Or grey. Whichever of those words
means the color plus the emotion. And it was chilly. Which
meant I'd completely bungled my packing. "I... My dad likes
to mess with me."

Ryder craned his head out the passenger window. "Dad
made us fly coach. He said it was good for us. He calls Iris
'Jaded Iris' because she acts so old."

"That's not very kind," Eamon said.

"Says the guy who called me a mountain troll," I snapped.
"And what do you plan on doing with Annie?"

"Say, who?"

"Her guitar!" Ryder yelled.

"Your guitar is called Annie? That's fairly cute." He smiled,
and part of me was tempted to smile back. I told that part to sit
down and don't even think about it. Instead, I focused on his
scrappy hair—I mean, really, it was the scrappiest dirty-blond
argument of a hairstyle I'd ever seen. At least it flopped over
his elf ears in a way that slightly camouflaged their weirdness.

Eamon held up some rope. "Let's tie Annie to the roof."

"Are you insane?" I cried out.

He laughed, slammed the trunk, and held open the driver's
side door, which was actually the passenger door, because the
car was inverted. "Annie'll have to ride on your lap."

I folded myself in and pulled my guitar after me. "Eleven days," I murmured, Annie pressed between my knees, my chin propped on the top of her case. "Ten after today."

Eamon's driving was all jerky gear adjustments on the serpentine, narrow roads, a problem exacerbated by Ryder's endless questions. Within minutes, I'd found out Eamon was eighteen, grew up in Dublin, and wasn't planning on going to college in the fall. Huh.

"So what are you going to do? For money and stuff?" I asked.

"Dunno," he said. "I'll figure it out when I get there."

Double huh. "Are teenagers allowed to do that here? In America, it's like, 'You're going straight to college, young lady, or you'll fail out of life.'"

Eamon laughed. "That's massive stupid. How're you supposed to know what you want to do as fast as that?"

I bristled at his use of "massive stupid," even if he seemed to be using both words differently—and even if he was right.

After singing the praises of every cow, sheep, and half-crumbled stone tower, Ryder started snoring. I craned my neck to look back at him. He was sweet and fragile when he was asleep, but even then, I could hear him chirping *Jaded Iris*. To be honest, I was feeling bad about being a giant grump. That's the thing about negativity—it gives you control and makes you ugly in one fell swoop. By that logic, my father was the ugliest, most powerful man in California.

And also the real reason I was crammed into this clown car.

"I want you to take Ryder on that Hollywood excursion to Ireland," my dad had said only a week ago, as if he were asking me to make dinner instead of cross the Atlantic. He didn't even bother to look up from his laptop. "I'll make it up to you."

"But you told Cate Collins we wouldn't be part of her movie," I said, stunned. "You swore at her."

"Yes, well, she won't stop calling, and your brother won't stop asking. Today I received a written notice that he'd like to trade"—my dad grabbed a piece of paper and read—"'five birthdays and Christmases for the trip to see the *Elementia* filming.'" He dropped the paper. "Also his therapist thinks it's a great idea. I'm overruled."

I was speechless. Particularly because my dad had spent the last seventeen years listing reasons why I should hate the nerd fantasy written by his mother and the last year monologueing about how much he loathed the film adaptation that was in development.

"I'm serious, Iris," he said through my shocked silence. "My book is overdue to my editor, your mom is deep in her writing, and I can't deal right now."

"Ah, the truth comes out," I muttered.

"Take him. Have one of those once-in-a-lifetime experiences. But no alcohol or flirting. Your job is to watch your brother."

"Watch Ryder? What'll that be like?" I snipped sarcastically. "However will I manage?"

"Don't give me that crap. Make the arrangements."

I took a deep breath. He was asking me to do something huge; I was going to ask for something huge in return. And I was ready. "I want to access my trust fund when I'm eighteen instead of twenty-five. I know you can change that."

My father finally looked up from his screen. "That money is purpose money. Tell me, Jaded Iris, do you have a purpose?"

"Yes." I did my best to sound as certain as he did. "I want to buy recording software and equipment. For my songs."

"Are you going to play for me?"

I paused. "No."

"Well then, I can't help you. If you're not ready to let me hear you play, you're not ready to record. I'm not letting you turn into one of those entitled, skip-the-hard-work-to-get-to-the-top, 'oh look at me, I'm a YouTube sensation' teenagers."

"Then I'm not taking him." I'd backed up, nearly out of his office before he replied.

"Speaking of your trust fund, Iris, you should thank Cate Collins. *In person.* Grandma Mae's book sales, a.k.a. the funds in your trust, are growing exponentially because of those films. Once you're done with college and find a real purpose, you can live however you want. Your kids can live however they want. Your grandkids can live however they want." He said that like it was a bad thing. Like it'd been a terrible idea for him to live however he wanted: writing ill-received detective novels all day and night in the darkest room in the house.

"Maybe I need money to help me find my purpose," I'd argued.

"I'll think about it," he said, "if you bring Ryder there and back again. *Safely*." He'd waved me away, leaving me to wonder if this was a real deal we'd made.

Eamon's tiny car shuddered while climbing a hill. I managed to reach my backpack tucked at my feet and pulled out my journal. I scribbled a few lyrics before I realized that Eamon was trying to read them. "Hey, *Shannara Chronicles*! Watch the road!"

He jerked the car back to the left. "You're a writer?"

"No."

"I hear your dad's a writer. Never read his stuff though."

"That puts you in the category of most human beings," I said. He looked at me askance. "No one reads his books, but he keeps getting contracts because of his last name."

"Ah, the Thorne legacy."

I frowned. "Everyone compares his writing to my grandmother's, even though it's not the same genre. He tried to publish with a pseudonym, but that left him invisible."

Eamon tapped Annie's case. "Are you going to ride the Thorne name into being a rock star then? Sold out concerts and platinum records?"

This boy had a lot to learn.

"Mind, I don't blame you. Everyone wants to be Taylor Swift. *I* wouldn't mind being Taylor Swift." He started singing "Bad Blood" in an unfortunately decent voice.

"Stop."

He grinned, and I dared to trust him with the truth.

"I'm a songwriter." There was something tricky about that sentence. Like the person I was saying it to might disagree—and maybe they'd be right.

"Can I hear a song?"

"No!" I was starting to feel nauseous, and it wasn't the windy roads. "I write songs for other people to play and sing."

"That doesn't make sense."

"Says the guy who gets paid to read lines someone else wrote."

"Touché, love." He shrugged, crystal eyes on the road. I knew people said things like that here, but it didn't make it any less strange.

The horizon was a patchwork of greens sewed up with zigzagging stone walls. It was pretty but rural. "So where are we going? And when do we get to a hotel with beds and showers?"

"How many showers does one young Los Angelino like yourself need?" His comebacks had amazing speed, but I gave him a side-eye instead of a compliment. "My orders are to bring you to Doolin, and then onto the ferry to Inishmore, where they're filming this week."

"Ferry?"

"It's grand. And wait till you see the set. It'll steal your breath."

"I like breathing."

Ryder's face popped up between the front seats, gleefully woken by the sounds of my horror, no doubt. "We're going on set? Today? In a boat?"

"Well, no," Eamon said, surprising me. "We're only going if your sister is up to it. After all, it's been a long night for both of you."

"Hotel," I said.

Ryder wriggled around the passenger seat, breathing in my ear. "Please, oh please, Iris? I will sit so still and not do a single thing I'm not supposed to."

I checked my brother's eyes for sincerity. He was eight now, and yet he still looked like the six-year-old who'd started screaming from the other side of the playground—a man's arm around his waist, dragging him toward a van. I'd never run so fast. I'd never been so scared.

I rubbed at the raised hair on my arms. Two years later, and I still got chills, which were always followed by my dad's voice in my head saying, *That's cliché description, Iris.*

Ryder's baby dragon breath was all over me—stale ketchup and bologna.

"You don't leave my side," I said. "Promise?" He nodded; I wasn't the only one who remembered every detail of what had happened that day.

Hours later, the frigid Atlantic sprayed my face every time the ferry crested a swell. Eamon and Ryder were overjoyed, skittering across the deck together, already brothers in mischief. At least the cement sky had cracked apart to reveal a striking blue.

"Cate reserved this vessel for the entire shoot. The captain said he'd take us 'round to see the filming," Eamon yelled over the engines. "Then we'll dock and meet up with the crew." I held the rail and tried not to breathe the dank mold smell of the ancient life preserver around my neck just as Ryder cried out, pointing at a great cliff wall topped by an ancient stone formation. "Dun Aengus," Eamon yelled. "It's a prehistoric fort dating back to the Iron Age."

But I wasn't looking at the ruin.

On top of the cliff, I squinted at a few dozen crew members, towers of equipment, a camera on a crane, and a woman wearing what can only be described as a Gandalf bathrobe. At the water level, a girl with massive hair gripped the sides of an old-world rowboat. It was tethered by bright-green ropes to a high-tech raft that ran its motor hard to keep the waves from pressing all of them into the rock wall. A helicopter buzzed overhead, and I whipped my head back to see a cameraman and his equipment leaning out of the open side door.

"That's so dangerous," I breathed.

"This will be the remains of Manifest," Eamon explained with a mischievous grin that actually made him look like an elf. "Imagine the CGI! There will be pieces of fallen towers and castles jutting up from the water like a watery graveyard of a city." Eamon pointed to the Gandalf woman atop the cliff. "And that's Maedina!"

"Who?" I yelled over the sound of the circling helicopter.

"What?" he yelled back.

"You're wasting your time, Nolan," Ryder said, most of his head swallowed by his life preserver. "Iris won't read the books. She doesn't know about any of it."

"No, serious?" he asked, crystal eyes wide and mouth gaping.

"Geez, I don't have cancer," I shouted. "I'm just not into fantasy."

"But your grandma—"

"Only met her once. She died when I was eight."

"But—" Eamon cut himself off this time, still peering at me like I'd told him I had two months to live. The ferry pulled away from the raucous shooting, and the thundering ferry engines no longer felt loud enough to fill the quiet.

I turned to the rail, gripping the bitingly cold metal and trying not to look back at the chaos of the filming, trying to stop the truth that now buzzed in my mind like that helicopter.

This wasn't going to be eleven days.

This movie was going to alter the rest of my life.

I now understood what had gotten my dad so fiery when we had first met with Cate Collins. Movies blew stories up. There would be posters, sequels, GIFs. Merchandise! Hot Topic would produce a trail mix of Thornian crap overnight. And that's if the movies were well received.

What if they were horrible?

I'd have a huge joke attached to my last name.

TROUBLES IN NERD PARADISE

WE DISEMBARKED FROM the ferry, my legs an odd combination of relieved and rubbery as we stepped onto the cement "quay," as Eamon called it. I would have said "dock" or "marina."

The quay ran quite a way out into the water, and we had a nice view of the small harbor village. The tight streets were crowded with brilliantly colored cottages huddled before the edge of a green and gray rise of stony land that spread out epically in all directions.

Moors, I thought moodily, caving to my Jane Eyre daydreams. Maybe I was about to become entangled in some brooding love affair. Or maybe I was here to suffer, to build my character before going back to LA, where my curse of a father waited to put me back in my place. Maybe I've always been a melodramatic soul…

"Did she get you?" Eamon eyed my no doubt enchanted expression. His hair was being manhandled by the wind, and at some point he'd slipped on a cable-knit, wool sweater, turning himself into a stock photo of an Irish boy—with fake elf ears.

"Get me?" I asked.

"Ireland. She looks like she got you."

"I don't know what you're talking about," I said fast, hiding a smile beneath the sudden bite of cold that came with twilight. "It's so quiet here."

"It's magic," Ryder added. "Can't you feel it?"

I smiled at Ryder. After all, this experience was his next five birthdays and Christmases.

At the end of the pier, Eamon loaded our luggage into a van parked on the street, groaning under the weight of my duffel. "There didn't even used to be cars on the Aran Islands. Not sure what we'd have done if we'd had to lug all the filming stuff by horse and cart. We'll walk from here. It's not much to the restaurant."

"Food," Ryder moaned. My stomach agreed; it'd been a long time since we'd eaten.

I wouldn't leave Annie behind to be stolen, so I hauled her past rows and rows of rentable bikes that weren't even locked up. *What a strange place.* Eamon and Ryder walked together in front of me, both of them overloaded with spritely enthusiasm. Ryder looked close to skipping. Eamon, well, I wasn't entirely sure about anything related to Eamon yet.

I lagged farther behind as Annie grew heavier.

Eamon stopped to stare back at me. "You want me to carry your girl there for a bit?"

"I got it." I switched my guitar to my other hand. "Why do you keep staring like that?"

"Anyone ever told you how much you resemble your grandmother?"

"Yes."

"It's that dark hair and the bright, almost otherworldly, dark eyes. You know, I think your eyes match your hair color. How often does that happen?"

I squinted my quite worldly eyes at him. He took the hint and turned around. I tied back my hair. Grandma Mae's author photos always showed her long hair down, so this was all I could do to set myself apart.

The sunset filled the sky with shadowy colors, and I finally felt more awake, most likely because it was now a valid time to be conscious back in LA. Still, I had to admit that Ireland had a strange charm. The night's glow had more greens and blues than the dry, red-orange sunsets I was used to, and the lack of people made the whole island feel like it was stuck in slow motion.

"How many people live here?" I called out.

"About a thousand, I'd say, but they have to contend with swarms of tourists." Eamon led us up the street to a restaurant that looked like an old, white barn surrounded by aged picnic tables. *Tí Joe Watty's* was scrawled on the outside above a violin.

"It's a fiddle," Eamon said like he was arguing with my thoughts. "Come on, then. Everyone is excited to see you."

Everyone?

He hauled open the outer door, and Ryder rushed for the inner one, and then we were staring at *everyone*. At least fifty cast and crew members, all holding up drinks. Petite Cate Collins stood on a chair at the center of the dim restaurant, raising a pint glass. "…not exactly a successful first day on location but—" Her words caught at the sight of us. "Witness our luck! M. E. Thorne's grandchildren have arrived to bless our production."

Oh, for crying out loud…

"Hey, guys!" Ryder yelled.

Everyone laughed, followed by a raucous call of "*Sláinte!*"

"It's Irish for cheers," Eamon said.

"I know," I muttered, although I didn't.

Cate rushed over. Her hair was tightly buzzed and beautifully gray. The laugh lines around her eyes were both sculpted and youthful. But all that aside, I bristled, recognizing the same intense excitement that had set off all my Thornian alarm bells back in LA months ago.

Dad, Ryder, and I had finally taken the bait and found our way to the Vantage Pictures lot and up to her office, where Cate had wept upon meeting us. "Elementia saved my life," she'd said while holding my hand like she wanted to steal it and keep it in an ornate box. She'd told us her vision for the adaptation that was days away from initial filming. Cate believed—fiercely—that the story should be celebrated as the feminist answer to Tolkien's male-dominated world, and that her home country of Ireland would benefit from the same tourist adoration that New Zealand had garnered in light of *The Lord of the Rings* films.

I glanced around the rustic interior of Tí Joe Watty's. Ireland might need to leave the nineteenth century if they wanted attention from the outside world, but then, the laughing, drinking production crew reminded me that a lot of people liked this sort of thing.

Cate was hugging Ryder too hard. I pried her off, trying to ignore the way Ryder hugged her tightly as well. "We're hungry," I said.

"Sure, sure!" She rushed us over to a table and soon meaty sandwiches and "chips" appeared.

"They're french fries," I said to myself, not exactly surprised, but tired.

"Oh, what a world that has different names for things," Eamon shot back, sitting too close. His crystal eyes threatened to do that snarky wink again, and I tried to scoot away without luck. Five of us were stuffed around a circular table meant for two. Besides Eamon, Ryder, and Cate, we were introduced to a thin man with a floppy hat, who was hunched over a notebook. "This is Henrik," Cate said. "He's the AD."

Henrik peered at me through darkly tinted glasses. "I'm here to make sure this movie makes sense to people who haven't memorized the books."

I liked him immediately. "Not a fantasy fan?"

"I have other allegiances." He pulled up his shirtsleeve, revealing J. R. R. Tolkien's stylized initials tattooed on the brown skin of his left forearm. *Good Lord, what is it with nerds and their tattoos?* "I'm a supporter of the original trilogy."

"Oh please, Henrik. M. E. Thorne was not a copycat." Cate seemed to fall headlong into an ongoing argument. "Thorne's story is about women saving the world. Tolkien went to the George Lucas school of 'one woman per universe.'"

"Galadriel, Arwen, Éowyn," Henrik listed.

"Oh? Three is it? Oh, that's much better. Three women per universe should do the job."

"Lúthien!" he snapped. "Or how about Haleth the Hunter? She killed thousands of orcs."

"*The Silmarillion* characters don't count," Cate said. "That's an entirely different book."

Ryder was smiling hugely at their debate, and I couldn't help weighing in too.

"I see Henrik's point," I said, enjoying Cate's growl. "Elves. Magic trees. A world in peril. That all sounds Middle Earth to me."

Henrik's satisfied grin was a bit trollish.

"This is anarchy," Cate said. "First, these fantasies, all of them, draw from *The Canterbury Tales*. Chaucer is the one who deserves the rights check from Tolkien, Lewis, Thorne, Rowling, et cetera. Secondly"—she turned at me—"how could you not see the genius of your grandmother's legacy?"

"I haven't read the books," I admitted proudly. "I'm—"

"She might be putting on a fair show, Cate," Eamon butted in, crossing his arms as he turned at me. "Ryder says your da read it to him when he was six. And you're saying that your da didn't read it to you as well? I don't believe it."

If I thought my face was red when we'd walked in, it was lava now. No, my dad had never read the books to me, and he'd only read them to my brother as part of Ryder's post-attempted-abduction therapy. My dad's voice filled my head, louder than usual: *Don't say a word, Iris. These people cannot be reasoned with.*

Cate and Eamon left me alone, discussing his elf ears before hauling over a girl who didn't seem much older than me. Her hair was shaved on one side and twisted into blond-and-pink spirals on the other. She wore fingerless gloves and laughed easily with her director boss. What I wouldn't give to be more like her. Artsy. Bold. Confident. People didn't mess with girls who looked like that. They messed with girls who looked like me—long hair without a committed style, enough makeup to seem like no makeup, decent clothes that didn't flare into any particular style. In short, girls who were a dead ringer for their dead grandmother.

"And this is Iris," Eamon said. "M. E. Thorne's grand-daughter. She's delighted to be here." In my defense, I was scowling long before that introduction.

The girl stuck out her hand. "Roxanne. Makeup artist." Great. She even had a cool name.

I managed a stiff smile and shook her hand across the tiny table.

"Roxy did my ears," Eamon said. "And she worked on that Shannara program you were talking about enjoying earlier." Roxanne beamed; apparently this was not a joke. Eamon's grin teased. "Lots of elves on that program, Iris?"

"We call them *TV shows*," I said. Oh my God, I was going to have to murder Eamon O'Brien, and I'd only just met him. Cate appraised me with a disappointed look, and I didn't like that either. "Yeah, I guess I only saw the commercials. Looked cool. I'll have to put it on my watch list," I added to Roxanne so that I didn't seem like a complete jerk.

Roxy gave me a half-smile. She knew I wasn't trying to insult her. She knew Eamon was messing with me. She knew that I had zero interest in being here. And she knew all that because girls don't get as cool as her without being perceptive about everything.

I made a study of my french fries...chips...whatever...

until everyone left me alone. The truth that had taken over my thoughts on the ferry—that this whole production was a lot bigger than I knew—made me scoot my chair closer to Henrik. He hooked an eyebrow at me. "Why was it a bad first day?" I asked. "What went wrong?" *Smooth, Iris.*

Henrik glared at his notebook and muttered, "Cate films in sequence. She believes it encourages the actors to feel the story, but it causes time constraints. And we only have two weeks to film a month's worth. We spent all day waiting for the clouds to lift for one shot when we could have set up another day and had it in an hour."

"We got the shot. Didn't we, Henrik?" So Cate was listening. He nodded, and she aimed that Irish accent—mildly tuned down after a few decades in California—at me. "Your father sent me an email about you, Iris. He says you can be rather negative." I bit my tongue, literally. If that wasn't the pot calling the kettle... "But I bet with a little focus and exposure, we can turn you into a wild-hearted Thornian."

Ryder laughed hard, coughing on a fry. I thumped his back, smacking hands with Eamon who was also trying to help. I pushed him away. This guy had gotten into my business fast. They all had. "So is this fantasy conversion camp or the set for a major motion picture?" I snarked.

Cate leaned forward. "Maybe it's both."

"Iris is a songwriter, Cate," Eamon interrupted. "She brought her guitar and everything."

Cate looked too interested, so I tried to head off whatever inquisition might come next.

"Where are the restrooms?"

"We call them *toilets*," Eamon said, still with the baiting humor, still unaware of how unfunny this all was to me.

"How specific," I shot back.

Eamon pointed, eyebrows raised.

I shimmied out from behind the table, while Ryder watched me with a tilted head that made him look like a terrier pup. No doubt trying to understand why his big sister made everything so awkward.

MEET CUTE: ENTER HOLLYWOOD
HUNK LOVE INTEREST
A.K.A. THE ORLANDO BLOOM EYE CANDY OF THIS FILM

THE RESTAURANT WAS louder by the time I got back from the bathroom. A three-person band had appeared in the corner, playing traditional Irish music that seemed invented to accompany laughing. Back at my table, Eamon was downing a pint, and I thought maybe I could jump on the alcohol train as well. Maybe that would make the room stop closing in.

The bartender stared at me for a full minute before I found the words. What did people drink here? Oh yeah. "A Guinness?"

"You're not eighteen," he said.

"I will be in seven months," I tried.

He shook his head.

"Fine." I slumped on a barstool. "Water, please?"

He filled a glass from the tap and set it down. The water

was cloudy and warm. I stared into the murkiness, looking for my life.

"Find any tadpoles? I definitely found a tadpole in mine."

The voice was like sudden sunshine, and I slipped off the edge of my seat. My legs caught me, and I looked up from a leather jacket—that probably cost as much as Eamon's car—to a chiseled, smiling face.

Julian freakin' Young.

"Hi, Julian."

"Hi…?"

He doesn't remember me. Why would he remember me?

"I almost have it," he said. "Give me a second."

"Iris," I said, and his smile broadened. His teeth weren't Hollywood caps—two of the bottom ones had a little lean to them. A perfect imperfection.

"Didn't we meet over a water cooler a few months back?"

Holy crap, he does remember me! "Yeah. Outside Cate's office. On the Vantage lot."

"One sec." He slipped his phone out of his jacket pocket and began texting swiftly while I recalled every detail of my first encounter with Julian Young, a story I'd regaled my school friends with at least a dozen times.

Cate had been mid-*Elementia* speech when my dad lost his cool and started dropping f-bombs. I'd taken Ryder to the bathroom, and while waiting in the hallway, filling a little paper cone with water from the cooler, I'd bumped shoulder to shoulder with Julian. His T-shirt hugged his biceps so hard my thoughts flickered with indecency.

"You're going to be in the movie?" I'd blurted, my eyes attempting to rip off said shirt.

"I'm the twin brother, Eager. Eric? Sorry, all the names sound the same, and I'm coming off a different production. My head isn't in it yet. Who's the brother again?"

"That's all right," I'd said fast. "I don't know his name either." A tiny lie. I knew the main characters and a few odd details. Couldn't avoid them once Ryder had become obsessed.

Julian leaned in, smelling of sandalwood. "Can I tell you a secret? I haven't read those books."

"I love you." Well, I didn't say that, but God, the words were right on my lips.

"But I'll read them soon. For the role. That would be professional, right?"

I'd nodded fervently. There were few people in this world who could make Grandma Mae's books seem legit. Julian Young, twenty-one-year-old movie star, was one of them.

"You two need bottled water?" the bartender asked, bringing me back to Ireland. Julian was still texting, the ghost of a smile on his lips.

"No, thanks. This looks great," I said. Julian laughed. I made Julian Young laugh.

He dropped his phone in his pocket and clinked his glass with mine. "You didn't tell me you were a famous grandkid."

"Well." I swallowed the earthy water. "No sense bragging. Plus, I'm like you." Pause for effect. "I'm not into those books."

"You've gotta meet Shosh." He took my hand—*whoa*—and pulled me to a dark corner booth where a stunning girl with wild, curly hair was holding court. I recognized her from the boat beneath the cliff. "Iris Thorne, this is Shoshanna Reyes. Our Sevyn."

A swift memory scan confirmed that Sevyn was the heroine of *Elementia*.

Shoshanna did an admirable job of looking interested in me, but we both knew we were different girl species. While Roxanne had made me feel plain Jane, Shoshanna's royal presence instantly had me questioning if I was an alien. She leaned back and cocked her head, proving that while she might be near my age, she was more comfortable in her body than I'd ever be in mine. Movie stars, I realized with a pinch. I was sitting at a table with movie stars.

"Shosh is my film twin," Julian said as if he were enjoying that detail too much.

"Yeah, I see it," I tried. "You do kind of look alike."

Shoshanna narrowed her eyes on me. "Are you racist or hopelessly naïve?"

I had been taking a sip from my glass and my mouth malfunctioned. Warm water poured down my chin, making Shoshanna bark a deep laugh.

Julian took my cup and actually wiped my chin with his thumb. "Seriously, Shosh? Why do you do that?" She shrugged, and I had no idea what was happening except that I had been doing far, far better at the table with the über nerds. "We're both part Filipino," he said.

"We're the studio's token attempt at putting some color in the cast," she added.

"That's…" A few choice words flashed through my mind. Nothing felt appropriate. "Terrible," I managed. "Of them. Sorry, I don't know what to say."

Shoshanna held up her palm triumphantly, as if I'd proved a point. "That's why I do it, Julian. Honesty in a hurry." She turned to me, her eyes wildly bright and her hair a halo of curls. "We meet a lot of empty heads in this business. I like to know right away who I'm dealing with. You seem all right."

I do?

"But you're also *the granddaughter.* Cate has been going on and on about how you and your brother are going to be our good-luck charms."

"That's so creepy," I said. Shoshanna laughed. Minor mission accomplished.

Julian leaned in. "See? She's not a nerd, Shosh. She's with us."

The rest of the evening got loud and blurry. And I learned a lot.

For one, Shoshanna had not been in that boat beneath the cliff. That was Jessica, her stunt double. Also, Shoshanna was going to murder Julian if he didn't quit calling her "Shosh." Most importantly, the Elementia fanaticism was keeping these two actors isolated—something I could relate to. Apparently the crew was made up of hardcore Thornians, working at minimum wage for the experience. Even after two months of soundstage filming back on the Vantage lot, Julian and Shoshanna still had no idea why everyone was nuts about Elementia.

So I told them ridiculous Thornian anecdotes. I even recycled the mishap with my in-flight boyfriend and his torso map. They didn't believe me when I said he'd asked to take me out for my birthday, so I slapped his card on the table.

"Fame leeches. Such a-holes." Shoshanna dropped the card in her empty whiskey glass. She quirked a smile at Julian before adding, "Julian's much nicer about his fans."

He leaned back, clasping his hands behind his beautiful head of dark hair. "My fans keep me working. I appreciate them." He was being so *earnest*, and I actually imagined Oscar Wilde sitting up in his grave to do a slow clap.

The cast and crew left the restaurant in a large group, and call it jet lag or being plain fed up with caring for an eight-year-old, but I sort of forgot about Ryder until we arrived at a circle of small production trailers. Ryder and I had been assigned to one, which wasn't the greatest news, except that we were right next to Julian's.

"Your brother is inside," Eamon said, pointing toward my door. "He's a bit homesick."

"Okay." I trudged up the steps. Julian had disappeared a few moments earlier, tucking his phone to his ear and speaking in a hushed voice. He hadn't even said good night.

"Missing something, Iris?" Eamon called out. I looked back, and he held up Annie.

"Oh my God, thank you!" I rushed forward and took it, shocked that I'd forgotten about her. Was it the star power of Julian and Shoshanna, or was I that far out of my element?

"I'm sorry I was slagging you back in the pub," he said. "It's odd, you being in the middle of all this and not caring for any of it."

I looked at Eamon for real. Past the fake ears and scrappy hair. He had no idea how to talk to girls, and I don't know where it had come from, but he was now wearing a backpack like he was waiting for a ride to school. How in the world was he supposed to blend in on-screen with his costars? Maybe I felt sorry for him. Maybe I related.

"I'm here for Ryder. This means the world to him. Up until about a year ago, he thought he was part elf." That was hardly the entire story, but there was no need to drag out Ryder's history with Elementia's rabid fans.

Eamon scrubbed his messy hair. "Why aren't your parents here then?"

I laughed. He waited, and I finally added, "Let's say they have other priorities."

Turning to go inside, his voice stopped me. "I'm in that caravan over there with about five crew guys. If you need anything, knock."

"Ah, thanks." I glanced over his head at the light inside Julian's trailer.

"Nice meeting you, Iris."

"Sure." Even Julian's pacing profile had star quality.

"Don't forget to breathe, Iris." Eamon walked away.

Who was Julian on the phone with? His agent? His mom? I'd looked him up on IMDb about forty times since we met on the Vantage lot. Acting since he was fifteen, star of half a dozen films—three blockbusters, including *Alien Army*—and best of all, no current girlfriend. I remembered the way he'd grabbed my hand in the restaurant, and my fingers tingled.

Cliché, Iris, my dad's voice chipped in.

I looked down at my hands. "But I'm tingly. Literally."

Stepping inside, the trailer was claustrophobic and covered with sterile white plastic, but it smelled okay. There was a small sink and bathroom, a tiny sitting area, and in the back, two narrow beds. One contained a whimpering Ryder. Eamon was right; my brother was a sleepy, emotional mess. I didn't even try to get him in his pajamas.

"I feel weird," he whined, his eyes tightly shut. "I'm going to throw up."

"No, you're not. You're fine. Sleep." I kissed his forehead and collapsed on the other bed. I checked my watch. Fifteen minutes, and I'd check on him. This was programming left over from when he was a year old. Sleep training, his doctor called it. I had been ten, old enough to know that my parents were not following instructions. They kept picking him up, which made him cry even harder and for longer. So I piled my pillows outside his door and set the kitchen timer on my knee. "You can't go in," I told my dad when he sleep-stumbled toward Ryder's door. "He has to cry for fifteen minutes. Then we check on him, but we don't pick him up. Then we set the timer again." He looked at me like I was nuts. "I was at his doctor's appointment too."

It had felt brilliant to care for my little brother that night. Like love and family done right. But it'd felt significantly less than brilliant to keep doing it for the next seven years.

Ryder quieted down, and I took out my phone and sent my father a message, not caring how much the roaming charges would be. He'd want to know that we made it. Most likely.

Sleep wouldn't come, and I felt deeply disconnected from reality. I was trying to sleep on an island off the coast of Ireland while my friends were getting home from school. Tomorrow they'd be creating Benedict Cumberbatch GIFs in study hall—a.k.a. CumberHour—while I watched nerds run circles around actors wearing glorified bathrobes. I pictured Shoshanna and Julian in such getups and flinched. They were great. Talented. Gorgeous. Why did they even want to be in this movie? Maybe I could convince them to quit. That'd shut down this nightmare. And then, having saved their careers, maybe we'd all become friends. Real friends.

I snorted into my pillow. Friends with movie stars? Now that was a true fantasy. I rolled over and scribbled lyrics and possible chords for the song that had been in my head all day. A tune about breaking out of your bubble only to find yourself hopelessly underground.

"Great," I murmured. "One day on set and I'm writing about hobbits."

Film: Elementia

Director: Cate Collins

On Location: Day 2

Aran Islands, Ireland

Filming Notes:

Morning establishing shots on the west end of
the island. Afternoon shots with SEVYN. No
dialogue.

Etc. Notes:

BRILLIANT CRAIC

BECAUSE IT'S NOT A STORY SET IN IRELAND WITHOUT IT

RYDER WOKE ME up, hopping around the trailer like a cricket. He pushed a note card in my face. "What is this?" I asked.

"Film stuff. Henrik said it's the *side* for the day."

"Okay, but why are we getting one with our names stamped on it?"

Ryder shrugged, and I commenced my daily battle to dress, groom, and get Ryder out the door. The picnic tables outside were bustling with crew members having breakfast. We collected some food from a small buffet, and Ryder bee-lined for Eamon and Roxanne, who were deep in conversation. I tried to sit silently, but Ryder yelled, "Hey, guys!"

Roxanne pointed to her plate. "You know they call this 'breaky' here? And this is somehow 'bacon.'" She held up a thick piece of ham on her fork.

Ryder was shocked. "But that's not bacon!"

"That's what I've been telling Eamon." Roxanne looked glorious this morning; she'd paired gold eye shadow with a dark hoodie. Man, I wished this girl would give me lessons.

"Yesterday Eamon taught me about 'the toilets' and 'slagging,'" I said, enjoying the way his ears—his real ears—turned red. Without the elf prosthesis, he no longer looked ridiculous, and I confirmed what I had suspected yesterday: he was, underneath the nerdisms, cute.

"Do you guys want to see the costume trailer?" Eamon asked. "It's great craic."

Roxanne snapped her fingers. "I know this one. *Craic* means fun."

"I want to have some crack!" Ryder shouted.

Roxanne laughed against the back of her hand while I gave Eamon a withering look. "Real funny," I said. "You can explain to my dad that he's not talking about hard drugs."

"What?" Ryder asked. "I can't go?"

"Eat," I said. "And you can go as long as Eamon promises to watch you."

"You don't want to come?" Eamon asked.

"I'm going back to bed. It's dead o'clock back in LA." I turned to my brother. "Listen to Eamon." My brother waved me away, and I grabbed my cold toast and headed toward our trailer.

When I passed Julian's, he popped his beautiful head out. "Hey, Iris, get in here. We've got real lattes."

"And a fruit plate!" Shoshanna yelled from inside.

Cue epic morning with Hollywood stars. If I'd written an honest email to my parents about my second morning in Ireland, it would have been all exclamation marks. I didn't, of course; they did not deserve to know how amazing it was to hang out with Julian Young and Shoshanna Reyes.

Last night, around the second hour of *why am I so tired and yet cannot sleep*, I'd looked up Shoshanna's IMDb page. She was eighteen and had three times as many credits as Julian. Mostly indies, but also a lot of TV shows. In short, she was a pro. They both were. And I spent an entire morning swapping favorite YouTube videos with them.

At some point, I tried to ask why they'd agreed to do a movie they clearly weren't into. I must've messed up the phrasing though because Julian got excited to show me the first cut of the teaser trailer. "They're going to add music, but it's pretty hot already," he said, pulling it up on his laptop. "Cate thinks we need to leak this early to rev up fan support."

"Brilliant move," Shoshanna said in a rather giddy Irish accent. When Julian and I looked doubtful, she added, "What? I want to beef up the special skills section on my résumé."

"Keep working on that accent, Shosh," Julian said dryly.

Shoshanna hit him with a pillow.

Julian used a remote to turn off the lights, and Shoshanna scooted in on one side of Julian while I claimed the other. The laptop screen lit up with a video. Black screen first, followed by Shoshanna's icy voiceover: "I was cursed by lightning at birth. Untouchable."

I snorted, and they both glanced at me, troubled. On screen, two hands appeared through the black, and I recognized Julian's long, lovely fingers. The hands almost touched, but then Sevyn's—Shoshanna's—crackled with static sparks, and Evyn's hand recoiled.

"That was only the beginning."

"That shot seemed cheesy," Shoshanna whispered. "But it looks good."

Julian shushed her as a montage of a rustic kingdom and a foul-faced king thundered across the screen. There was a deer in the woods, and then Sevyn was running, angry, branches tearing at her clothes. She fled through a tunnel, coming out behind a mammoth waterfall. Evyn appeared behind her, pleading, but a great, clawed hand reached through the veil of water. Julian's best acting face filled with dread in the moment before he was ripped through. Gone.

It was pretty affecting, to use Dad's favorite word, and when the screen went black, I had a bizarre urge to whack the computer to make it keep playing. "That's it?" I asked. "Evyn was kidnapped? Is that why Sevyn ends up on a quest?"

Shoshanna crossed her arms. "If we've made M. E. Thorne's anti-fantasy granddaughter curious, we're golden, Julian. This is going to be the big one. I told you."

"Shosh…" He winced as she gave him a murderous look.

"…anna, the trick is not to get your hopes up. I've shot scenes covered in blue slime, which felt like the end of my career, but then *Alien Army* was twice as popular as *Starship Troopers*. You can never tell, but don't jinx it."

"Blah, Julian. You sound as paranoid as Cate Collins." Shoshanna kicked her feet up. "Why haven't they called us yet? Did something else go wrong? There has not been a single seamless day on this production."

"Yeah, and talk about the lack of press interest," Julian muttered.

This was my chance to drill up some negativity, which according to my dad was my specialty—but he wasn't here and I wasn't actually Jaded Iris. "What's the special skills section on your résumé?"

"Well, normal stuff like riding a horse, juggling, foreign languages," Shoshanna said. "And also odd stuff. Like the ability to flip your eyelids inside out or speak pig Latin."

"I can make my pecs dance to 'Twinkle, Twinkle, Little Star,'" Julian said. "I got a commercial once because of it."

Shoshanna sat up, way too excited. "Show us. Now."

"Only if you sing," he said. And that's how Eamon and my little brother found us, sitting in the dark in Julian Young's trailer, singing "Twinkle, Twinkle, Light Star" while a shirtless Julian made his pecs dance. Eamon clapped a hand over Ryder's eyes.

Julian clicked on the lights and started texting. God, he

was a ninja texter. One minute he was talking, the next: *BAM*. Forty messages fired.

"What, Ryder? We're busy." I braided my hair, hopefully looking less conspicuous.

"They're filming out on the west end of the island. Cate said we could go watch. I got these out of your bag." My brother held up my hiking boots—and my heart stopped.

A pair of lacy underwear was stuck to the Velcro of one boot. Not just any pair either.

I lunged, but Shoshanna was faster. "Julian!" she shrieked, thrusting the skimpy cloth in Julian's still-texting face. "Your face is on Iris's undies!"

Julian dropped his phone in his lap and grabbed the lacy abomination.

"Those aren't mine!" I shouted. "My school friends gave them to me as a joke because they knew I'd be hanging out with you. See? The tag is still on them. I wouldn't wear them!"

Julian and Shoshanna slumped on the couch in hysterics while I died of embarrassment. I closed my eyes, picturing my headstone:

IRIS MAE ELLEN THORNE

2001–2018

KILLED BY NOVELTY PANTIES

After a minute, Julian surprised me by handing the underwear back. "This is not the first time I've seen underwear with my face on it, Iris. It'd only be a problem if you were wearing them and wanted to show me."

Oh my God.

I turned fast, pushing Eamon and Ryder out of the trailer. Shutting the door behind us, I threw the underwear in the nearest trash can and stomped toward my brother.

"Say, take a breath, Iris. He didn't mean to do that," Eamon tried.

"Shut it, elf."

"Certainly, mistress." He bowed, and I almost kicked him in the shin. Ryder did have a rather paralyzed look on his face; he hadn't meant to embarrass me. That didn't help though. And something else caught my eye. I ruffled his hair back, finding fake elf ears. "Ryder! You did not ask to do this. What if you have a reaction to the chemicals?"

"They're not glued!" my brother said. "I told Roxy about my skin sensitivity."

"He did," Eamon said. "It's double-sided tape." I cooled; that actually was rather responsible of Ryder, even if he was now the spitting image of yesterday's Eamon. Today's Eamon pointed at one of the production vans. "We're headed to the west end. Come with us."

I looked back at Julian's trailer. "Ryder can go, but watch him. I'm staying here."

"But it'll be brilliant," Eamon said. "You'd trade that in for Hollywood brownnosing?"

Aghast. I believe that's the right word, Dad.

Even worse, Eamon was holding a small camera. "What is that?" I asked, pointing.

"I'm making a video blog of the production. Cate said it will help get fans excited. I've already got twenty thousand subscribers on my YouTube channel."

I got closer to him than I'd ever been. Not face-to-face. Face-*in*-face. His eyebrows rose up into his tousled hair, and I was glad I'd stunned him. "My brother and I don't show up on your blog or you will learn the wrath of Henry T. Wittmeijer, my family's lawyer."

Eamon's scowl was his cutest look. I could give him that. "What is your problem?"

I grabbed my little brother's chin. "He's not an actor, Eamon. He's eight. He's trying to have a normal life. Don't put an X on his back for all the crazy fans to target."

Eamon understood. Maybe. He stepped back at least.

"Does this mean I can go?" Ryder asked.

"Only if Eamon promises to watch you," I said.

Eamon gave a stiff nod.

I pretended like I was inspecting Ryder's ears, adding, "Remember what Dad wants you to think about while we're here?"

He nodded and sighed like a forty-year-old.

They headed for the vans, and Ryder regained his bounce after a few yards. Eamon dropped his camera in his backpack and slung it over his shoulder. From behind, Eamon was so skinny I couldn't figure out what was holding up his pants. And then I had to chastise myself for spending any amount of time contemplating Eamon's butt. *Where's your head, Iris?*

⌐ᴏ⌐

I couldn't step back in Julian's trailer after the underwear nightmare. I went to mine instead, where a short nap made me feel even worse. I turned to Annie.

My all-black Martin was the best thing I owned. I'd tuned each peg down three turns for the plane ride and fixing her back into singing shape took a little fussing. Annie felt hesitant, but then, I knew that was my hesitation. Two things always happened when I picked up my guitar.

One: I felt at home. Two: I felt like an impostor.

Logic might say these sentiments don't coexist, but logic is useless when it comes to art. My dad had been demonstrating that for me since birth. I was younger than Ryder is now the day my dad sat me down and said, "Iris, passion is just an obsession with the thing you can't seem to get better at."

I wished I were a great songwriter, and somehow with that driving desire came the overwhelming feeling that I wasn't good. That I never would be. To date, my best song was about how I could hear my dad's voice in my head. How it confused me. Told me I was wrong. Which explained why I couldn't play it for him—especially because my dad wasn't a bad guy. He was preoccupied and obsessive, but he wasn't cruel.

The dad voice in my head, however…that guy was after me. He was the one who told me I wasn't going to break out from my family's shadow. He was the one who reminded me that all this fantasy crap was my own personal, and yet somehow universal, nightmare.

The chords I'd been strumming died away. How thick were the trailer walls anyway? Someone might hear. Looking around, my eyes caught on a movie poster that Ryder must have just hung up over his bed. A huge lightning bolt split a dark picture: Sevyn's angry, powerful face on one half and Evyn's fire-lit expression on the other. I could barely recognize Shoshanna and Julian in those images—the emotion was too strong. Too dire.

"Fantasy," I cursed.

Eamon/Nolan didn't make the poster. Did that bother him? My eyes trailed the silver *Elementia* title treatment, followed by *Based on the novels by M. E. Thorne.*

"How'd you do it?" I asked the dead air in the trailer. "How'd you write your heart into those books and then share them with everyone?"

No answer.

I'd be the shadow of the shadow of M. E. Thorne, and with the advent of this stupid movie, that shadow would be more like a permanent gloom. I nestled my face into the curve of Annie's side. *You should give up*, Dad said on cue. *Think about how happy I'd be if you became a literature professor.*

When Eamon rushed into the trailer, I tossed my guitar on the bed and started yelling. "What's wrong with you? You can't just burst in here!"

"He's gone."

"What?"

"Ryder. He was with me one second. Then he was gone."

IN WHICH I SPROUT GRAY (OR GREY) HAIR

EAMON AND I jumped in a production van and raced down the narrowest road in the world. Seriously, Siberian summer mud roads have nothing on the Aran Islands—which was actually what I was thinking about because I couldn't let myself imagine Ryder wandering off a cliff or being taken by… No way. That guy would be living in an institution in New Jersey for two more years.

"Sorry, sorry," Eamon said for the twelfth time. "I don't know—"

"Stop saying you're sorry. I'm not mad at you."

"You're not?"

"This is my fault. Ryder is swift and impulsive and my responsibility." The words tasted sour, and my eyes watered. "I should have gone with you."

"The whole crew stopped to look for him. They'll have found him by the time we arrive." He paused. "He's probably wandered off, Iris. I'm sure of it."

I closed my eyes. "I know."

You don't, my dad's voice thundered.

The sun was setting when we arrived at the random, gorgeous field that had become a graveyard of film equipment. The crew was spread out as far as I could see. "You know him best," Eamon said. "Where would he go?"

I scanned the green fields, piled rock walls, and the glittering edge of the ocean. The sunset was so beautiful it felt sarcastic. "Over there." I pointed to a stone barn in the distance.

"That far?" Eamon asked, but then he shook his head. "Right, we go."

We ran, weaving around boulders and stone walls, until my breath burned in my chest. The structure I'd seen wasn't a barn after all, but a small stone house left over from another century. The roof was missing, and trees grew tall inside. "Ryder!"

No answer. I walked all the way around, finding the only doorway bricked up and the window ledges out of reach. "They don't want tourists messing around in there," Eamon noted.

"What if he climbed through a window and hit his head?" I took a deep breath. "Ryder!"

"How could he get up there? You can barely reach the ledge."

"Eamon. He climbs the two-story banister at home like a spider."

"All right," he said, walking to the nearest window. "I'll give you a boost." Eamon linked his hands, and I stepped in them, using his shoulders to balance. I peered inside at nothing but overgrown grass before Eamon grunted and wobbled. We fell in a heap, and I sort of flattened his face with my boobs. He sat up with a wild expression, pressing his hair back with both hands.

"Not there?" he asked.

I shook my head.

"Let's see if anyone else found anything."

We tried to jog back, but we were both sweaty and out of breath. Our pace slowed, and I growled, "I knew this country was too dangerous. Did you ever read *Angela's Ashes*? Every kid dies in that book!"

Eamon laughed, a quick, deep sound. "You are so ridiculous it's adorable. This is an island that barely boasts electricity. What harm could come to him?"

"What harm? This island is currently full of fantasy whack jobs. You guys believe in elves and controlling the elements with your hands. And you think my brother and I are extra special because of our dead grandma! One of you probably stole him to drink his blood."

"Drink his blood?" Eamon asked, stunned. "You call us fanatical, but you have the most overactive imagination of anyone!"

"It's happened before!"

Dead silence, and then Eamon said, "What do you mean?"

"His name is Felix Moss, and when he was twenty-four, he heard M. E. Thorne's voice in his head, telling him to abduct her grandchild and drink his blood like the characters in *Elementia*. I wish he'd found me first, but he found Ryder, who was only six! He dragged him into a van, and I ran…I ran…"

I couldn't take one more step. I started to hyperventilate.

"We'll find him, Iris," Eamon said firmly, but I was lost in the memory of that day on the playground. My baby brother screaming. My heart ripping while my mind filled with hot rage.

Ryder's therapist had told me I should be proud. *Fight or flight, Iris*, she'd said. *Most people don't know what they'll do when faced with such a test. Now you know you will fight.*

But what about now? I wasn't fighting; I could barely breathe.

A loud echo reached across the stony field. Back at the center of filming, someone was yelling over a megaphone. "What are they saying?"

"They must've found him," Eamon said.

We ran again, and I was stumbling by the time we reached Cate. She was kneeling in front of Ryder, holding his shoulders at the center of the crew member crowd. I nearly knocked her over, wanting to hug my brother, but I shook him instead. "Where were you?"

"I met a man. A real-life shepherd!" Ryder pointed across the field. My brother looked tired. Small. A fine-boned replica of my stunning mother, and I shook him again because I wanted to shake my parents. The people who had dropped this wild person into the center of my life.

Ryder was surprised by my anger, his brown eyes wide. "Iris, I'm okay. He gave me some tea and helped me come back. The tea was all black and gross, but I'm okay."

"You know better, Ryder! Do you have any idea what that guy could've done to you?"

Ryder blinked. He didn't know; he didn't have my imagination. He hadn't seen *The Lovely Bones* or learned how to look up registered sex offenders like I'd started doing compulsively two years ago. I didn't want to hurt him, but he couldn't think it was okay to go off with a stranger, let alone without telling anyone.

"Look." I turned him in a circle so he could see the faces of the crew members. "They dropped their work to find you. You probably cost them thousands of dollars and ruined this shoot."

"I wouldn't say that," Cate tried, but I shot her a death look.

Ryder's face was finally filling with the gravity of his actions, but it wasn't enough.

"We're going home. As soon as possible. Tomorrow morning if we can get a flight."

His shock twisted into a scream that made people cover their ears. His tantrum came fast, and I couldn't lift him anymore; he was too big. His legs went limp, and when several people tried to help, I warned them back, feeling feral. I had found Ryder safe, and yet I was still pounding all over with fear and anger.

We made it to the van, and I buckled him in the back, mad that my life was so tangled with his, that whatever he did avalanched on me. Loving him this much was downright infuriating. It always felt like a punishment for something I hadn't done.

~

Eamon drove us back. The sky was black, and the road jarred the van with endless bumps. Ryder sniffed in the back, and I crossed my arms, imagining the phone call home.

"We have to come back," I'd say. "Ryder won't listen and he nearly got himself killed."

"Why weren't you watching him?" my dad would ask.

"It's not my job," I'd snap once and for all. "You two shouldn't have had him if you didn't want to raise him. You shouldn't have had either of us."

"Your mother and I feel that way too."

I gasped. Even for a make-believe argument, that cut deep.

"You can't leave," Eamon murmured. "You'll break his heart."

"What about mine?"

"What about yours?" he asked. "What is it that Iris Thorne wants, then?"

I closed my eyes and rested my head against the window. "To play my guitar in a place where no one can hear me. No responsibilities. *No* elves."

"That's escapism, Iris. That's not real life."

"Coming from a Thornian, that's rich."

He was driving slower and slower, like he didn't want to get back too fast. "Iris, when I was a kid, I wanted to find a portal. Desperately. No more this world, time for a new one. I thought every cabinet was Narnia's wardrobe or Alice's rabbit hole. I even made my own subtle knife." His eyes twinkled in the dark as he looked at me. "You probably don't get that reference."

I did. But I couldn't tell him. That door was locked tight inside.

"What was wrong with your world?" I asked.

"A fair amount of disappointment. Loneliness. My da is a piece of work, and my sister moved out when I was still little. Mam worked long shifts." He paused, and I wondered why he was telling me this. Was Eamon opening up because I'd told him about Felix Moss? This was new ground; no one outside of my family knew the truth. Not even my school friends.

Eamon cleared his throat. "Mam said I was reading the

stories all wrong. It's not about disappearing. It's about experiencing a new world so you can understand the real one. That's what *Elementia* is about. Sevyn leaves home to find her brother, and she finds her life instead."

This was either too deep for me or I was too exhausted. "Okay, sure."

"That man…Moss." Eamon's voice turned hard, his accent sharper than usual. "He must've had a psychotic break. Not all Thornians are like that. There are a lot of us who simply appreciate the story."

"If you say the books saved your life, I'll have to stop talking to you."

"The story saved my life," Ryder said, his voice scratchy from screaming.

I glanced back at my tiny brother in the huge back seat. "No, it didn't. You didn't need to be saved. You were fine and happy. The story's terrible fans messed up your life."

That's right, my dad's voice slipped in.

Ryder replied even louder. "Byers took Evyn because he was sick. He didn't hurt him."

Eamon smiled at Ryder via the rearview mirror. "And Byers saved Evyn in the end."

"Byers?" I asked. Fantasy talk was so isolating. You either knew everything about the fictional world, or you knew nothing. I grasped to understand. "The clawed hand that reaches through the waterfall and grabs Evyn…that's Byers?"

"Yes," Eamon said. "And considering your brother has been part of a kidnapping, you might want to read the book he's identifying with."

"*Attempted* kidnapping. I stopped it. And considering you want to be my friend, you should stop asking me to do something that's against my nature."

Eamon squinted, more mischievous in the dark. "Who said I want to be your friend?"

"He does," Ryder supplied. "He called you 'rascally cute.'"

I laughed and snorted and sort of choked all at once.

"Now that was cute," Eamon said. We pulled up outside the circle of trailers. I tried to ignore Eamon's mild flirting—because I honestly didn't know what to do about it—and marched Ryder up the steps.

"Iris, a minute?" Eamon called.

"Pajamas. Teeth. Bed," I said to my brother and shut the trailer door behind him. I turned to face Eamon O'Brien. He wasn't Julian Young, but there was something about his smile and sandy, wavy fistfight of a hairstyle.

"He's a great kid. Don't be too hard on him."

"Thanks for the parenting advice." Despite my snark, my voice fell. Eamon motioned for me to follow, and we sat at one of the empty picnic tables. I turned my face up to the very black sky with its silver stars and fiction-quality silver moon. "Ryder's therapist thinks this fantasy stuff is good for him, but he's stopped caring about anything real. It's all costumes and weapons. At school, he signs his name in that phony elf language. Kids tease him. A lot."

"Iris, how did you stop him?" Eamon cleared his throat. "Moss, that is."

My words stuck in my throat. "I don't think anyone has asked me that since the police."

"Do you mind?"

I shook my head and started talking. Remembering. It was easier this time because I was choosing it. "Ryder was screaming, and I ran. Moss had shut him in the back of a van, but he'd left the driver's side window down. I climbed through and clawed his eyes while he was trying to drive away."

Eamon flinched.

"Yeah," I agreed. "Gruesome. Apparently I blinded his right eye. Our lawyer said that was unfortunate. It gave Moss sympathy points with the judge." I looked down at my hands, nails so short they often hurt, but it did make it easier to play guitar. "You know what he said when they put him on the stand? 'I wanted the Thorne family to read my manifesto. I'm Elementia's biggest fan.'"

"No wonder you hate us." Eamon's shoulder bumped mine.

"It's not hate. It's more complicated than that. Ryder has been disappearing in this fantasy world since my dad read the books to him. It was supposed to show him that Moss isn't a monster, just a disturbed fan."

Eamon faced me, shadows playing with his cheekbones, making him starker. Lovelier. From this angle, I could see what Cate Collins must see: a diamond in the rough. "So what about you?"

"I'm fine," I said.

He scoffed.

"Hey, I excel at *fine*. I'm going to have to major in it in college at this rate."

"Iris, do you always act like this happened to Ryder and not to both of you?"

"I was older. I could handle it better."

"Could you?"

I laughed, which felt odd but not unwelcome in my still-reeling body. "You're a piece of work, Eamon O'Brien." I stood to leave.

"Stay." Eamon's voice cracked, which was bizarrely endearing. "For the rest of the shoot. It's only for, what? Nine more days? You'll regret it if you don't."

"You'll regret it if you don't quit telling me how I feel."

Apparently Eamon and I had leveled up to flirty threats. His brand-new smile turned my heart into a kick drum, playing the rhythm to a song I'd never heard before.

THE SAN ANDREAS FAULT AND OTHER POTENTIALLY DISASTROUS FAMILY FORMATIONS

RYDER SAT AT the back of the trailer, staring into space. "Are we really leaving tomorrow?"

"I don't know," I said. Somehow I wanted to stay. Mostly because of Julian and Shoshanna, but also Eamon. I'd be lying if I didn't admit that I wanted to see him in the morning. And maybe even the next day...

"Why did you have to say all that stuff about me ruining the shoot? I got lost."

"You don't understand how movies work, Ry. They're all about budgets and money and time, time, time. You stole their time today. I knew I shouldn't have let you go without me."

My brother eyed me coldly, reminding me that it didn't matter if he looked like our mom. He had our dad in him as well. "Then why'd you let me go?"

"I don't know." Except I did. I'd wanted to hang out with people my age instead of feeling like the single parent of a third grader.

Ryder pounded a tight fist against his leg. "I mean, why would you let me do that? Do you want to go home that bad? Is it killing you so much to be here with me?"

"No…" I fought for words through the knots in my heartstrings. "This isn't my thing, Ry. You know that."

He blew out a frustrated sigh and then whacked himself in the face. Hard.

"Stop!" I held his wrists and put my face close to his. "Don't do that."

"I can't listen!" Ryder's cheek was bright red with his little handprint.

"That's crap. You can do it."

"I can't! You and Dad tell me all the time I'm so much trouble. All the time! My therapist says it's a self-filling proph-ecy. And prophecy means I can't stop it!"

I tried not to smile at his jumbled phrasing. "Hey, no prophecies, pal. This is real life. All this fantasy stuff is a hobby." I scooted closer on the bed, pushing his foam weapons out of the way. "This is a movie. It's not real." I pointed at the poster on the wall. "See how fake that is? Think about Shoshanna and Julian. They're not these characters. They're actors."

"You said I ruined their shot. Will Cate Collins hate me?" Tears filled Ryder's eyes. I pulled him to my chest, furious with myself. I'd yelled too hard. Scared him. *You had to make sure he understood the gravity of his actions*, my dad's voice spoke up, only to play devil's advocate a second later. *Except you were over the line. You shouldn't have embarrassed him.*

I shut down my thoughts with some serious effort. "Come on, Ry. What will make you feel better? I'll do anything."

He wasted no time, slipping out of my arms and down from the bed. He searched through his suitcase, returning with something behind his back. "Read to me?"

I knew which book. This was his oldest trick. "No."

"I want to hear one scene. The one we saw yesterday. With the boat and the cliff."

I breathed four breaths in one go.

"Please?"

"Only if you don't tell anyone," I said. He jumped on the bed, handing over the worn paperback copy of the Elementia trilogy. The book was wider than it was tall, all three novels smashed into one mass-market binding. "Find the page."

He flipped through, and I was surprised that he made it about a hundred pages in. "I thought Cate was filming in sequence."

"They shot all the scenes for the island kingdom of Cerul back in LA. They're going to do all the shots for mainland Elementia here. So Ireland is Elementia. Isn't that a great idea?"

"Sure."

He handed the book to me, the binding falling open, evidence of a well-read section. Glancing over the words, I disliked them immediately. All fantasy lingo and thesaurus-inspired color descriptions.

Before I could stop myself, I slipped into my sole memory of Grandma Mae. A snapshot. She'd taken me for a walk in the park and told me that the sky was not blue. *It's azure.*

She died a few months later. "[Expletive deleted] cancer," as my dad would say.

"Iris?"

I glanced at my brother. "You won't tell anyone that I read this? Especially Dad?"

He nodded solemnly.

MANIFEST

Sevyn eyed the drunken old man with disgust. She moved away from Coad, edging along the boat and pulling her cloak tight. The wind sought to push her to Elementia with a cool hand, so unlike the air her father commanded on Cerul.

She imagined this wind came from the north, somewhere with snow. She had seen drawings of snow, and Evyn had told her about his trek to the top of Eyelit Pass, where he scooped handfuls of white powder until the burning touch of his fingers made it disappear.

I glanced at Ryder. "So Evyn and Sevyn are twins. Unfortunate naming there. Where's scrappy Eamon slash Nolan?"

"We don't meet him for a while." My brother's smile was blissful. "Sevyn was cursed by lightning. No one can touch her. Evyn was blessed by the power of fire. Sevyn's dad—who can control the wind—hates her and loves Evyn. He has some issues."

"Clearly." I remembered the teaser trailer, the sparks jumping between the two hands in the dark. "You're serious about the lightning?"

He scowled with his eyes closed. "Keep reading. It'll make sense."

Remembering Evyn made her ache with fear. She stared at the midnight sky with its coin-faced moon and prayed that wherever he had been taken, he was safe. Alive. No matter how small the chance. "I'll find you," she whispered. "I'll go to the mainland. Survive its poisons. Somehow…"

When sleep finally came, she dreamt that she was an eagle, soaring over Elementia. She surveyed an ancient, dense forest and an argent river. She turned in wide arcs, shifting her wings until she could see the coastline. A beautiful woman stood upon the cliffs, her chestnut hair waving as it caught the wind.

Wake, *she told Sevyn.* You are astray.

A thunderclap rang in her ears, forcing Sevyn's eyes open.

"This isn't what we saw yesterday. Sevyn wasn't an eagle when Maedina was on the cliff. She was in the boat," I said, trying to line up what we had seen with what I was reading.

"Cate said they have to change things to make it a better movie. There's no Coad too. And you know Sevyn and Evyn are supposed to be thirteen, but now they're eighteen, so they could cast Julian Young for sex appeal."

"Ryder!" I blushed, although I couldn't argue. "Cate Collins is onto something. The casting of Julian Young is the saving grace of this whole experience."

My brother's grin was joyous. "Can I ask Cate to give us bit roles? Please?"

"Absolutely not, and you know why." I kept reading to cut off that line of questioning.

Bump. Bump.

Sevyn struggled to sit up. She had slipped into the bottom of the boat. It was early morning, and the sun scalded the water with golden rays. Her mouth was parched and her skin was crusted with a fine layer of salt.

Coad still slept at the other end of the boat. His head was thrown back, exposing the stringy ligaments of his neck.

Bump. Bump.

The boat was caught on something. Sevyn swung

her head over the edge to behold a hand projected from the water, outstretched and ghostly white. She stifled a scream, remembering the clawed fingers that had ripped Evyn out of her life.

But then, the bleached appendage was not a real hand; it was the raised limb of a sunken marble statue. Beneath the surface, Sevyn could make out the armored head and body of a soldier. The raised hand gripped nothing, its sword long lost.

All around, the azure water was a graveyard of statues. Most were broken beyond recognition, but she made out the headless bust of a royal woman, barnacles blotching its ivory surface. Beyond that, two child figures held hands against a large marble slab. They appeared frozen, their small faces pointed toward the sky.

Sevyn swept the scene, eyes catching on a rock. It was strewn with bird droppings and seaweed, but underneath, it had the distinctive shape of a castle battlement. The white marble had been cut into massive crenels, carved with the images of men and elves.

"Manifest," Sevyn whispered. Her favorite stories had been about this great city. This was where the kings and queens she had descended from lived and ruled—before the exodus to Cerul. Before Elementia

had started to die, the trees burnt, the ground break-
ing apart and creating great rifts.

The flat, wide wall of white rock showed how
the earth had split, and her bedtime stories had
never truly encapsulated the horror. Manifest had
once been a bastion larger than the entire island
of Cerul. And it had tumbled into the sea in one
cracking moment of fear and loss. As Sevyn looked
out over the half-sunken ruins, she could hear the
cries of all the lives the sea had swallowed that day
as if they were still in the air.

"So it's a sad story," I murmured.

Yesterday on the ferry, I'd seen the wide, tall, harsh stone wall below the old fort. It had been impressive, true enough, but how would it feel after the CGI littered the scene with the remains of a fallen kingdom?

"Ryder, what..." My brother was asleep, his mouth open. I straightened his legs and pulled the blanket over him. He flopped on his side, and I was a little sorry he hadn't stayed awake until the end of the chapter. I was now wide awake.

Before I closed the book, I noticed some pencil scribbles in the margin.

San Andreas Fault parallel—obvious.

It was my dad's handwriting. Old and faded. Was this his copy? Wait, he owned a copy? I shut it and carefully placed the book next to Ryder, as if it had turned into a land mine in my hands. My dad's feelings about these books were something I avoided out of a biological sense of self-preservation.

I crawled into bed, picturing fictitious Manifest falling into the sea, wondering if it would look like all the wretched blockbusters where LA cracks off the edge of the continent and gets swallowed by the Pacific.

Parallel—obvious… Is that where he got the idea?

To date, my dad's only true moment of literary fame hadn't come from one of his books, but a rather infamous obituary he wrote for the *New York Times*. In it, he'd described his mother and himself as being "on opposite sides of the San Andreas Fault. Always grinding against one another. Always threatening disaster."

I'd read the obituary more times than I cared to admit. It had fascinated me. Made me wonder how my dad could have been at odds with his own parent—although after the last few years, perhaps it was just research on Thorne family tendencies.

My dad and I had been pushing against each other since way before Felix Moss came into our lives. Since before Ryder, even. All the way back to the catastrophic event with my literary tutor. That was, what? Nine years of resentment and frustration building underground between us? I kept stuffing my feelings down, but I was running out of room. What would happen if I told him how I hated being my brother's stand-in parent? Or that my music wasn't my "little hobby"?

I imagined the earthquake would be a ten on the Richter scale. Fire and flood. No survivors.

FILM: ELEMENTIA

DIRECTOR: CATE COLLINS

ON LOCATION: DAY 3

ARAN ISLANDS, IRELAND

FILMING NOTES:

A.M.: SEVYN's docking in Elementia and introduction to MAEDINA.

P.M.: EVYN's initial conversation with BYERS.

After dark: One take burn of MAEDINA's tree.
BE READY.

ETC. NOTES:

Ryder Thorne is joining the crafty crew.

Iris Thorne is meeting with Julian Young for
lunch.

Make sure to give Eamon O'Brien brief interviews on your Thornian background for his
"Making Of" blog series.

MEANWHILE ON SOME LITTLE-KNOWN EDGE OF THE WORLD...

I WOKE TOO early, groggy and stiff, to the sound of some-one knocking.

Ryder slept through it, snoring lightly. I checked my watch. Ten o'clock at night in LA, which was what in Ireland? Through the blinds over the tiny trailer window, the sky was dawning with slivers of orange. The knock returned, louder this time. I shot out of bed before it woke up Ryder, only to find Cate Collins—in a full-body, black spandex suit.

"Filming CGI this early?"

"Funny, love. Your father said you run."

"You talked to my dad? When?" I tried to keep the irrita-tion out of my voice. Tried and failed. He hadn't even replied to the text I'd sent two days ago.

"Last night after the excitement." Oh great, now Cate

had told my dad what happened before I had a chance to spin it. "Get dressed. I'm rather serious about running."

"I don't run on vacation," I said.

"This isn't a vacation. It's time you and I talked that through." She walked away, stretching her arms over her head. I changed into my workout gear, curious but also confident that this forty-something-year-old would not be able to keep up with me.

Wrong again, Iris.

A half hour later, we were running along a cliff walk that veered within feet of a twenty-foot drop to the ocean. Inishmore was silent except for the occasional screech of gulls and the tussle of the waves against the gravel beach below. It was beautiful, but more than that, it was different. How could LA's congested vibrancy exist on the same planet as an island missing from time and seemingly pleased to be so lost?

Ordinarily I ran with headphones, drowning out the world, but Cate kept her nose high, eyes searching the landscape. I followed suit. She sprinted on the uneven ground, while my stride shrunk until my sides hurt. Cate slowed and looked back. "We can power walk now."

"Great. Thanks."

She was taking pity on me, but maybe she was ready to talk. After all, we weren't out here for the epic scenery. "I read your grandmother's books when I was out of film school, still digesting LA. I missed home, and this is what I pictured. In my heart, Elementia will always look like Ireland."

"Isn't that weird though?" I asked. "Isn't Elementia all collapsed stone cities and burned forests? Isn't it abandoned?"

"It is until the second book, when it begins to flourish." Her light tone proved she was surprised that I knew this much; I didn't tell her I'd learned it last night. She sighed and her emotions shone on her face: wistful longing with veins of deep sadness. I looked away. Thornians always wanted to tell me what they'd discovered in Grandma Mae's books, but they didn't need a reaction. When I was Ryder's age, I pretended to go invisible when people began this speech. No one noticed; I was that good. "Iris?"

"What?"

"I asked if you truly think you're on vacation."

"I'm here for my brother," I said. Last night had been an acute reminder. "This trip means the world to him, and his therapist thinks... How much do you know about his situation?"

"Your father told me the harsh details last night." Cate looked annoyed. "I would have appreciated knowing earlier. I could have helped."

She was being earnest, so I tried not to laugh. "Unless you have a time machine and can remind my dad to pick us up instead of leaving us at the mercy of a mentally unhinged stalker, there is no help."

"*Iris.*" She said my name like a mom. Like a person who

cared about me deeply, which was weird and misleading because we barely knew one another. "That attitude will kill you."

Jaded Iris, reporting for duty.

"I know," I admitted. The sun cracked over the eastern horizon, and I turned my eyes away, toward the west and the sudden jewels of light popping across the deep blue ocean. Azure?

Blue.

Cate flexed her hands in the rays. "I assure you yesterday did not go as planned for anyone, but I want you to stay. To become part of this production community."

"Because we're your Thornian luck charms?"

Oh, I'd gotten to her. She scowled. "Because this is your family's story. Whether you like it or not. Whether you know it or not." She picked up the pace, and I had to hustle. "I have jobs for you and Ryder. Perhaps if you feel more involved, you'll seek out less trouble."

"Look, Eamon should have been watching Ryder like he promised and—"

"Eamon O'Brien is one of the stars of this major motion picture, not a babysitter. And I'm speaking of the trouble of you and Julian and Shoshanna huddled up in Julian's trailer, making fun of everyone on set."

"But—"

"I'm very sharp, Iris. *Very*," she said in a way that left me wondering if there was an Irish mafia. Did she bring me out here to dangle me over a cliff and tell me to watch myself? "I know you haven't read your grandmother's books, and high fantasy is not your literary style. You're a, what, *Pride and Prejudice* kind of girl?"

"No," I threw back just as snappish. "*Jane Eyre*."

"Oh, Iris. That is a true fantasy." Cate's accent crystalized in a way I hadn't heard before. She sounded more like Eamon, like this country. I already felt foolish for thinking the accent was exotic when I arrived. It was far better: welcoming, honest, and, well, *sharp*. "Regardless of your reluctance, you can be no stranger to the feminist themes in Elementia."

I rattled off my dad's dry elevator pitch on cue. "Male chauvinist king who denies his daughter's birth rite in favor of his son ends up killed by said son while the whole world gets saved by said daughter."

"That sounds like a man's interpretation," Cate said. "Your father's?"

I nodded, wondering what had given me away.

"You need to know this story is more complicated. Like this world. What does your mother say about the books?"

"She hasn't read them either. She's a poet. She…" How much to say? When it came to my mom, the outside world didn't understand, and we Thornes rarely asked them to. "She's a bit of an Emily Dickinson. Instead of an attic, she hides in her greenhouse. All day. Every day." Cate's pitying look made me ache. "It's okay. My dad does the heavy lifting."

"From my point of view, *you* do the heavy lifting."

"Yeah, maybe."

Was I relieved or embarrassed that my situation was so transparent?

We were approaching what felt like the northern edge of the island. A towering silhouette loomed on the pinnacle of the cliff wall, and I squinted but couldn't make it out.

Cate took off her running headband and rubbed a hand through her short, grey hair—I felt pretty certain now that Cate's hair was grey, not gray. Whatever she was about to say took a back seat to Julian jogging down the cliff walk, shirtless. He wore huge headphones, shout-singing the wrong words to "Hooked On a Feeling" at the top of his voice.

He caught sight of us and waved like a five-year-old. He was all sweaty and glistening, and if I hadn't had such a glorious view of his chest yesterday, I might've fainted. We stepped to the side, and he hollered, "GOOD MORNING," his headphones throwing off enough "ooga chackas" to drown out the ocean.

My laughter came from somewhere deep. It rose up and up, until I couldn't hold it in.

Cate smiled, and then her smile cracked open, and she started laughing rather musically. "Well, after such an interlude, I don't know how to continue." The crinkly laugh lines around her eyes were inviting, joyful, and I dared to like Cate Collins for a moment.

"I've set Ryder up with a job in craft services. Food prep.

He'll be busy and involved, and under the supervision of Mr. Donato," she said. I opened my mouth to object to a stranger watching my brother for the next nine days, but Cate added, "He's a father of five, and he's already been approved by your dad to watch your brother."

"Ryder's going to mess up," I countered. "He can't even load the dishwasher, and when he gets frustrated, he throws tantrums like a toddler. You saw him last night."

"You have to trust him to take on more responsibility. Otherwise, he never will."

I could see the chaos now. Whole trays of food dumped on the ground. Water coolers doused with brain-numbing amounts of sugar. "All right. It's your production."

"It is," she said, mafia style. "As for you—"

"No cameo appearances. I'm not ending up as an Easter egg joke on some deleted scene."

She waved her hand in dismissal. "I have a problem you're uniquely qualified to help with." I don't know why, but I pictured Eamon. Was she going to make me help him with his lines? "Julian Young is a mess. When I finally got through to him that he's no one's love interest, he started playing Evyn as a pathetic child, which is just…" Her voice dwindled to a growl. "If he doesn't turn this around, I'll have to fire him."

I stopped walking. "You can't fire Julian! You've already filmed so many of his scenes!"

Cate kept going, and I had to jog to catch up. "I will do

what I need to do. I am directing this film and will not be bullied by any big-shot producer." The conviction in that sentence had little do with me. What was going on behind the scenes of *Elementia*, the major motion picture? "I want you to talk through his character with him, Iris. Make sure he understands the story."

"How? I don't even understand the story."

"Evyn—Julian's role—has been kidnapped by a damaged creature," she said. "You have some experience in that department."

I searched the horizon for a focal point—anything to avoid the sudden mental picture of Felix Moss. We were getting close to the pinnacle where the sun lit up a massive tree. Part of me wanted to say, *How dare you, Cate Collins*, but a larger part was relieved to be surrounded by people who didn't shy away from what had happened. They asked questions. They wanted me to face it. Which was…what, exactly? *Refreshing* definitely wasn't the right word.

"Will you do this?" Cate asked. "It'll mean quality time with Julian Young, which seems like something you're mighty interested in." I couldn't say she hadn't pinned me there.

I looked at Cate anew. She was short and so skinny the black spandex suit made her look like a luger. My gifted imagination now pictured the weight of this production across her shoulders. She was the new Atlas—a fantasy globe about to crush her. No matter my hang-ups and desire for this movie to disappear, I didn't want it to come at her expense. "I'll help Julian."

"Good." She took my shoulder with one hand. "And so you know, that boy is head over heels in love with some girl. Don't let him lead you on."

Crap.

"Men. Always keeping secrets," I said, a joke to cover my sudden letdown.

She sighed and seemed even more disappointed in me than ever. "This is why you have to read the books, Iris. Your father is wrong. The story isn't about punishing a king who makes a sexist choice. It's about a girl who discovers the sheer power of her courage."

"As if courage is that simple." Jaded Iris had come back strong, the words scalding my throat. "You can't order courage on Amazon Prime and simply unbox it." I thought about Grandma Mae. About me. "Some people have it. Some don't."

Cate Collins looked like I'd spit at her, and I waited for her to correct me. Scold me. Even say my name in that motherly way. But she didn't, and my dad's voice whispered, *Nice one, Iris.*

I couldn't tell if he was being sarcastic or not.

IF I'M BEING HONEST, I HAVE SOME INTEREST IN BEING HONEST

WHEN CATE AND I reached the great old tree, I gasped. The base was hollowed out while the ancient branches reached high and huge. Beautiful skeletal arms grasped for the heavens.

"Hello."

I jumped. Eamon stepped out from inside the tree with a grin on his face. The grin was aimed at me, and my body flushed with mixed signals. I felt like smiling back and turning around and sprinting away.

"Did you get a few shots with the sunrise?" Cate asked.

Eamon nodded. My eyes trailed down to his handheld camera, and I had a strong desire to toss it off the cliff. At least that squashed my crush for the moment.

"Design has been building this tree for eighteen months,"

Cate said to me. She knocked on the side and it made a hollow sound. Then she stepped inside and showed off the small living space within. "This is Maedina's home." I recognized it from Ryder's drawings. Cate stared lovingly. "Tonight we're going to burn it to the ground in one take."

"Why?" I asked, startled.

"Because that's what happens in the book. Sevyn can't control her affinity with lightning, and when she finds out that Maedina was the one to curse her, she calls down the mighty bolt."

That would probably be pretty cool on screen. I tried not to look too impressed.

Cate turned to Eamon. "You're the director right now. Tell me where."

"Ah, here?" He motioned to the gnarled roots. "I can get the tree and the ocean in the shot." Cate sat where Eamon had pointed, and Eamon set up his camera on a small tripod.

"Should I leave?" I asked.

Cate looked at me with those hard, blue eyes. "I think you should stay and hear the story of how your grandmother's books saved my life. Eamon is recording it for his blog series."

I laughed, falling headlong into one of my dad's favorite sayings. "The only way my grandma's books could save your life is if you were in a Wild West gun fight, and you had the book in your vest, and it stopped a bullet from entering your heart."

Eamon and Cate stared like I'd grown horns. "Not a morning person?" he asked.

"She's parroting her father's beliefs. Let's move forward."

How did she do that? I thought about storming off but didn't want to appear even more petulant.

Eamon started recording and scurried around the camera to sit beside Cate. "Here we are on gorgeous Inishmore with wonder director Cate Collins. Cate, *fáilte* and *go raibh maith agat.*"

"My pleasure," she said.

"You have said in several interviews that M. E. Thorne's Elementia books saved your life." Eamon tossed a brief but potent look at where I stood off camera. "Care to elaborate?"

"Well, twenty years ago when I started film school, becoming a female director was a pipe dream. They didn't seem to exist. And we don't even have to go that far back. Four years ago, a study showed that eighty-five percent of all movies released in 2014 had male directors. Eighty-five percent. The zeitgeist over the years about hiring more female directors is nice, but the thing about large-scale filmmaking is that you've got to earn your spot. You can't pluck a female director out of film school and hand her a half-a-billion-dollar project. Still…"

She paused, and I could tell that sharp, intelligent Cate Collins was debating what she would say next. She cracked a knuckle and kept going. "Peter Jackson directed five movies before his vision for the Lord of the Rings films was green-lit. I directed sixteen feature-length films before Vantage Pictures would meet with me about discussing the possibilities for an *Elementia* movie."

"That doesn't sound quite fair." Eamon's innocence shone when there was a camera on him. Maybe that's what had drawn Cate's eye during casting.

"My gran had a saying. *Fairness is fantasy.* That's rather apropos, come to think of it." Cate smiled; she wasn't looking at me, but it felt like she was. "But you were asking how the books saved my life. Well, in film school, I had a mentor, a wise, talented man who had been in Hollywood for decades. He has since passed."

"I'm sorry," Eamon said.

"Don't be. If he were still alive, I doubt I'd have the courage to tell this story." She rubbed her hands together. "Straight out of film school, he selected five of us as interns. I was honored because I was the first woman he'd ever picked. We all worked our asses off. For years. The boys kept getting promoted. They got their own productions. I did not. And one day, I marched into his office and demanded to know what I was doing wrong. He gave me a glass of water and asked me not to get hysterical—as if that were something I often did. 'You're the most passionate director I've ever met,' he said. 'But you're a woman, and the studios don't want women. They're too emotional. Too unstable. I'm sorry.'"

She paused. "So I quit."

Eamon had gone downright green, and she patted him on the knee. "I felt dead after that. I was broke and living on a friend's couch. She put a copy of *Elementia* in my face and said, 'This is a story about girls kicking butt. Read it.' And I did. And it inspired me to fight back."

"How?" Eamon asked. "What did you do?"

"The first thing I did was change the name on my résumé to C. Collins. Like M. E. Thorne or J. K. Rowling, I hid my gender with my initials, slipping past that hurdle. I immediately started getting calls from producers who assumed that the C was for Charles or Conor. After all, my résumé was impressive. Sometimes the producers were pleasantly shocked when I walked in the door. Sometimes they pretended like the position was already filled."

Cate turned her face toward the rising sun, basking in the gold glow. "I made ground an inch at a time, shooting indies for peanuts. Living on nothing. I kept going, like Sevyn. I didn't let anyone stop me, and I called down the lightning when I needed to. After all"—she turned, pinning me with her sharpest look—"courage is quite simple. First, be honest. Second, don't back down."

～

I slumped back to the trailer by myself only to find Ryder on the phone.

There was only one person he'd be talking with.

"Iris is back. Yeah, okay." He touched the mute button. "Dad wants to talk to you. He knows what happened, and he doesn't think we should come home."

"Okay." I took the phone.

"I don't want to leave either." He sat on the edge of his bed and tied his sneakers.

"Where do you think you're going, Ry?"

"I'm going to help the food people. Dad already said it's okay, so don't try to stop me." He slipped out the door like he did this sort of thing all the time, and I stood with the phone in my hand, racking up a bill I couldn't even imagine.

I touched the mute button to disengage it. "Hey, Dad."

"Your brother says you want to come home. I'm going to finish my draft in the next day or two. I'll fly there and take your place. You can come back."

What?

"Iris?"

"Well…" The words piled fast. "Cate gave me a job. I think I should see it through." Granted this was about Julian Young, but I also thought about Eamon sitting next to me on the picnic table last night, his shoulder bumping mine.

"Are you scamming money? The production is skin and bones, from what I hear."

"No, of course not!" I snapped. Dad didn't like it when I spoke sharply, and I pictured him in his pajamas—

writer's uniform—standing with the phone outstretched.
"Sorry."

He sighed, and I swear I felt it gust across the Atlantic.
"I'm about to finish my draft."

"Congratulations."

"Thanks. I'll come relieve you. I'm sorry I sent you into
that Thornian hell in the first place. Has Ryder been listening?"

Apart from getting lost and nearly dying yesterday?

"He got himself dressed this morning. No hassle." I reached
for the cup of toothbrushes by the tiny sink and felt Ryder's.
Wet. "He even brushed."

"You should email his therapist. Mark the achievement.
Or I can do it later." He paused for a long moment, and I
remembered that it was midnight back home.

"How's Mom?"

"She's still green. You're better with her than I am when
she's like this." *Green* was the term we used for the weeks
or months when Mom went into her greenhouse and didn't
come out. She had an apartment in there; she didn't need to
come out.

"I see." The situation now made sense. Dad was about
to finish, and Mom was in her own world. He was lonely.
"Maybe you could come see this with us. It's…something
else." What was coming over me? These words had not been
sanctioned by my brain's overthinking committee.

"Oh, don't go changing sides on me, Iris. You're my

literary-fiction girl. I raised you so I could have a nonfantasy ally in this damn family." This was a joke. Sort of. But it was also true, and for the first time, I didn't like that I'd been raised to be on his team.

I paced until I found my voice. "You know I'm not into elves and crap, but being here makes me wonder what was going on in Grandma Mae's head. How did she have the courage to write her guts into those stories? What if the world had hated it?"

"Your grandmother didn't care what people thought about her. Not even her son." My dad's voice was on the edge, and I held my breath. "Iris, she was a classic writer— whiskey and neglect. Don't need more of those in our lives, do we?"

"No." He didn't hear the edge in my voice. He never did. "You'll call back in a few days?" I asked. "When you're done?"

"Soon as I've sent my draft to my editor and the coast is clear."

The snippiness of his voice worried me. "Dad, are you staying off Goodreads?"

He almost growled. "Who reviews a book about a dead FBI tech director and gives it one star for..." I pictured him leaning forward, scrolling, quoting. "'Not having enough dogs and cats in it.' What is wrong with this world, Iris?"

He hung up before I could attempt an answer, which was in line with our longstanding relationship. He lobbed

questions like grenades, and I sat in the crater of the aftermath, pondering.

"What's wrong with this world, Dad?" I thought about
everything that had transpired since we arrived. "Enough to
need a fantasy one."

Ryder's—or my dad's—old copy of the Elementia trilogy
was still sitting next to my brother's pillow. I picked it up
and flipped to the last page. To the bio and headshot showing off Grandma Mae's long, dark hair and the eyes Eamon
hadn't been wrong about. They had a dark brightness to them
that felt bold beyond this world. But Eamon had been wrong
about me. Mine might have been the same color, but they
were flat and sad. My dad's eyes.

I pushed away the thoughts and read the short bio.

> *M. E. Thorne was born in San Francisco in 1945.*
> *She is the author of the Elementia trilogy. She lives*
> *in Ireland.*

Wait, she lived in Ireland?

AN IRISH INTERLUDE

OUTSIDE, THE MORNING sky was turning brilliantly blue. I went in search of breakfast and maybe to have a few words with Ryder. He'd been strange earlier—getting dressed and calling Dad all on his own. He'd even left without pleading with me to go with him.

A tall, angular man stood beside a griddle, popping silver dollar pancakes in the air. Apparently, this was Mr. Donato. Ryder stood next to him holding out a plate. He caught three in a row before he missed one, and I was about to speak up, but Mr. Donato's response was to toss a pancake onto Ryder's head. My brother's cheeks were bright red from laughing, and all I could think about was how he'd slapped himself last night. I'd made him snap.

Only Dad pushed him over the edge at home.

I grabbed a banana and sat at an empty picnic table with my empty thoughts.

"Hey, I've got something for you." Eamon appeared next to me like he actually did have sneaky elf powers. He held out a closed fist, and I put my cupped hand beneath it. He opened his fingers, and nothing but air appeared on my palms.

"Oh look, it's an excuse to talk with me," I said.

"Magic elf dust, Iris." He winked. "You have to believe in it to see it."

I pretended to sprinkle it on his head. "You need it more than I do. To help you get a comb through that hair." He pretended like he was offended, and I pushed his shoulder. Someone snorted behind us, and I turned to see Henrik with his dark glasses and floppy hat and clipboard.

"Something funny?" I asked.

"Yes. Puppies are hysterical." Henrik handed small pieces of paper to Eamon and me, our sides for the day. I noticed that Cate had already put Ryder's job on there. God, she was quick. My meeting with Julian was there as well.

"Why is my name stamped on this?" I asked Henrik.

"In case it gets leaked on the internet. Then we know it was your fault." He walked away, heading for Cate's trailer. It was identical to the others apart from a small Irish flag by the door.

"What's Henrik's story, Eamon? Cate and him are an unusual pairing. He's such a grump and she's so can-do."

Eamon shrugged, and I glanced at his T-shirt and jeans. He'd changed since the interview this morning. Now he looked like he'd fallen out of a 1990s music video—which reminded me that one of these days, I was going to see him in full makeup and costume. Acting. "When are you shooting scenes?"

"I've got a few more days. Still just enjoying the general splendor on set."

"And doing your blog series."

"Ah, yes. But I promise not to bring that up while you're around. I know how you feel about cameras." Now Eamon looked at his side. "What are you doing with Julian Young?"

I leaned in. "I've been assigned a special mission: make Julian Young a better actor."

"You're going to need that magic dust then." Eamon leaned in too, and his crazy hair brushed my forehead. "So you're staying around after all?"

"Don't get too smug about it." We were oddly close, and I studied him. He was cuter today than yesterday. Some boys were like that. One day they were sort of odd, and the next they had noses and grins and eyes that seemed manufactured in a *fall for me* factory.

"Do I look strange?" He wiped his mouth, a dash of shyness making him even cuter.

"No, you look like you."

"I do work hard at that," he said.

Ryder shrieked gleefully, sending laughter through the

line of hungry crew members. Huh, my brother didn't need me, which meant I was free, which was weird. "According to the side, I have hours before I meet with Julian. What should we do, Eamon?"

Eamon's face lit up. "We could go down to the quay. Or the sweater market."

I lifted an eyebrow. "Really? That's what you've got?"

"What would you want to do?"

Oddly enough, I found myself thinking about the scene I'd read to Ryder. About the cliff and the remains of Manifest. "Did you know that my grandmother lived in Ireland?"

"I did. Did you know that she came to this very island many times? I've got a picture of her up at Dun Aengus."

I blinked at him. "What? How?"

He swung his backpack off his shoulder and pulled out a torn-up biography titled *M. E. Thorne: A Legacy in Magic & Grief*. I knew biographies about my grandmother existed. The doctoral candidates always came knocking, and my dad loved giving them "the real story" that he wouldn't tell me, but I'd never been close to one before. I poked it with a wary finger. "Why do you have this? Oh no, you're one of those die-hard Thornians, aren't you?"

"It's research for my role," he said. He flipped to the middle of the book, to the glossy chunk of pages containing all the pictures, and then held one out to me. It was a gorgeous picture of Grandma Mae. She was maybe forty. Smiling at the camera with her long, black hair blowing out around her. Her toes were on the very edge of a cliff drop.

"I wonder who she was smiling at," Eamon said. "Your grandfather?"

"Not likely. They never married. My dad barely knew him."

"Who then?"

I shrugged. "I don't know anything about her. My dad says it's not my business."

"You could read this." Eamon held out the book, but I leaned back.

"Would you want to find out all the ugly things in your family's past from a book?"

He shook his head; at least he understood. "But then how do you know they're ugly?"

"Because I'm not dumb," I muttered. I looked at the picture again. "This is here?"

"That's Dun Aengus," Eamon said. "The fort we saw from the ferry."

"You mean Manifest?" I asked.

"Yeah." His grin sparked. "You want to see it? You can stand where she stood."

I leaped up. "Let's go."

⁓

A half hour later, I was breathing like a beast, seriously

doubting this decision. I was riding the oldest purple bike known to man, and we were in the middle of nowhere, stuck on a low-grade incline. All around, the green land was set into patches by crumbling stone walls.

"Is it…uphill…forever?" I called out.

Eamon was a few yards ahead, riding his rusty bike with ease. "There." He pointed toward the top of a great hill, the backside of the ancient fort we'd seen the day we'd arrived. We kept pedaling until the road dead-ended and then parked our bikes. Eamon pointed up the grassy slope. "Dun Aengus. Three thousand years old!"

"Dun Aengus." I struggled with the pronunciation. "Is that Gaelic?"

"No. That's the English version."

"Is it really that great? It looks like a cliff and a bunch of strategic rock piles."

"It is really that great," he said without missing a beat. He started climbing and I followed, glad I had put on my hiking boots. "I've been thinking we should get to know each other better, Iris, so I've sorted out a question for a musician. What's your top song?"

"My what?" I asked. "Do you mean my favorite? I don't have a favorite song."

"Rubbish. Everyone should have a favorite. It's says so much about a person. Tells you where their heart is."

"My heart is in my chest."

"There's that comedic literalness I've come to admire, but what else have you got inside you?" He stopped climbing the hill and faced me.

I nearly bumped into him. "What's your favorite?"

"I was hoping you'd ask." He pulled out his phone and started a track.

I recognized the bass rhythm, shaking my head. "Oh no. Queen?!"

"Freddie *and* Bowie. Pure magic." Eamon bobbed his head and sang "Under Pressure." It had been a while since I'd given the song an honest listen, and it actually was better than I remembered.

We kept climbing, this time our steps set to music. When the song ended with its odd finger snapping, I glanced at Eamon, which was starting to get tricky. Maybe I was growing used to his face, but every time I looked at him, I liked him more. "So what is that song supposed to tell me about you?"

"I suppose that I'm old fashioned, like the tune. And I'm great under pressure. Mam says it's my superpower. No matter how crazy things get, I'm groovy."

I tried not to giggle. "Groovy, huh? You're definitely old fashioned." We were nearly at the top, searching the outer wall for a doorway.

"You should have a favorite song, Iris. You could always change it. I hear it's a fine acting tip. Always have favorites. It means you can make decisions on your feet."

I laughed. "That sounds like the first terrible acting tip that comes up when you google 'How to act.'" It was a joke, but Eamon looked away. Was he embarrassed? "I didn't mean—"

"No, you've caught me. I searched 'how to act.' I'm a phony. Never been in an audition or even a school play before this." For a moment I thought he was kidding. His bleak expression proved otherwise.

"Wow." I tried not to sound too surprised. "It's, uh, exciting you've won such a breakthrough role."

"We'll see." He frowned, his hair covering his eyes like a cloud. "Maybe I'll fail then."

Oh God, I'd sunk the grinning, adorable, self-professed "great under pressure" guy in a few minutes. Maybe that was my superpower. Jaded Iris, a villain.

"'Rabbit Heart,'" I blurted. "By Florence and the Machine. That's my favorite."

"I know that song." He pushed his hair back to look at me. "I did not have you pegged for drama rock, Iris Thorne." I charged ahead, and he called out, "Hey! That's a fantasy song. Like kings and magic. And gold!"

I ducked through the narrow doorway of the prehistoric fort. Now I could see why this place was perfect for filming make-believe. The horizon dashed across the sky, green on blue meeting in swift, stark lines.

"Tell me something I don't know about Ireland," I said because I was staring at the scenery like I was in love, and I didn't want Eamon to ask if the beauty had got me again. "As an American, what should I know that I don't?"

"Quit saying 'Gaelic.' The language is called Irish. *Gaelic* is the Irish word for *Irish*." Maybe he could tell that I was confused because he added, "That would be like calling German '*Deutsche*.' Everyone says German. Right?"

"Okay. I'll spread the word." I paused, amused by his abrupt candor. "Can you say something in Irish?"

"What? No."

"Why not?"

He leaned toward my face and squinted. It was too cute. "Because I'm not a performing leprechaun." I turned, mostly to hide the way he made me smile, and walked toward the cliff's edge. "Also because I remember an embarrassingly small amount from primary school," he added.

"I was pretty impressed this morning," I said.

"What'd you think about all that?" he asked, making me suddenly nervous. "About Cate's interview and all that sexist shite she goes through with the film industry?"

"I think she was trying to get to me," I muttered.

"What?"

"Nothing." I didn't want to tell him that Cate made me itch. All of her "fist-up, face-up, and fight" feminism wasn't my style. Or maybe it wasn't allowed to be. Her words trickled through my thoughts. *Courage is simple. First, be honest. Second, don't back down.*

Flawed logic, my dad whispered. *Honesty is complex.*

We approached the cliff's edge, and I gasped. The height of the fall was grand, and the surf below was so far away that the waves were a solid heartbeat ahead of the crashing. I couldn't even get within five feet of the drop, scared that the wind might reach up and steal me.

Eamon held up his phone. "Can I take your picture like hers? We can put them side by side."

"No way. You'll say it won't ever end up on the internet, but it will at some point, and then I'll have to hate you and send my lawyer after you."

"So severe, Iris Thorne," he teased. "Here I was, wanting a picture to remember you by since you're going to vanish from my life in a week like an elven princess."

I held down a smile. "Very smooth. Nerdy, but smooth." At least now Eamon was blushing too. "Okay, you can take the picture, but this is a big deal. Remember that."

I thought about my grandmother's image, her hair blowing back. I untied my ponytail. The drop was still a yard away and already terrifying. I took a step. Then another.

When I was a foot from the edge, Eamon said, "That's close enough. I'm no small amount frightened for you."

"She was standing on the edge. *Toes* on the edge." I felt the wind sweep up the cliff, but I stepped forward again, sick of being afraid.

You're going to fall, Jaded Iris.

"Just tell me I can do it for once," I said to that dad voice, inching closer.

"You can," Eamon replied. "I believe in you, but please don't die in front of me today. Seventy years from now, sure. But not before my big-screen debut."

"Don't make me laugh!"

Another two inches…

When my toes reached the edge, I shrieked. "Take the picture! Take the picture!"

Eamon fumbled with his phone, and then I was smiling at him like Grandma Mae had smiled at whomever took her picture.

"Got it."

I collapsed backward, grateful when Eamon's hands were on both of my arms, pulling me to the ground. I flattened myself on the hard rock, shaking. And laughing. Eamon fell over beside me. "My heart is storming!" he yelled. "That was awful stupid!"

I laughed even harder and stared at the sky. Security and gravity came back with each slow, pounding heartbeat. When I felt like I had finally returned from my conversation with mortality, I looked at the picture Eamon took. "But I look scared," I said. "She looked so bold."

"She had a few years on you." He sat up and looked down at where I lay. It felt a little like he was trying to read between my lines, searching for whatever I wasn't saying.

He really needed to stop doing that; I was getting used to it.

"You were right, Eamon." I sat up, taking in the way the ancient fort made the very sky and ground feel timeless. "This really is that great."

QUALITY TIME WITH JULIAN YOUNG

THAT AFTERNOON, JULIAN and I sat shoulder to shoulder on an epic white sand beach before crystal-blue waves. He wore his incredible black leather jacket and dark sunglasses, which helped to balance out the Frodo wig, fantasy urchin clothes, and makeup that made his cheekbones stand out like wings.

He pointed to where the crew was setting up the scene, putting down tracks on the beach for the camera. Henrik was directing the setup. "Things must not be going well. Cate should be back from the other location by now. And look." He nodded toward the production vans where a woman stood with a notepad. "Reporter. I can smell them a mile away."

I squirmed and pulled my hair over my face.

"If she comes around, say 'off the record.' That's the magic phrase with these people, but you have to say it before you say something, not after. And she doesn't have a camera. Cate would eat her if she did. Come to think of it, she must have permission to be here. Something is up." He sighed and stared between his knees. "Down to business. Cate thinks I'm messing up my character, doesn't she?"

I answered his question by not answering it. "She thinks I can help, but I don't know."

"The real problem is that I should be Nolan," he said. "That's a great role! All my best reviews are when I'm the romantic lead. Who is Eamon O'Brien anyway? I mean, I like the guy, but do you think he can act?"

I shrugged. Picturing Eamon as the love interest did feel odd. What was he going to do? Seduce Sevyn with his scrappy hair? I pictured Shoshanna kissing Eamon and got sort of angry. "Maybe it's not supposed to be romantic. They were thirteen-year-olds in the book."

"Only in the first novel. They grow up a lot in the second and third. If those sequels stay green-lit, Shoshanna and Eamon are going to have to get *physical*."

My brain flatlined, unable or unwilling to picture it. "Let's focus on Evyn," I said. "On you. What's Evyn's emotional journey?" Writing-craft talk. My dad had primed me for this conversation from the womb. "Tell me how you see it."

Julian took his side out from his jacket, flipping through

his lines. "Evyn's born weak, blessed with fire but sickly. Unlike Sevyn, who sends bolts of lightning after people every five minutes. Evyn's power draws the attention of the bad elves. One of them—Byers—abducts Evyn and takes him to the Blackened Wastes of Thornbred."

"The blackened what?"

"I know." Julian took off his sunglasses, his green-brown eyes piercing. "Honestly, I don't get Evyn's reaction. He gets abducted but doesn't try to escape or fight back! I have nothing to work with. He should at least be terrified. I can do fear, but Cate says I'm misreading the heart of the character."

"Let me see." I took his script and read.

Ext. Elementia Beach
BYERS flies across the water on dark wings. He's a divided creature, part-elf, part-eagle. His elven parts are attractive but sinister, his torso and head very human. His skin is ivory, but occasionally pulses with black veins. His hands and feet sport talons and dark feathers, and he's carrying an unconscious EVYN by the arms.

They have been flying since Byers pulled Evyn through the waterfall, and Byers drops Evyn on the sand. Evyn doesn't stir. Byers collects

driftwood and starts a small fire. He pokes
Evyn awake. Evyn sits up, confused.

I looked out to sea. Byers was the character who reminded Ryder of Felix Moss.

"What…" I rubbed my eyes, my throat dry. "Who is going to play this creature?"

"CGI. My whole scene this afternoon is me talking to a tennis ball on a stick while someone reads Byers's lines off camera. If only we could afford Andy Serkis and his magic suit."

I looked back at the script, but when I started reading again, I didn't picture Julian. I saw Ryder trembling before Moss.

                    EVYN
          (stammering)
          Are you going to hurt me?

Byers shows Evyn the flames he built.

                    BYERS
          For you. Can I call you Fire,
          Little Fire?

Evyn edges closer to the fire and eyes his
abductor.

                    EVYN
Do you want to know my real name?

                    BYERS
Names are dangerous, Little Fire.

                    EVYN
You are dangerous. You are a
mighty predator.

                    BYERS
(cocks his head, amused)
You speak truth. I will give you
my name, but you mustn't use it
against me. You may know me as
Byers.

Evyn reaches into the fire, letting the flames
grow up his arm. The light and heat builds,
and Evyn breathes easier. Byers is entranced.

                    EVYN
Come sit with me, Byers.

                    BYERS
(cringing)

Can't maneuver a sit. Only stand
or fall.

*Evyn looks over the creature. Byers's bird-
like qualities have given him no waist, and he
crouches. His eyes are drawn to the pointed
elf ears. Byers shuffles closer, watching Evyn
move his hand through the flames.*

BYERS
You are torn in two. Like me.

EVYN
(startled)
What do you mean?

BYERS
Like me, yes. You are a boy and more.

EVYN
You are a boy and more?

BYERS
I am more and more.
(sad)
And less and less.

                    EVYN
What do you want from me?

                    BYERS
A warm friend, Little Fire. I am
tired of cold. I miss the heat of
the fires that made me. And I will
not feed on you, I won't. I will
tell you about the world, and you
will tell me I am right.

                    EVYN
Are you taking me to Thornbred? To
the burned forest?

                    BYERS
(pained)
Do not speak of such destructions.
They will hear you, and they are
angry. They will feed on you,
little human. They will drain you,
and I will be cold, and alone.

*Evyn straightens, attempts to be as commanding
as his father, the king, or his bold, harsh
sister.*

                    EVYN
          (nobly)
          Take me home, Byers. I demand it.

Byers's face scrunches, and his veins pulse
darkly, drawing a spiderweb netting across his
complexion. He bares his sharp teeth.

                    BYERS
          Bloodsuckers, demons. You are mine!

"I forgot there were vampire creatures in this story," I said,
although I hadn't. I didn't have the luxury of forgetting after
Moss had screamed, "Let me drink his blood!" while the cops
cuffed him to the ambulance's stretcher. During the following
weeks, Ryder had acted like Moss was a monster coming for
him at any moment. His therapist had my dad read the books to
him as a first step—and then we'd all gone to the institution so
Ryder could see Moss, a schizophrenic fanboy. I went as well,
watching my brother develop a strange bond with his would-be
abductor as they discussed their favorite parts of Elementia.

Afterward, Ryder was relieved. "Moss isn't scary. He
loves the trilogy like me."

Julian had his phone out, but for once, he wasn't texting.
He was watching me. "You went to a dark place when you
read that," he said. "Your face got very old."

"I'm sure that was attractive."

Julian mimicked my dark look as though he were adding it to his acting library. "One reviewer said I look like I'm forty when I act sad. That's why I took this fantasy role. It was supposed to be light and fun." He dragged a hand through his hair and his bicep popped. "But I have to be honest with you. This feels like a career ender. Shoshanna is starting to think so too." He looked at the time on his phone. "We're an hour off again."

My dad's voice reminded me that this was what I'd wanted only yesterday. For the movie to fall apart. How did I feel now? I didn't even know. "But you said *Alien Army* seemed that way, and it turned out great."

"Yeah, well, *Alien Army* didn't have to worry about fans with ridiculously high expectations. The people you call Thornians? They hate the movie already. They've been blowing up my Twitter with asshole comments, and they *hate* Cate Collins. Everything is always her fault."

"Oh. That is bad." I glanced over at the crew, working hard to make sure that the shot was ready for when Cate arrived. "I hope she proves them wrong."

Do you? my dad's voice asked, but I ignored him.

I held out Julian's script. "Cate's right. You don't need fear for this. Evyn's not afraid of Byers. They have too much in common. They're both misunderstood. Lonely. Sick."

"But how do I play that? How do I have something in

common with a CGI creature?" Julian bit his lip and squinted, deep in thought. It was his most honest look to date, and I found myself thinking about Cate's prescription for courage. Honesty first, then, follow-through.

"Julian, you have to pretend like you're acting with yourself."

"Really?"

"I think so."

Cate Collins arrived, and the crew buzzed with action. I watched her inspect the shot and make adjustments. It was strange to think of the Thornians turning on her. I'd thought she'd be their fan club president. She was fearless. She'd strut to the edge of Dun Aengus just like Grandma Mae, no problem.

Henrik called, "Last looks!" and Julian stood up, texting again.

I brushed the sand off my butt and decided to go for it. "Julian, do you have a girlfriend?"

"Did someone say I did?" He put his phone away fast. "Off the record," he added as if I were a reporter, "Elora's not my girlfriend. She's my fiancée." His grin shone twenty watts brighter than I'd ever seen. "Wow, it feels great to say that aloud. Shoshanna knows too. Although really, don't tell anyone."

I surprised myself by having zero jealousy. "Why is it a secret?"

"Elora doesn't want the attention. My fans are intense."

"I understand that." I stared at the jeweled water, waves cresting white. Henrik hollered again, and I added, "Remember, you're talking to yourself. Your saddest self."

"Got it." Julian squeezed my shoulder and headed over to Roxy and her makeup case. I watched him take off his sunglasses and leather jacket, turning into waifish, starved Evyn.

Cate caught eyes with me across the beach. She nodded as if she already knew that I'd done something good. I hoped she was right.

BURN, BABY, BURN FANTASY INFERNO

MY THIRD GOLDEN sunset in Ireland found me alone, which might not seem noteworthy except that I was never alone. Ryder was still helping craft services, the crew was preparing for the one-take burn of Maedina's tree on the pinnacle, Eamon was somewhere being Eamon—and I was playing Annie on the cliff walk I'd pioneered with Cate that morning.

I sat on the rocky edge, the gravel beach only ten feet below. Not too scary this time, but not negligible either. Baby steps.

Yesterday I'd told Eamon that I wanted to play my guitar where no one could hear me. No responsibilities, no elves. Strangely enough, I had the first part—and I already wanted to make an exception for the second, as long as it was a scrappy, fast-talking Eamon elf.

For once, I didn't feel like strumming an energetic, belting song. I warmed my hands and tuned, discovering a lovely fingerpicking pattern that made me feel like an honest-to-God songwriter. I tried to put words to it, but they weren't there yet, so I sang the notes. Slow and quiet at first, but then I let the melody out.

All around me, Ireland felt like a private world. No people. A few gulls. The wind tugged at my braid and fishing boats dotted the bluest horizon. Some part of me felt at home here, and that had me reaching for Grandma Mae. For my sole memory of her, walking in the park by our house. My dad had refused to come, and she'd held my hand, which made me nervous because I didn't know her.

I changed two notes in my fingerpicking pattern, and the song brightened and filled with sadness—the good kind, not the messy, pent-up stuff. It made me smile and hum my nonwords a little louder. *What is this song about? Being alone. Cut free from all of this nonsense.*

I thought about Eamon's childhood portal-searching. I wish I'd told him that I'd felt like that too, and the way he'd described being small and lonely had kissed a nerve. Particularly his *The Subtle Knife* reference. I wanted to tell him I loved Will and Lyra, but that love was buried so far down in the muck of my regrets I'd never be able to bring it to the surface.

Eamon said fantasy stories were about helping people

connect to reality, not bury it or escape it. But then, when it came to the Thorne family, I didn't even know what was buried. And when it came to me, I didn't know how to ask for anything except escape.

⌇

That night, I stood near the pinnacle as the crew prepared to burn the massive fake tree. The wind whipped cold off the black water, and I was downright excited. I hadn't actually watched the cameras roll yet.

Tonight I would.

Everyone was charged. The whole "one-take" deal was more pressure than I could have imagined, and the hustle and bustle of the crew was nervously wired. I stood back and watched it all unfold, worrying something might go wrong and that the cost of remaking the tree would bankrupt the production. Not that I wanted that to happen, but I couldn't stop my imagination from going there. Did anyone else see the worst-case scenario in everything? Or was this a Jaded Iris specialty?

The crew set up a perimeter for fire safety. Ryder ran by, and I grabbed his elbow. "There's a cliff right there and thousands of wires on the ground. I don't want you to move when they light that tree up, you hear me?"

He tugged away. "Yes, mother!"

I froze. In all my years of taking care of Ryder, he'd

never pulled that one on me. Before I could respond, Eamon approached, filming the behind-the-scenes with his little camera.

"Don't worry. I've not got you on video," he said, staring through the screen.

"Are you really making these videos to boost fan support?" I asked, my voice rough from trying to hastily pull it together after Ryder's stunning outburst.

"Cate says we need the Thornians to band together as soon as possible."

"Julian said they're banding together against the film," I said. "I'd like to smack them."

"Careful, Iris Thorne. Someone might think you're pulling for us to succeed." He winked sassily and shut his camera with a sigh. "The studio could cancel the film at any time. Send it straight to DVD or sell it to the Syfy channel. Right now it looks like the sequels will get axed."

Ryder gasped. "They couldn't! The first book is only the beginning of the story!"

"They've done it before." Eamon's tone was stiff. "Look at *The Golden Compass*."

"When do you…get your big break?" I asked.

He dropped his camera in his bag. "We're moving lock, stock, and barrel to Killykeen Forest tomorrow. That's where I'll have my first scene."

"Nervous?" I asked.

He glanced at me and quirked a tight smile. "What do you think?"

"I think you are," I murmured. They were dousing the tree with flammable liquid, and I got a bad feeling. It had to do with the whip of the wind and the grass field all around... but a costumed woman eclipsed all of that. I hadn't seen her since that first day, and up close, I couldn't believe the nerve of Cate Collins.

"You've got to be kidding me." I pointed at the woman. She had long, dark hair and a face I'd recognize anywhere— and not because she was a famous actress.

"That's Maedina. I mean, her real name is Nell Waterson," Eamon said. "Classically trained and used to West End. I think Alec Guinness was more comfortable cruising around with a wookiee than she is in that getup."

"Doesn't she look familiar?" I asked.

He shrugged. "She looks a little like M. E. Thorne. Like you."

"A little?" I asked. "It looks like Cate Collins scoured the planet for my grandmother's doppelgänger. This is too far!"

"Why? It's *Mae*dina. You think your grandmother didn't name a character after herself? That's got to be on purpose. Look"—he motioned to Ryder's nodding—"he agrees with me because he's read the books."

"You get your pretty from Grandma Mae, Iris," Ryder piped in. "That's what Dad says."

"He's right," Eamon said, and for once I didn't mind the connection. I might've even enjoyed it.

Henrik called for "Quiet on the set!" and everyone turned to stone. Even Ryder.

Shoshanna stepped out of a group of people who had been fussing over her makeup. She looked like a fantasy refugee, all wraps of cloth and wild hair. They started in the middle of a scene, Shoshanna—Sevyn—charging out of the tree before Maedina.

"You ruined me!" Sevyn yelled. "And then you tried to take me in like a pet." A foghorn blared and the actresses glanced at the sky, imagining the CGI lightning we'd been promised.

"I never meant to hurt you. Not when you were a babe or now. There is much you don't know." Maedina glanced around. "We're not alone. You must sense that."

Maedina reached for her, and Shoshanna screamed like a feral creature. I had to admit it; the girl was good. Anger sparked from her skin without digital enhancements.

A searing flash dazzled my eyes, and when I'd blinked away the brightness, the tree was already burning. It lit up the actresses, who dashed away. It lit up the branches and the cliff's edge, and then far below, it drew an orange halo on the dark water. The fire grew and cackled and surged into the sky, and I looked around at the delighted faces of a hundred people.

On my left, Ryder's joy was pure wonder, and on my right, Eamon was boyishly charmed. He glanced at me, and

I waited for the smile. A smile always came with him. Only this time, his lips stayed still, and I felt his fingers slip against mine.

And then we were holding hands. Together. In front of everyone. Only no one was looking, and we both turned back to the blaze. Sort of. I watched him out of the corner of my eye. He stood close; he always did. Was that an Eamon thing or a liking-me thing?

"Cut!" rang through the night, and as fast as the fire had caught, it burned out. A huge hose appeared, dumping foam over the brittle remains of the tree. White floodlights replaced the orange madness, and the crew cheered when they checked the gate and announced success.

I stole my hand back from Eamon before anyone noticed.

"I've got to help Mr. Donato hand out cake!" Ryder said, but I held on to him before he could scamper away. "Listen and don't mess anything up," he said for me. "I know! That's all you ever say."

My brother stomped off, and I stared after him. "He's mad at me."

"He's mad at you," Eamon agreed.

"He's never been mad at me before. Not like this."

Eamon didn't hold back. "You embarrassed him last night when you yelled at him in front of everyone."

"He scared the crap out of me! And this is a ridiculous double standard. If I were his real mom, no one would question how I parent him." My mouth hung open after the last word, stunned.

Eamon wasn't fazed. "Come with me," he said. I started to object, and he continued. "You're going to say you can't because you've got to keep an eye on Ryder, but he's doing his job now and he needs some space, and so do you, so come with me and see what I found today because I think it'll delight your musician's heart."

My nerves lit up like that tree and not in a bad way either. "I think that's the most Irish you've ever sounded."

"You liked it," he quipped.

I did.

Eamon led me down the cliff walk until the celebratory sounds of the crew died away in favor of the rushing surf over gravel. He walked ahead, and the floodlights ebbed until his back and shock of hair sealed into one lean shadow.

"Eamon, are you going to move to LA?" I called out.

"Why would I do that?" He looked back over one shoulder.

"Because you're going to be a famous actor when this comes out. Don't you want to do other movies? LA is the heart of film."

"I haven't thought that far out." He waited for me, and I took a few hurried steps to catch up. "Iris, will you play guitar for me if I promise not to say anything?"

"I don't play in front of people."

"Never? Why?"

I sighed. "That's how you lose control. My dad loves each and every story he writes. Loves them fiercely. Then he sends them to his editor who comes back with notes, and then my dad starts hating them. He doesn't even open the boxes of finished copies when they arrive anymore."

"That's awful sad, Iris, but that's your da. Not you."

"You don't know how similar we are. It's like a curse." I honestly couldn't believe I'd said the words. They were too fantasy. Too true.

Eamon dug his hands in his pockets, and we walked in silence.

"How was your date with Julian Young?" he asked out of the blue.

Hello, jealousy.

"I never said it was a date. I was helping him for Cate. Besides, Julian has a fiancée." I clapped a hand over my mouth. "I wasn't supposed to tell anyone."

"Oh, I've known since I met him. What's the American saying? He's losing his religion."

"If that's American, it's not from my side of America. You mean that old REM song?"

"Means he's so far gone on this girl he'd lose his religion for her. My best friend Charlie went Protestant for his lady." He looked at me. "Have you ever done that?"

"Gone Protestant? No way. The Thornes are strict atheists."

He cringed. "No, I mean, go wild for someone."

Was he asking if I'd ever been in love? I shook my head, feeling sort of strange.

"So no one back home should object to my feelings for you?"

I shook my head one more time, dazed.

"Grand." With that, he disappeared.

Gone.

"Eamon!" Good grief, had our relationship talk literally pushed him off the cliff? I sunk down to my hands and knees to look over the edge.

He was scaling down the rocks to the beach. "There are steps here. A bit. Come on, girl."

ELEMENTIA
A FAMILY HISTORY?

I CLIMBED DOWN the rock wall to the beach, my shoes crunching on the wet gravel.

Eamon was sitting on a large rock in a hollow space, the cliff yawning up and over us. "I think I found a portal to another world this afternoon." He tapped his ear and gestured to the way the waves hummed inside the cliff's overhang. "It's even got music."

I sat beside him and realized I was staring at his soft profile a little too obviously. I turned to the black glass of the water, tiny slivers of white moonlight reflecting on the surface. There was no way around it; I was developing a crush. And to date, my crushes had, well, *crushed* me.

Plus, they made for very bad songs.

"Tell me why Sevyn ended up in Elementia," I asked. "What happens before chapter fourteen?"

His smirk drew a tiny shadow on his chin. "Do I start at the beginning?"

"Give me the abridged version. We don't have all night."

"I bet we do." His words made my chest swell, and then I kind of wanted to smack him for being slick. Or for getting away with it. "That was so smooth!" he said, breaking the moment and making me laugh.

I bumped my shoulder into his, lingering a tiny bit. "Get on with it."

When Eamon spoke again, he used that low, storyteller voice that made him sound older. "It's starts off a familiar story. On an island called Cerul, off the coast of a cursed land, a medieval people have a monarchy, complete with king and queen and castle. They also have an island to the north run by a monastery of women who worship the elements. The Draemon. It's more than worship. They harness individual elements into—"

"Orbs. You're going to say orbs. It's not a ridiculous fantasy without orbs."

"Say orb once more."

"Orb." I laughed, and he moved his leg closer until our knees kissed.

"They can harness energy into…round balls of concentrated power…and gift them to the heir to the throne. Which is why the king can control the wind. He's also knocked up his wife, and she gives birth to a large, healthy girl. And a runt of a boy. The queen dies giving birth because it's not a ridiculous fantasy without the queen dying while giving birth to twins."

"Naturally."

"The Draemon come to bless the new heir with fire, only the king refuses to acknowledge his daughter, choosing his sickly son instead, even though the girl was born first."

"That's bullshit."

"It is." He turned to face me, crossing his legs under him and looking delighted. "When they're doing the ritual, one of the teen Draemon, a supremely gifted girl, is up in the tower with the baby Sevyn, and she's pissed about the sexism. She tries to do the ritual to bless Sevyn with fire, only she calls down the lightning. From that day on, Sevyn can't be touched. She's pure energy."

I thought back to the tree and Sevyn screaming. "The girl Draemon was Maedina."

"Well spotted. But that's later. We're still on Cerul. When the head Draemon, Bronwyn, finds out what Maedina did, she tries to help Sevyn but gets struck." He clapped his hands, and I jumped. "Dead. Maedina is horrified and disappears. Sevyn is labeled a killer and spends the next thirteen years in the tower except for visits from Evyn. And that's where the story begins."

He paused, and I stared. "You mean this was all backstory?"

"No, no. Prologue."

"Fantasy," I cursed. "Okay, how does she end up on the boat?"

"When the twins turn thirteen, there's this big ceremonial ritual. The prince is supposed to use his elemental gift to catch a special deer that's been marked by the king. A passing of the torch sort of thing. Evyn, who is still sickly and can't do much with fire, ventures into the wood, but Sevyn busts out of her tower and sneaks into the woods too, determined to win back her rightful spot as heir. She finds the deer first, and there's this scene where she touches it."

I was tempted to laugh, but Eamon's face was too serious. "She touches it?"

"Yeah, remember she can't touch people, but she figures out how to control her feelings and touches the deer, and it's nothing short of beautiful. And then her brother scares her and—"

I grabbed Eamon's hand to stop another clap. He laced his fingers with mine, and my head rushed. *Well that's plain cheesy*, my dad's voice broke in.

Don't care, I said right back.

"You're a little bold with the hand-holding, Eamon."

"Am I now?" Cue mischievous grin. "You don't seem alarmed."

I definitely wasn't alarmed, but I wasn't cool and calm either. Every time his fingers tightened around mine, I felt a bit overcharged. "So…she kills the deer?" I redirected, hearing the nervousness in my own voice.

Eamon nodded. "It's awful. She runs away behind this waterfall. Evyn follows her, feeling rightly wretched, but before they can make up, a sinister hand comes through the water and grabs him. Evyn vanishes from Cerul, and no one believes Sevyn. Her father and the whole kingdom think she killed her brother. The king banishes her to the Draemon's island, only she hijacks the boat and ends up in Elementia, looking for her brother for the rest of the story."

"Does she find him?"

"You'll have to read to find out."

I pushed him in the shoulder. "You know I won't do that."

"Suit yourself." He stole the hand that pushed him and now we were double holding hands. His head dipped into the space between us, face hidden by his wild hair, as if he were nervous too, and I couldn't stop staring over the line of his neck to his ears.

"Iris, do you ever wonder how much literature resembles real life?" Eamon asked, starling me out of daydreaming about lips on skin. "Like with your dad's twin sister, Samantha?"

My ears popped like my mind had tuned itself. "*Samantha? My aunt? They weren't twins.*"

"According to my biography of M. E. Thorne, she had twins. Michael and Samantha."

I felt a little snarled inside. "Why didn't my dad tell me he had a twin?"

Eamon bit his bottom lip. "I feel like I shouldn't have said that."

"What else don't I know about my own family?" I asked. He shook his head.

"Well, I know she's dead. She died when she was a kid. Sick from birth." I sat up. "Cystic fibrosis." I'd heard my dad begrudgingly talk about how we had CF in the family with my pediatrician, but I'd never put it together until now.

Eamon nodded, so still and silent that my feelings burst. "I hate that he doesn't trust me to know any of this! It's like he's the asshole king father, and I'm Sevyn locked up in my bedroom with a guitar and permanent babysitting gig." I looked at my hands, woven with Eamon's. "But I'm touchable. I'm not Sevyn."

"Not by half. You're your own kind of power." He risked a smile. "But angry, ambitious Shoshanna? That was good casting."

My mind slipped back to the scene on the pinnacle. To a cursed girl who burns down that tree simply by screaming out her pain. "The feminist answer to Tolkien indeed, Cate," I murmured. "Eamon, why is that tree so special?"

"It's Maedina's mother," Eamon said. "Maedina is part elf. And the elves are in the trees. The trees are the elves. Sevyn runs after the fire and ends up lost in the woods." He brought our conjoined hands to his chest to point at himself with both thumbs. "That's where I come in."

"Wait, you're a tree?" I laughed. "What kind? Poison oak?"

"That's a vine, but yeah, I'm a tree. Definitely oak or ash, aged and mighty."

What a ridiculous boy, and yet I could see why Cate thought he'd make a great love interest. He couldn't help but be his earnest, mischievous self, no matter what. Eamon smiled at me with such an intense expression that I couldn't help but stare at his lips. "I'm going to ask you for a favor now, Iris Thorne. And I don't want you to say no straight-away, per your usual candor."

"No," I said. He gave me a pleading, sweet look and tugged me closer.

Holy crap, he's going to ask to kiss me.

My lips tasted salty, and my pulse sped. "Okay…what?"

"Will you be on my video blog?"

I blinked long and hard, my brain coming back from kissing daydreams with sluggish effort. "*What?*"

"Please? It could help us so much."

"Help *us*? The movie, you mean?" I pulled my hands from his, growling, "Oh, I get it. You want video of me smiling on set so all the fans think M. E. Thorne's family is on board, huh?"

"Well, it was Cate's idea. And it didn't sound half so bad before you said it in that Lex Luthor tone of voice."

"Did she tell you to flirt with me too? Did she tell you that'd make it easier to convince me?" The words sounded angry, but all I could feel was pain. It pulled every muscle tight and made each breath prick at my throat. I got off the rock, dropping straight into knee-high water. The tide had been coming in while we sat, and now we had to sludge our way out.

"Iris, what's so terrible about a minute of video if it helps people?" he asked, following as I trudged my way back to where we'd climbed down.

I started breathing too fast. Why didn't he understand? He'd seen that gross, old Thornian try to touch me at the airport—and I'd told him about Felix Moss. "Google my name, Eamon. In a world where every girl has posted a thousand selfies, my face doesn't exist on the internet. Ryder too. You don't understand how nervous I am that you have a picture of me."

"You don't trust me?"

"I want to, but it's not that easy. I don't even take pictures with my school friends because I'm too scared of losing my phone and someone finding it. Which makes it hard to open up enough to even make friends. My family has to be private for good reason."

"And what is that reason exactly?"

"I already told you," I snapped. His inability to understand was making me boil.

"Remind me."

"So you fantasy freaks can't hunt us down!" I'd whispered

the words, but it sounded like someone was holding a knife
to my chest. My voice rumbled with deep aches, the kind of held-
back feelings that caused earthquakes…or lightning storms.

Eamon looked away, stunned and burned, like I'd struck
him.

And in a way, I guess I had.

~

We walked back on the cliff in silence, heading for the circle
of trailers. The tension between us was dead weight, and
when Eamon finally spoke, it didn't lift in the slightest.

"Cate didn't tell me to flirt with you, and if she did, I
wouldn't have."

"But she told you to get me involved. To help with the
movie."

"Before you even landed. Before we found out about your
history with kidnapping psychos, Iris. And you know it was
hard for me to ask for that favor, because I knew you'd blow
your top. I thought we were…starting to like one another."

"And you were happy to use that advantage, huh?"

He threw his hands up. "Things are going downhill for
the movie. The producers have been on Cate, checking her
dailies like they're waiting for her to screw up. I've been
trying to get the blog up and make it popular. I'm trying to
help. Don't you want to help?"

I thought about that day on the beach with Julian, talking

through his character with him. It had felt good, sort of. "I do want to help but *not* online."

We paused in a shadow between two large trailers. Several yards away, the picnic tables were full of celebrating crew members beneath white, hot flood lamps. I held myself back in our shaded, secluded spot, not wanting to leave Eamon until we were done fighting. He paused too, and I hoped it was because he felt the same way.

"Sorry, Iris," he said, his shoulders hitched toward his ears. He touched my wrist with careful fingers. "Sorry. Truly."

I leaned closer, his hand traveling up my arm in a way that warmed me straight through the chill of the night. When my face was an inch from his neck, I stopped. I heard singing.

Strange singing.

"Eamon, do you hear that?"

He looked toward one the trailers beside us. "The bad music?"

The sound grew louder. *Sharper.* I started to recognize it as if I were slipping into a nightmare. I walked to the doorway, looking up the steps of the makeup trailer to where Ryder was holding out his iPad.

And there was laughter—lots of laughter—but it wasn't loud enough to drown out my strangled voice coming from the video. I was singing my worst song. The one that had been too influenced by Florence Welch, and in which I screamed "absent" at the top of my lungs. I stepped up behind Ryder and looked at the screen. The video had been taken through a cracked open door, and you could see me wailing my heart out on my bed.

"*Ryder*," I said.

He jumped, trying to hit pause, but wasn't fast enough. I ripped the iPad from his hands and threw it out the door and over Eamon's head. Far enough to barely hear the glass break.

"Hey!" Ryder yelled and scurried out of the trailer after it, leaving me with the worst feeling I'd ever had. I didn't even know how to describe it.

Julian and Shoshanna were giggling, sitting in captain's chairs and still wearing their fantasy garb. Roxanne was there too, using a Q-tip to loosen the scalp line of Julian's Frodo wig. She *wasn't* giggling, and that kind of hurt more than if she had been. She knew this was bad.

"Don't get mad, Iris." Julian sat forward, and Roxanne hissed. "We wanted to hear you play."

"Can't believe I liked hanging out with you guys yesterday," I managed, feeling choked. Shoshanna quit giggling first; she smacked Julian until he stopped.

I left, running straight into Ryder. He was pouting over his broken iPad. "I can't believe you, Ry! I can't even…" I broke inside with one of those ugly hiccup sobs, and then Eamon was there, trying to touch my back, and I snapped, "Leave us alone!"

I grabbed Ryder's arm and hauled him away. When we

were inside our trailer, door shut tight behind us, he pulled out of my grip. "Stop dragging me around, Iris! I'm not your baby!"

"Of course not! You're my responsibility. And *how could you?*"

He shrugged, avoiding my glare.

"So you wanted to embarrass me because I embarrassed you, is that it?"

He kept looking away.

"That's such a stupid, little-kid thing to do," I said even though I knew it wasn't. It was a very teenage, backstabbing thing to do. "Why do you have that video?"

"I came home early with Dad, and we heard you playing, and he said, 'Let's tape her.'"

My hands shook as I picked up Annie and put her in her case. I wanted to break her. To never pick up a guitar again after hearing that terrible hate strumming and my harpy wailing. Was I really that bad? No. That video had to be six months old, but still... I thought about the melody I'd fingerpicked on the cliff earlier. I'd thought it was beautiful, but how could it be? I was a hack. I sat down, holding my stomach. Too stiff to cry.

Suddenly, my music wasn't about the music. It was Shoshanna's and Julian's giggling faces. And Eamon's *oh shit* expression. It was even Roxanne and her stupid, half-shaved hipster haircut. They were all talking about me, no doubt. About how funny that video was…or how I'd freaked out.

But honestly, only one person mattered. The one who'd made it all happen. I looked at my tiny, skinny brother. "What'd Dad say when he saw it?"

Ryder shook his head.

"Tell me!"

"He said you've got a lot of secret anger in you. He thinks you should see my therapist."

I squeezed my eyes and rocked a little. The whole world was burning inside. "Sometimes I hate you," I said to my dad.

"What?" Ryder asked.

My eyes popped open, and I sighed. "I didn't mean you, Ry."

His face erupted in that devastated-kid way. His eyes welled up and his cheeks flashed scarlet. "Maybe I hate you too!"

I stood. "Hate *me*? I'm not the one who ruined your life. You ruined mine!"

"It's just a stupid song," he said, sounding exactly like a miniature version of our dad.

"I'm not talking about the song. I'm talking about me and Dad. Before you, we had *plans*." I couldn't believe the door I'd opened—or the fact that I was now stepping through it. "We were going to leave Mom to her poems and start a real life in New York City. Dad was going to get me real music lessons. We were looking at apartments when Mom found out she was pregnant with you. And now look at me! I can't write a decent song, and I can't even go to college because who will take care of you? You'll starve or get stolen by a psycho."

I regretted the words in a bright, silver flash.

Ryder stood frozen. I thought he'd break into pieces, but instead he puffed his chest like a tiny Tarzan. "I know how much I'm not wanted, Iris! I'm not in your club with Dad!"

He left, slamming the door behind him.

I collapsed on the bed, hands over my ears, trying to drown out my own voice screaming that damn song. In the imposed quiet, my dad started talking. *What'd I say the day you bought that guitar, Jaded Iris? You'll never be as naked as your feelings set to words. It'll make you hate everyone who hears them.*

He'd never been so right, and I didn't want to face any of them again. Not Julian or Shoshanna. Not Eamon. I found my phone and typed a fast email.

> Dad—I can't believe you told Ryder to video me. You cold, mean, negligent asshole. I'll never forgive you.

I shook for a minute before deleting the words. If I sent that, he'd only taunt me about being *Jaded Iris*. Honesty

never worked with him. I blinked back my tears and wrote a
new message.

>Dad—When you buy your ticket here, get me
>one home.
>>I'm done with these people.

I hit send.

Film: Elementia
Director: Cate Collins

                          On Location: Day 4
Aran Islands & Killykeen Forest, Ireland

Filming Notes:
No filming today.

Etc. Notes:
A.M.: Moving house to Killykeen Forest. The
ferry leaves on the hour until noon. Leave
nothing behind but footprints!

IN WHICH FLORENCE SAVES THE DAY...WITH MY HELP?

I PLANNED TO lock myself in the trailer until I heard back from my dad, so I could pack up, hold my head high, and leave. Ryder had gotten up in the morning and left to help Mr. Donato without saying a word. I wanted him to apologize for the video, but I think he wanted me to apologize for smashing his iPad—and for telling him he'd ruined my life. Impasse.

I slumped on the bed, listening to Florence + The Machine on repeat, full volume. Maybe I should have been peeved at Florence for inspiring the song that had swiftly ended my music career, but I couldn't. She was too great. And boy, did she sing anger well. I got up and read the film side for the day. Nothing but moving locations.

Someone knocked on the door hard, but instead of answering, I checked my email. Nothing from Dad. Why hadn't he responded? Did he break the router again? Sometimes when he was on deadline and couldn't keep himself off-line, he broke the internet for the whole house. The knocking grew louder, and I peered through the shades at a burly man.

I looked down at my pajama pants and slippers. My hair was in a state of wild disaster. "Sorry, buddy. I don't answer the door when I look like this," I muttered.

The guy hollered something, and the ground rumbled. The whole trailer lurched, and I yelled in a panic and flung the door open to leap out.

The burly man laughed and slapped his thigh. "Told you that'd get her out, Sol!" he yelled to the driver of a huge truck that was now hooked up to my trailer.

The other trailers were gone. Only the picnic tables remained. There were no people either. I crossed my arms over my chest and glared at Mr. Burly. "Where is everyone?"

"Gone," he said. "Packed and moving on to Killykeen. We left you last because we heard you were having a tantrum in there."

My mouth hung open. That was it, huh? I was going to be Jaded Iris, no matter what country I was in. "Don't move," I said, pointing a finger at him. "I'm going to get dressed and then you can haul this trap away."

"You have two minutes." Mr. Burly sat on the picnic table and smirked. "And I mean two. I've got a fifteen-year-old daughter who could challenge you in attitude, girl. And let me tell you, she doesn't win with me."

I slammed back into the trailer. Why did everyone act like I wasn't mature? I was the most mature teenager I knew. I was raising my brother, wasn't I? Speaking of, where was Ryder? It wasn't like me to forget about him even when I was having a tan—no. This was not a tantrum. It was a serious infraction on my mental well-being.

Mr. Burly hollered out, "One minute, sass pants!"

I threw on some jeans and kept on my black shirt that said "NO!" It was a pajama top and not my usual, carefree invisible style, but I didn't care. My hair was a bigger problem. I'd need at least ten minutes to detangle and straighten it back out. I tied it into a wild knot and stared at Annie in her sleek, black case.

I didn't want to leave my guitar in the trailer; she could be stolen. But I didn't want to touch her either. To be honest, it hurt to look at her. The trailer jerked into motion again, and I jumped out, pushing my headphones into my ears so that Mr. Burly knew I wasn't going to talk to him.

I walked to the quay. The ocean was a brag artist of sparkles beneath a bright sun, and the production crew was loading up the huge ferry with equipment vans and trailers. I found Shoshanna siting on a rock wall down by the water, skipping stones and watching an eighty-year-old skinny dip in the near distance.

"Is that really happening?" I asked, popping out my earbud in slight shock.

"Yes," Shoshanna said without looking at me. "I'm disgusted and yet I can't turn away. Who knew skin could drape like that?" Shoshanna glanced over her perfect shoulder and motioned to my clothes and hair. "That's a good look on you."

I couldn't tell if she was being serious. My scan of her tone only provoked the feeling I'd had when I first met her: that she was royalty and I was a lowly creature.

"Sorry for being a dick last night," she said, surprising me.

I wanted to say something cool back. I didn't. I kicked some loose stones and felt my chest tighten. "Where is everybody?"

"Almost all gone. Cate and your brother are at the restaurant. Roxanne went off with the rest of the crew. They're going sightseeing on their way to Killykeen."

I wasn't sure why Shoshanna was telling me where the makeup artist went, but I left it alone. "Everything okay?"

"There's been some drama about the teaser trailer. This damn production…" Shoshanna picked up a rock from a pile and threw it at the water. As much as my mouthy pajama top was a different look on me, Shoshanna's distress altered her fierce, confident facade, showing deep cracks. "How come when your dreams come true, they come true all effed up?"

Another rock hurtled at the water, making a *bank* sound when it hit.

So she wasn't skipping stones. She was cannonballing them.

I hurried to Tí Joe Watty's, vaguely noting how much I'd gotten used to the quiet, unhurried motion of Inishmore. When I ducked inside the restaurant, my eyes adjusted slowly. Ryder was sitting at a table in the corner with Eamon. He waved but pulled his hand back like he shouldn't have done that. Eamon looked over and then away, which stung.

I turned from both of them. The restaurant was mostly empty, the crew members gone. Cate held court at the biggest table before three different laptops, a printer, and stacks of paper. Henrik sat next to her, talking on the phone in a hurried rush.

I walked to Cate, and she glanced up, her gaze heavier than usual.

"I wanted to tell you that I'm leaving as soon as my da—"

"Sit," she said. "We have to talk."

Henrik started yelling on the phone. He left the table while Cate and I watched him go.

"What's happening?" I asked.

"You don't like Elementia," Cate said.

"I think we've covered that much," I tried.

She swiveled one of the laptops so I could see the screen. "Watch. Tell me what you think as a nonfan."

I paused Florence who was still wailing through my iPhone and plugged my earbuds into the computer. Cate looked at me a little strangely but pressed play. I watched the same trailer I'd seen with Julian a few days ago, only this time it was more finely cut and orchestral music swelled along with it. It didn't feel as powerful as it had during the first viewing, but then, I wasn't snuggled up to a movie star in the dark this time.

When the minute forty-five was over, I pulled out my earbud. "It's good."

"*Good* is the kiss of death." Cate shuffled some pages. "The focus group of non-*Elementia* readers found it to be 'okay.'" She rubbed her grey hair with both hands. "Okay is not good, and even good is not okay. We don't have fan support, and now we don't have nonfan interest either."

I wondered if she was the sort to cry, but instead she slammed a gold-tinted beverage in a whiskey glass. When I eyed it, she snapped, "It's ginger ale, Iris. Sugar is my preferred poison."

She tried to take back the laptop, but I held on to it. "Can I try something?"

"Oh, by all means." Cate grabbed her glass and headed for the bar.

I had a weird idea. I reclaimed my headphone cord and put it back into my iPhone. Then I synced the Florence song that had been in my head all morning with the trailer on mute. It sounded good. It felt good. When Cate came back, I handed my headphones over, turned the laptop and played it for her with my song choice. She listened and watched once, and then twice.

When Henrik came back, she grabbed his arm and handed over the headphones. He listened twice as well. Then they stared at me.

I shrugged. "You want to appeal to non-nerds, you've got to choose cool music."

"What is that song?" Cate asked.

"'No Light, No Light,'" I said. "It always felt like a fantasy to me."

Cate looked at Henrik. "Did it make you feel feelings?"

Henrik nodded. "And you know I prefer not to. But…we do not have the budget for the permissions to a song like that."

"Find out how much and take it out of the account we discussed," Cate said.

"Cay, no…"

She waved off his concern and snagged the phone out of his chest pocket. She left the restaurant, dialing.

Henrik started typing on the laptop. "Congratulations, Iris."

"Did I save the movie?" I asked, surfing the uplifting feeling that came with being helpful.

"You saved the day," Henrik said. "And when you're making a movie, someone has got to save every single day." He said this sourly, like *Elementia* wasn't going to make it. Like this was simply the close call before the real death. He kept typing, and then sat back, holding his hands over his face. "Damn, that song is expensive."

"Do you have enough?"

"Maybe."

"So that's good, right? You can cover it?"

He looked up at me through his dark glasses, and it felt like he was deciding to trust me. "Between you and me? Cate cashed in her paycheck. She mortgaged her house. This movie is not only going to crush her career, it's going to leave her homeless." He took off his glasses. "What are the odds the Thornes would invest? We could get your dad a producer credit. I know that's impertinent, but that's how low we've sunk. Plus, if the movie does well, your family would be bound to see immense returns in book sales and new editions."

"You want my dad to help fund the movie?" I tried not to laugh. "He won't even give me money. He loathes Grandma Mae's financial legacy. *Personally*," I added, only realizing how true those words were as they slipped out.

Henrik removed his floppy hat, dropping it next to his glasses. He was going bald, which jumped out at me when he de-accessorized, even though he was probably only thirty. He had a well-worn Batman watch—the kind with the old school *pow bam* on it—which somehow sweetened every impression I'd ever had about him.

"What if the movie doesn't crush her? What if it's good?" I asked.

"No one sets out to make a bad movie, Iris. It just happens. We gamble. We win or lose." He scowled at his screen, and I realized Henrik was talking about his career as well. And Julian's, Shoshanna's...Eamon's. Everyone's career was on the line. They were all taking risks to make this movie happen, and here I was upset about a bootleg video of me playing guitar on my bed.

Maybe it *was* a tantrum.

I felt like a coward all of a sudden, slipping out of the restaurant with my head down. I'd already told my dad to get me out of here. He wouldn't let me change my mind again. I'd have to go back now, whether I wanted to or not. Did I have one more day? Two? How could I even fix this?

I stepped outside.

Overhead the soft, brilliant-blue sky seemed like an omen of strength I didn't deserve. "Okay, Grandma Mae. It's azure," I said quietly. "Now what?"

THERE IS SOME KISSING IN THIS CHAPTER

ON THE RETURN trip to mainland Ireland, I wrestled surprisingly weighted feelings about leaving Inishmore. I stood at the back of the ferry, leaning on the rail as the green land with its odd cliffs, unconventional beaches, and colored cottages disappeared.

When the island was gone, I watched the propeller stir up trouble, throwing the water into fits of ice blue. They reminded me of Eamon's film-friendly eyes.

"I accept your apology." Eamon leaned on the railing next to me.

"I wasn't…but I…" My more pleasant thoughts about him turned into a hard scowl. "I don't know what to do with you."

"Ah, so you are thinking of doing something with me?"

He grinned, and I relaxed. If he was back to flirting, maybe I hadn't ruined things last night. "Someone wants to talk to you." Eamon motioned with the tilt of his head, and I glanced at my brother. Ryder sat on one of the benches.

"I don't know if I'm ready. We were harsh with each other."

"He's sorry. And if you break it down, it wasn't his fault. It was your da's idea to take that video." Great. Eamon didn't like my dad, and they hadn't even met yet.

"It is my dad's fault, but he's got this weird sense of morality. His law is creativity. His writing sets the rules in our house—what he gets excited about, when we get to eat dinner, et cetera and so forth." Eamon frowned, and I shook my head. "When I try to explain, it sounds worse than it is. Ryder and I have each other."

"What about before Ryder?" he asked like he wanted to know everything about me. I looked at him, standing close, and remembered our hand-holding on the beach. How much of this was real flirting and how much was just Eamon? "Your age difference is ten years, yes?" he added. "What were you like before you had to play guardian?"

"It's nine years." I tightened my hold on the railing. "And I was the perfect daughter, I'll have you know. My parents threw dinner parties every week, and I'd sit quietly at the table between poet laureates and National Book Award winners. My dad would say, 'Look how our girl can behave anywhere!' I'd eat filet mignon next to forty-year-olds and talk about the melancholy downturn of literary fiction. When it got too late, I'd put myself to bed, and they'd all be so impressed."

I couldn't help but smile. Remembering how much those people praised me still felt good. "Then Ryder was born, and he *never* stopped crying, and they'd leave me upstairs with him. When I couldn't get him to stop crying, they had the parties at their friends' houses."

"Oh," Eamon said, ruffling the back of his hair. "That's…"

I shook my head. "It wasn't bad. Life was more fun with Ryder. We watched Disney movies. Built forts. I taught him his letters and how to count. We actually did feel like big sister and little brother back then."

"Before Moss?" he asked in that way he had of cutting straight into a matter.

"Before Moss." I turned from the waves and looked at Ryder, still waiting on that bench. "Did he send you over here?"

"He did." Eamon turned around too, and we watched Ryder, whose eyebrows were raised hopefully. "He wants you to drive in the van with Mr. Donato and the rest of craft services out to Killykeen. I think he wants you to meet his new friends."

"Who are you riding with?"

Smooth, Iris.

"I'm driving the queen herself, Lady Shoshanna." He crossed his arms, moving several inches away from me along the railing. "She's going to give me some acting tips."

"So you're going to be an actor after all."

He got riled fast, his eyebrows turning into a hard V. "Wouldn't know that, would I? Maybe I'm like that girl who played Luna Lovegood. Maybe I *am* Nolan, but not a real actor." He pressed his palm to his forehead and then cooled off with a sigh. "I think I've come this far on my good looks alone, Iris. It's such a curse."

I laughed, and he looked delighted with himself.

Cate stomped along the deck, not losing an inch of intensity in her expression when a swell made her steps go all helter-skelter. She pointed at Ryder and me. "There are reporters waiting in Doolin, so you two need to do your 'Michael Jackson's kids' no-face thing."

"Hey!" I'd never heard our hiding referred to as such. It did sound bad.

She turned to Eamon and Shoshanna, who had appeared from the other side of the ferry. "And you two need to find Julian and stage a photo op. Something compelling."

"Where is Julian?" I asked. I hadn't seen him since last night in the makeup trailer.

"He's belowdecks, then," Shoshanna said, throwing on her Irish accent. "Fighting with his girlfriend. She's got him in a tizzy."

"Don't do that," Cate said, while Eamon added, "No."

Shoshanna shrugged, and Cate pointed to me. "Get Julian and tell him he's got to have his charm on when we dock. He's got *five* minutes."

I swayed down the stairs, through the tiny door that led to the cabin. It wasn't hard to find Julian, even though it was rather dim. He was sitting on a small cot that was bolted to the floor.

"Julian? Cate says some press are waiting at the dock…"

Julian looked up, his eyes bloodshot and his nose running. "Elora's going to break up with me, Iris. She's going to dump me because she's afraid of my fans."

I sat next to him and patted his back. I thought about telling him that he was too young to be engaged, but ended up sighing deeply instead, still annoyed about Cate's *Michael Jackson's kids* line. "Well, Julian, she'll have to live a certain way if she wants to avoid the attention. It's a lot of work. And it sucks." The captain's voice echoed down from the deck. "But we should talk about this later. Right now, you have to act like the happy, sexy Julian everyone loves."

His face sunk into his hands, and he messed up his beautiful, dark hair—which I'd never seen him do. When he looked at me again, he'd gotten worse, not better. "Can't do it."

"Of course you can. You're a great actor." He laughed, but I continued. "Pretend the cameras are rolling. From what I hear, there *are* going to be cameras rolling."

"You're right." He blew out a long breath and looked at me. He was awfully close and the dim light was sending the wrong messages. Hollywood-hunk alarms. "Kiss me?"

"What?"

"I have to get in my acting brain. I need to do something that doesn't mean anything."

I stood up fast. "First of all, that's terrible. Secondly, I'm not an actor."

"True." He glanced away, deterred but unashamed. "Get Shoshanna for me?"

"You're not serious."

"Please, Iris?" His puppy-dog expression was too much. This guy was no longer the starlet I'd had a crush on for years. No longer Julian freakin' Young. He was simply Julian, a regular guy whose nose ran like a faucet when he cried. And I surprised myself by liking him even better this way.

I fetched Shoshanna, and Eamon followed. The four of us packed into the tiny cabin while I explained Julian's predicament and request.

Shoshanna looked over Julian's miserable face. "I won't do it. I'm slightly method, and you're supposed to be my *brother*." Julian started to complain, but she grabbed Eamon's shoulder and hauled him front and center in the cramped space. "He'll do it."

"Oh no." Eamon's bewildered expression was adorable.

"You want to see if you're a real actor?" Shoshanna said. "Well, this'll do. Pretend you love Julian. Pretend you've been waiting to get your lips on his for ages."

Eamon shook his head.

"*No one* wants to kiss me?" Julian blurted. "This is just great for my self-esteem, you guys."

"Fine." Eamon jammed forward and planted one on Julian, so fast I almost missed it.

"Yeah, you're not an actor, Eamon O'Brien," Shoshanna concluded.

Eamon's face got much redder than I'd ever seen, and I could tell he wanted to be able to do this.

Julian stepped closer to Eamon, and the room got smaller. He stared intensely. "I think I love you, Charles. I think I have for a while."

"Why am I 'Charles'?" Eamon asked, but Shoshanna shushed him and motioned to Julian's emotive face. His eyes were still red, his hair fussed, but I could see the change in him already. The acting switch had been flipped to *On*.

Julian put a hand on Eamon's cheek.

"Okay. Kiss me," Eamon said.

"No!" Shoshanna said. "*Act.*"

Eamon groaned and turned his back. He shook his arms and shoulders, rolled his neck. When he faced us again, I didn't recognize him. He was serious.

"Line, Julian," Shoshanna whispered.

"I love you, Charles. I think I've always loved you." Julian touched his cheek, and Eamon closed his eyes. In relief? Pain? It was a strong emotion, whatever it was. When

Eamon opened his eyes again, he was there with Julian…in some moment Shoshanna and I were not part of.

"Okay," Eamon said. "You should kiss me, then. If you care so much."

It was a line, but *wow*, it was well delivered.

Julian moved forward. He kissed Eamon, and Shoshanna and I both made small, breathy sounds. They looked beautiful together. In love. And I felt, well, great at first and then incredibly jealous. That's what Eamon looked like when he was kissing? Where could I sign up?

They jostled apart as the ferry bumped into the pier. Julian rubbed his hands together. "Good. This was good." He left the cabin with that hundred-watt smile, and Shoshanna followed, clapping Eamon on the shoulder with admiration.

Eamon stood there stock-still, a statue of himself.

"You still in scene?" I asked. He looked like he might need a shake back to reality.

"I'm here," he said. "That guy has lips like a pretty, pretty girl."

"He keeps them well moisturized, I bet." People were hollering above, and I began to worry about getting Ryder off the boat incognito. I tried to step past Eamon and up the stairs, but he touched my elbow, leaned down, and kissed me.

His lips. On my lips.

And we lingered there. Not pulling away.

"Sorry," he finally said. "I think I needed to…reset?"

Something inside me had stopped ticking when he put his mouth on mine. I tried to say a few nonchalant words, but the kiss had been so soft, neat. The kind of kiss two people share before the altar at their wedding rehearsal. It left me wondering if it had been another acting thing, or something else entirely.

"I think…" I managed. "I think I just kissed Julian Young vicariously?"

Eamon laughed and touched the side of my face with hesitant fingers. "He'll take it wrong, so don't tell him, but your lips are far better."

SET 'EM ALL UP, KNOCK 'EM ALL DOWN

TWO HOURS AFTER Eamon lit me up in a dim, cramped ferry cabin, I was being thrown about the craft services van. The seat belt did nothing to combat the whippy, windy roads, and Mr. Donato drove like a fiend. Beside me, Ryder tossed his weight into each turn with delight.

"I think I'm going to be sick," I muttered.

"Peppermints for Iris!" Mr. Donato called out. The person in the passenger seat, Susan, handed back a fistful of wrapped candies. I popped one in my mouth while Ryder beamed. I'd never seen him so proud of a set of people. There was Mr. Donato—a passable stand in for Stanley Tucci—Susan, his second-in-command and a stout, fierce blond. And then Bob and Dean in the back who were definitely smoking hash during the breaks. They were quirky and fun, a bonded subset of the crew family.

"Mr. Donato has five daughters, Iris. Five!" Ryder said.

"Alice, Hero, Deirdre, Ryan, and Sierra. The eldest is nineteen and the littlest is nine," Mr. Donato said. "The hormones in my house could wipe out a village, so when Cate Collins said, 'Come on to Ireland with me, Paul Donato,' I said, 'My bags are packed!' Oh, but I miss them," he added, and Susan *awww*ed. "My wife is going to shoot me when I get back."

Ryder laughed hard. I gave him a peppermint, enjoying how entertained he was by this Mr. Donato. I parted his hair with my fingers, and he leaned into my hand like a puppy needing a scratch. We were back to normal with one another, but also...not. It would be hard to forget how we'd both gone for the jugular yesterday. Our dad snapped like that all time, but we'd never done it before. Speaking of my dad, I checked my email. He still hadn't responded to my message about wanting to come home, and after everything, did I still want to?

No. I wanted to be real friends with Julian and Shoshanna. More than friends with Eamon. We'd all stepped off the ferry together, and it'd felt unbelievable—even if I was hiding behind a craft services crate. The three actors had posed for the press and answered questions, and Shoshanna had winked. Eamon glanced at me too, and I wanted him to blush so bad that I think he did.

The memory of his lips was bright, leaving me warm. Was

that a real kiss? Something he wanted, or did the moment just…happen? More importantly, how could I make it happen again?

When my attention came back to the car, Ryder was giggling at Mr. Donato's lively story about the time Sierra painted Alice's toenails with jelly. "The moral of the story is that kids get wiser as you go. Sierra stole all her sisters' secrets, so you don't mess with Sierra. Ryder back there probably knows all of Iris's biggest fears. Siblings are dangerous."

Ryder was beaming. I couldn't resist. "All right. What's my biggest fear, Ry?"

He wiped stray, happy tears from his cheeks with the back of his arm. "You're afraid of people hearing you play guitar. Oh, and that Dad'll make you stay home for college and take care of me."

I tried to laugh, but the humor lodged in my throat, making it hard to breathe.

An hour later, we arrived at Killykeen Forest Park in County Cavan. The trees painted the horizon in scallops of green, while a meandering lake wound around everything. Then, right in the middle, a crumbling, old tower sat on a spit of island. It *was* Elementia. I pictured the map—the one my in-flight boyfriend had tattooed on his chest—and I was surprised to know where this very real place belonged in that made-up landscape.

We climbed out of the van, and Mr. Donato loaded

my arms with sacks of potatoes. I searched everywhere for Eamon's car, but the red rust bucket was nowhere in sight. I helped the crew set up and watched as the trailers were placed in a circle, similar to their arrangement on Inishmore, which felt sort of like…home.

The evening sky was a warm stretch of pastels as I slumped on a picnic table and watched two people in a rowboat by the island tower. They were laughing so loud that disembodied shrieks shot across the water, messing up the ambiance.

Julian sat beside me. "Thanks for your help earlier. You're a lifesaver. Get it? Boat. Water. Lifesaver?"

I nodded.

Julian cleared his throat. "I'm sorry about last night. I shouldn't have laughed at your guitar playing."

"Of course you should have laughed. It was ridiculous," I said. Admitting this aloud helped. "That video shouldn't exist, but…not all my songs are that bad," I dared.

"You've got talent, Iris. We can see that. You just haven't found your feet yet." He pulled out his phone and thumbed a quick YouTube search. He held out the screen. "Watch. Laugh."

Over the course of the next thirty-two seconds, I watched the most ridiculous commercial I've ever seen. First a girl tried on different swimsuits only to realize she'd gotten her period with a terrible *oh no* face. The girl's mom came to the rescue and handed her a box of tampons—and then cut to the girl on some California beach, smiling at a boy playing volleyball. And then for the final shot, they were waist-high in the surf, kissing.

"Is that…"

"Me," Julian said. "Yes, my very first acting gig was Hunky Beach Guy in a tampon commercial. I'd be thrilled if you didn't share this with other people, although some a-hole put it on my Wikipedia page." He fixed the sides of his hair with careful fingers. "Well, I'm out of here tomorrow for the week. Any words of wisdom as I head home to face the girl who's about to break my heart?"

"What?" I turned to him, almost shouting, "You can't leave!"

"All my interiors are going to be shot on the sound-stage in LA, but I'll be back for the grand finale in Dingle." He glanced over the water with me, sighing dramatically— *Julianly.* "Bonding exercises, ugh. They get extra points for the rowboat. I'm actually surprised Cate waited this long to get on their case, Eamon needing to act like he's in love with her and all."

"What?" I asked again like a sound clip.

He motioned to the people in the boat. "Eamon and Shoshanna. Shosh thinks she's method. You might want to give our boy Eamon a heads up. She's going *after* him."

I squinted at the rowboat, now understanding the silhouette that was Shoshanna's mighty hair and the lean mark of Eamon's body, rowing. So Julian was leaving, and Eamon was now Shoshanna's plaything. *Great*. My earlier hopes about making real friends and finding love sunk so hard I doubled over.

Julian was trying to read my expression. I suppose it wasn't hard. "You like him? He's a decent kisser, I can tell you that much." We both sort of laughed, but it was painful on my end. "So is this a crush or true liking?"

"What's the difference?"

"A crush is obligatory—new scene, new people, new crush. Elora says I always get a 'work crush,' which she teases me about nonstop."

"Your fiancée teases you about having crushes on other people?"

"Hey, I'm in the business of kissing. It's not love *in* the movies. It's love *and* the movies. If the actors don't love me, the audience doesn't love me." He smiled, and again, I had a flash of how different the real Julian was from the on-screen person I'd idolized.

"So a crush is a crush, but real liking is…what exactly?"

"Hard. Impossible. You've got to have serious courage to make it work."

I hung my head. "Yeah, I wouldn't worry about me then."

Julian hooked his hands behind his head. "You know why I wanted to be Nolan, Iris? It's not only that I'm good at romantic roles. Nolan is a great character. Your grandma must have had incredible love in her life to write a guy who gives up body and soul for his girl. If we pull this off, fans are going to fall for Eamon. They're going to tattoo *Nolan* on their wrists."

I honked—a sarcastic laugh turned pained goose.

Julian stared at the sky over the lake, looking for said waterfowl, no doubt. "I want to be that courageous with Elora," he whispered. "I want to be her Nolan."

I couldn't help him there. Not even a little. And I had to work hard not to call Julian a Thornian. Maybe this was the fantasy conversion camp Cate threatened back on the first day.

I squinted at the rowboat. Shoshanna and Eamon stood together, making the boat tip, yelling and laughing. I stood up too, ready to give up, and Julian patted my shoulder. "Don't look hopeless. Especially if you keep this up." He gestured to my clothes.

"This is my messy look," I said, surprised to have my second compliment on this outfit.

"Well, messy is a good look on you." Julian grinned. "Badass Iris."

Henrik walked over like he was on a rather serious mission. "Cate wants to see you." Julian stood up, but Henrik shook his head. "Not you. You." He pointed to me.

⁓

Cate called, "Come in, Iris!"

Her trailer was identical to the others, except that it was

overflowing with office equipment. She sat at the tiny table, reviewing a script on her computer, and pointed for me to sit on the chair across from her. First I had to move a stack of different editions of the Elementia series, which was a little like cradling my trust fund.

She glanced up, all steely eyed—a bird-boned, Irish Vito Corleone. "I have two reasons to thank you. First, Julian's delivery yesterday was finally in character. He said you gave him new perspective. Secondly, the music for the teaser trailer smashed expectations with the focus group. You have a gift, Iris."

I shrugged one shoulder, trying not to remember the spectacular gift of Ryder's iPad flying through the air, my wretched singing coming to an abrupt *crack*.

"Have you ever thought about becoming a music supervisor?" she asked.

"A what?"

"Someone who selects music for films, TV, et cetera. A soundtrack artist."

"My dad would freak if I tried to work in Hollywood," I said. "He's not a big fan of...you guys."

"I did notice, but I asked *you*, not him." Cate shut her laptop. "Speaking of, I've had an email from your father."

"What? When?"

"About an hour ago."

I whipped out my phone, fully aware that she was giving

me one of those *your generation doesn't know about social courtesy*
looks. I checked my email but there was nothing from my dad.
"He messaged you but he didn't even bother to reply to me?"

Cate frowned. "Do you want to know what he said?"

I shoved my phone in my back pocket. "When's he going
to be here?"

"He changed his mind. He's not coming."

"Of course," I muttered. "Why would he keep his word?"

"He's having trouble wrapping up the book he's writing."
She said this like writing was an exotic, fragile, sacred business. It wasn't—not for my dad. He was an industrial word
factory, all pounding keys and fuming snorts. "I know you're
anxious to leave, but this might be a blessing in disguise." She
said *disguise* like the most Irish person on the planet. Which
made me think of Eamon. Which made me want to get the
heck out of Ireland before my crush turned into the scary kind
of liking that Julian talked about.

Cate didn't say anything, but I could feel her eyes. "Are
we so bad, Iris Thorne?"

"You're actually growing on me," I mumbled.

"And you've been growing on us. Eamon and I have
come up with a plan for you."

I ignored her name-drop of the boy I was trying to pretend didn't exist. "Another job?"

"You know that scene in *The Return of the King* when
Pippin sings to Denethor—it's one of J. R. R. Tolkien's

poems. Billy Boyd, the actor, wrote the melody, and I think we can all agree it made for one of the most powerful moments in that final movie." She paused. "Don't tell Henrik I said that. He'd like it too much."

"I haven't seen those movies." Lie. "I'm not into elves." More lies. "Wait. You're not going to ask me to write a song for one of my grandmother's poems, are you?"

Cate raised her nose in the air. "I might be."

"Well, ask Julian, Shoshanna, or even Roxanne—I can't sing or play guitar. They heard me. They laughed." My voice scratched.

"I don't know what you're talking about. I've heard you play and sing, and I know you are good." Cate proffered Eamon's handheld video camera. She opened the view screen and hit play. Eamon ran the gravel beach, talking to the camera, giving facts about Inishmore. Then he stopped. He zoomed in on the cliff above. Or, more specifically, my foot dangling over the edge. I was playing my song—the pretty, moving, fingerpicking melody that had stumbled out of me when I felt like no one in the world was listening. I took the camera, turning my ear toward the tiny speaker to hear the song over the shush of the waves. "What a girl," Eamon half whispered, and my heartbeat banged in a rush.

Cate was eyeing me, and I shut the view screen, forcing nonchalance.

"Eamon only gave this to me after I assured him I would

not let you destroy him for taping your foot and song. I don't know what you said to that boy, but he lives in fear of your wrath." She said that with the fierce, *just be a courageous woman* attitude I remembered from our run yesterday. Was that only yesterday? Every day here felt like a lifetime. "I'm glad to see you've got the reins in that relationship," she added.

Ha!

"So yes, Iris. I am asking you to write a song for one of your grandmother's poems. It'll be for the most important scene in the movie—when Sevyn meets Nolan." She handed me a piece of paper. "I'd like you to record the song you were playing on the cliff. That was perfect. Match the lyrics to it however you see fit."

"Record? Record where?"

"In a studio in Dublin. Tomorrow. Julian needs a ride to the airport, and I've already made an appointment for you." I opened my mouth and a croaky protest came out instead of words. "Eamon says you want to have a songwriting career. This would be a serious step toward that goal. And you will be paid. I don't believe artists should volunteer their skills."

Record a song? For the movie? *Tomorrow?*

"But my dad will be so—"

"Your dad is not here, and that was his choice. You're, what, seventeen, Iris? Your time in his shadow is coming to an abrupt end. It's time for you to make your own choices, and I know how tough that can be. I had to wrestle my future out of the grips of my controlling, small-minded grandmother who thought going to film school was the equivalent of setting myself on fire." She paused, and her whole face smoothed, relaxed. "Iris, I see you trying to be more. I know that fight. I want to help."

My negative thoughts crept up and up and out. "You're only offering this because I'm M. E. Thorne's granddaughter."

"True," Cate said. "But I'm only here because I'm one of the Coppola cousins."

"You are?"

"No!" She leaned forward, aflame. "But if I were, you better believe I'd be calling them right now and asking for a little support. Don't turn your nose up at friends, Iris Thorne. You helped my production, and now I'm helping you. This is what women should do for one another. We are a continent. We stick together. We all rise up, or we all go down. Now go practice."

Two days ago this speech might have made my eyes roll. Today all I could think about was standing on that cliff's edge, feeling connected to Grandma Mae. To knowing the grief and love that made her write—and somehow set her free.

PHILIP PULLMAN WILL BREAK YOUR HEART

BACK AT MY trailer, I got Ryder into bed, assuring him that, "Yes, I like Mr. Donato," and "Yes, he's very funny."

"I bet he's the best dad," Ryder said through a yawn. "I wish we had a dad like that."

I bristled all over. "Dad is all right. Mom too."

"He said he was coming." Ryder turned away, face to the wall. "I bet he doesn't show."

I didn't have the heart to tell him he was right. "I'm here," I said. "Although apparently I'm going to Dublin tomorrow to record a song for the soundtrack. I'm supposed to use one of Grandma Mae's poems for the lyrics."

Ryder shot up and fastened his arms around my neck. "That's amazing!"

I couldn't help but laugh. "I'm glad you think so. I feel super weird about it."

He grabbed his worn copy of the Elementia trilogy and rifled through the pages. "Is it for Queen Seeria's Prophecy? I bet it is. That's Sevyn and Evyn's grandmother. She can control water, sort of. She sees the future through it."

"Ah, yeah, that's the poem. The song is for the scene where Nolan and Sevyn meet."

My brother dog-eared a page and handed it to me. "Take this. It's the *best* scene."

I took the book and watched him crawl under the covers. He still felt like my puppy, but he was getting bigger, and I was getting older. And he'd been wrong in the van today. I wasn't afraid of Dad making me stay home for college. I was scared I would make that choice. That I would stay because of Ryder and then resent him for it.

"Ry, do you…" I paused; it was hard to go back to last night, to the harsh truths we'd exchanged. "Do you honestly feel like Dad and I have a club you're not part of?"

Ryder was quiet for a few breaths. "You guys never invite me to those concerts or the theater. You leave me with Mom, and she says we're going to hang out, but as soon as you guys leave, she goes to her room."

"Dad and I see historical war dramas together, Ryder. It's not fun. I would skip, but it makes him happy to lecture me on the inaccuracies afterward." My brother stared like an owl; I'd never considered he might be jealous of an activity I loathed. "It's not fun or easy to be in Dad's good graces. At least he doesn't call you Jaded Ryder."

"At least he doesn't call you stupid for liking Elementia."

"Ryder! He's never called you stupid."

My brother gave me a look that said, *He doesn't have to say it.*

"Dad is…" I'd never tried to talk to Ryder about this before. Would it help? Was he old enough? "You know how Mom is different from other moms?" He nodded. "Well, Dad is just as different, although he's better at hiding it. There's something big in him. Something—"

"Sad?"

So Ryder was old enough to get it.

"Yeah." I brushed his hair out of his eyes. "You know those lessons he's been asking you to think about?" He nodded. "He wants you to have interests outside of fantasy. Something he can buy lessons for you to pursue, so he can feel like a good dad. It can be anything. Martial arts, Mandarin, or how about engineering? You like building things."

"What if I got cooking lessons and become a chef like Mr. Donato?"

I laughed too hard, too fast. "He won't go for that. He wants you to do something special with your life. Nothing blue collar or, heaven forbid, fine arts."

Ryder rolled to face the wall. "Everything I do is wrong."

I touched his back. "Ryder, look at me please." He didn't. "Okay, well, when I was your age, Dad wanted to get me lessons too. I picked literature because it made him happy. Every week I read a new book with this tutor named Mr. Sams. We read Charles Dickens, Mary Shelley, *Moby Dick*. I mean, in hindsight, it was way beyond my comprehension level, but it was fun, and Mr. Sams acted out roles and we had the best talks."

Ryder rolled back over. "Was he like Mr. Donato?"

"Yeah, a bit." I chewed my bottom lip, wondering how much I could tell him. I decided on an abridged version. "One day he gave me a new book, a fantasy trilogy like Elementia."

"What was it?" my brother whispered.

"*His Dark Materials* by Philip Pullman. It changed my whole life. It was amazing. I can't even—" I cut myself off. This was where the memory turned sour, and I had to have enough courage to tell Ryder the truth. "Dad got upset when he saw how much I liked those books. He accused Mr. Sams of turning me into a little Thornian, and he fired him. Dad took over, giving me books to read, but we never talked about them together. And it wasn't fun anymore."

My brother was stunned, his eyes bright.

I was stunned I'd told him, but I pushed on. "Ryder, if you choose lessons that make Dad happy, well, it might make you unhappy. And vice versa. We'll try to find something that makes you both happy. How about that?"

He smiled wearily, and that's what I hated most. All this stuff with Dad made both of us so old.

"Okay, now I've got to go practice." I stood and grabbed my guitar.

Before I could slip outside, Ryder called out. "Eyeball?"

It had been years since he'd used his little-kid name for me. "Yeah, Cowboy?"

"You think you could get me those Dark Materials books?"

"Definitely."

Slipping outside into a chilly, late-spring Irish evening, I couldn't stop thinking about how Ryder and I had the same parents but such different experiences. Sure, I'd had my hands full raising him over the last eight years, but I had also been my parent's precocious sweetheart, an only child for nine years. Ryder had been treated like a wild animal since birth, and what was worse, looking back, I'm not sure my parents even tried.

I turned the corner and ran into Eamon, but the pillow he carried cushioned the crash.

"Hiya!" he said way too enthusiastically, like he'd forgotten I was on this set. He clutched the pillow to his chest. Then he looked at my guitar. "Did Cate talk to you about the song?"

I nodded. "I guess I should say thanks?"

He blew out a sigh of relief. "Taping you was the scariest thing I've ever done. I sort of thought that you might, you know, kill me and harvest my organs."

I held down a smile. "I thought about it."

He edged around me as though he was late to get somewhere and didn't want to be rude.

"Where are you going?"

He pulled a hand through his hair. It stuck in his fisticuffs of curls, and he had to back it out. *Smooth, Eamon O'Brien.* "My big first scene is in two days. Shoshanna is helping me loosen up. I'm sleeping in her trailer tonight."

If the blood rushing to my face could make a sound, it'd be howling like a train whistle.

"It's for my acting," he added, like that made it better.

"Of course," I said, surprising myself with a cool tone. "Julian told me to warn you, by the way. He said Shoshanna is trying out method acting, so if she seems like she has feelings for you, she's pretending." Somewhere in the middle of my speech, my tone went from cool to ON FIRE. Eamon froze, and I had another flash of Sevyn and her ability to call lightning down on anyone who pissed her off. That did actually make her a pretty badass heroine.

"You're upset because we shifted," he said, and when I blinked like he'd spoken Latin, he added. "Because I kissed you. I should have asked first."

No, I'm upset because you haven't been doing it every minute since.

Shoshanna leaned out of her trailer across the circle and called Eamon's name. He hollered back before turning to me. "Got to go, but we'll talk later. Just us. Right?"

"Sure," I whispered.

He hugged me, and I hugged my guitar case. "It's for my acting," he said again.

"I thought you weren't an actor."

He scowled, reminding me of our initial, not-so-pleasant interactions. "I don't know—not yet. I'm trying to find out." Eamon left with his pillow, disappearing into Shoshanna's trailer where he'd be "sleeping" all night or "acting." It didn't matter which, because both of them were "smashing my feelings into smithereens."

Needless to say, I did not practice.

Film: Elementia
Director: Cate Collins

On Location: Day 5
Killykeen Forest, Ireland

Filming Notes:
A.M. & P.M.: SEVYN running through the forest
moments.

Etc. Notes:
Iris Thorne will be recording a song for the
soundtrack from 12—4 at Dublin Recording
Studio.

Julian Young flies out on Aer Lingus Flight
2059 from Dublin Airport at 11:40 a.m.

HOW COME WHEN YOUR DREAMS COME
TRUE, THEY COME TRUE ALL EFFED UP?

"JULIAN!" I SHOUTED. "You have to *listen* to her!"

The driver put up the screen between the cab and the back of the short limo. Julian and I were getting loud on the drive to Dublin.

"But she doesn't listen to me!" he said. "She worries about these specific things. 'I don't want people to take my picture.' Or 'I don't want people following us on vacation.' Do you know what she pulled yesterday? 'What if we have kids, Julian? We'll have to hide their faces.' Kids! So, I said, 'I'm twenty-one years old. Why are we talking about kids?' And she said, 'You're so shortsighted, Julian. How can I marry you?' And hung up."

He took off his dark, dark sunglasses, which were pretty pointless because the whole of Ireland had turned grey—definitely not gray—today.

I checked our progress. We seemed close to Dublin, and soon Julian would be gone, and I wouldn't get to see him again until the end of the shoot, if we all made it that far. "Look, I know what I'm talking about. I've spent my whole life hiding with my brother. You don't have that luxury, but Elora doesn't want to be hounded just for loving you."

"You think she should dump me as well? Great. Thanks, Iris."

"Work harder to see this from her perspective. Girls are going to be mean when they find out you're with her. Like *mean*. You have no idea what they'll say. When you were dating that girl, the one from *Alien Army*, my school friends and I said all kinds of stuff about her."

He looked up, so horrified that I was ashamed. "Bella? Why? She's the sweetest."

Good question. Why had we been wretched about that famous actress? We picked apart her body like she was a dissection in science class. We made up insulting nicknames. We'd raged with empty jealousy, as if her dating Julian was a personal affront.

"We just, well, Bella was dating you, and we loved you, and that meant she wasn't good enough for you." I found myself thinking about Cate's "continent of women." How connected were we after all? And what did tearing down one woman do to the others?

All of a sudden it felt like self-sabotage.

"You and your friends loved me?" Julian sniffed and tried a small smile.

"Julian, I was so happy when I ran into you at Cate's office, I nearly cried. I might've even told my friends I was going to seduce you, which is why they gave me Julian Young underwear." I couldn't believe I'd said that. I waited for him to laugh.

He didn't. He looked sort of strung out, hopeful but exhausted.

"But then I got to know you, and you're great. And you love Elora. You just have to be more sensitive to her fears."

He nodded.

"Eamon's terrible at this too. He thinks I should do his video blog to help the movie." *He's also sleeping over at Shoshanna's.*

Julian nodded. "A show of support from the Thorne family? Yeah, the movie needs that. The fans would be so happy."

"Well, I can't do it. You see that, right? People will come after me, whether or not the movie ends up being good. I'll never be able to blend in, in college or anywhere else." I left out my raging fear of people like Moss. "And I'll never be able to start my music career on my own terms." I glanced at Annie's case next me. I was on my way to a recording studio to lay down tracks for a song that I could not—for the life of me—remember how to play. This was already not on my own terms.

"How do I be more sensitive?" Julian asked. "I'll do whatever. I've already spent a year not dating her, and it ate me apart inside. She only agreed to date me again if I promised to keep it a secret, but at some point, someone is going to catch on. I'm terrified that that'll be it for us."

Oh, Julian. His nose was all slimy and somehow still adorable.

"Plus, I don't want people to think I'm hiding her. I want her on my arm at my next red carpet. I want people to know she makes me damn happy, and I'm *so* proud of her."

Tears sprang into my eyes. "You really are good at being romantic, Julian."

He grinned. "Yeah?"

"You know what you said yesterday? About Nolan and courageous love? I think I can help you." I leaned forward. "Someone told me that courage is two things: being honest and not backing down. You need to go to Elora. Tell her everything. Say you're scared, but you can't live in the dark. You're right. At some point, people are going to find out, and the only control you have is how they find out. You won't have that control forever."

His smile faded into a slow understanding. "You don't need to be afraid either, Iris. Imagine what might happen if people know who *you* are."

I laughed. "Here's where we're different. I'm nobody. My grandmother was the star. I'm an immediate disappointment to anyone who's excited to meet me." I'd never thought about it that way before, but it was true. "The first time Eamon met me, he called me a mountain troll."

"That guy." Julian shook his head. "He could use a lesson in being a love interest."

"I'll say."

We pulled up outside the Dublin airport. Julian looked out the window and then took my hand in both of his. "Iris, I want you to think of your fans—" I gave him a withering look, and he shook his head. "They are your family's fans whether you like it or not. *Your* fans. And if you let them know who you are, some will be extra nice. Some will be extra mean. But the majority? They'll want a smile and a picture for their Instagram feed, promise."

He let go of me and straightened his leather jacket. Popped on his sunglasses. "Imagine what it would be like if you didn't have to hide? It's freeing."

I wanted this to be the whole truth, but I already knew it wasn't. "What if some of the fans are cruel? Unstable? What then?"

Julian looked at me over the top of his glasses. He knew what I meant. "Give me your number." He pulled out his phone and began thumbing fast. I gave it to him, yet was still pretty shocked to hear my phone receive a text in my pocket. "Thanks for everything, Iris. We're real friends now, right?"

"Yeah. Of course." Considering I'd been hoping for this, I sounded very cool.

He got out and grabbed his bag from the driver. "See you in six days. Wish me luck."

"Good luck!" I missed Julian the second he turned his gorgeous, leather jacket–clad back and walked into the airport. I glanced down at my unread text.

This number is Top Secret 😎

A second message popped up. A URL. The preview was a photo of the back of Julian's head with a tiny bald spot and the title "Young Gets Snipped By Fan at Florence + the Machine Concert."

I clicked on the article and read about a girl who'd shorn a spot on Julian's head while he was on a date. She'd nearly cut off his ear. I wrote him back in a hurry.

This is EXACTLY what I'm afraid of! This is terrible!

His reply was ninja fast.

Are you kidding? It was the best concert of the century!

And another one:

Imagine if I missed out on this:

The next text was a picture of Florence Welch glamour-glaring beside Julian, a python around their shoulders. I sent off my own series of rapid-fire texts.

This picture is amazing. Where'd she get the snake? Tell me she pulled it out of her dreams.

You like Florence?! WHY HAVEN'T WE TALKED ABOUT THIS YET?

Can you introduce me to her?!?!

Never mind. She's a god. I'm not worthy.

I waited a few minutes for his response, the biggest, dop-iest smile on my face the whole time. I pictured him at the counter, checking his bag. Finally, he shot back:

ROFl Gonna miss you

And:

You got this, Iris. Play your heart out.

Conor clicked the button and his voice reached through the speaker over my head. "Iris? Do you need a minute? If I'm making you nervous, I can set record and head out for a coffee. We'll trim the excess when I get back."

I nodded stiffly. He set the record, the red light glowing from the ceiling bulb, and left the sound booth. I repositioned on the stool, fiddled with my tuning, but it didn't matter. The song wasn't in me anymore. I'd tried to recapture the fingerpicking pattern I'd played on the cliff, but I couldn't remember the notes that bolstered it—that made it sing-able. Also the poem Cate had given me was ridiculous:

THE FIRE PROPHECY OF QUEEN SEERIA

Ultimately Cerul will touch
The land's blackened despondency.
The verdant Ertha, dry and rust,
The trees plagued by sterility.

Need of life and hope will not trust
The ties that bind Water to sea,
And Wind's breath will choke with dust,
Hope chilled with solemnity.

Then a childe will be born in two,
Both blessed and cursed with Fire's heat,
Will feel and bear the threat of doom
To weather loneliness's defeat.

Till need regrows in Erthen hue
And life springs forth from foliage pleat,
Till Wind binds both star and moon
And Thornbred's curse is truly beat.

That was some Grade A Fantasy Bullshit. *Sorry, Grandma Mae. Not your best work.*

My palms were damp as I fitted fingers to strings. I glanced at the glowing red light above my head and tried not to cry. A desperate, hard feeling lodged in my throat, nearly choking me. I had about fifteen minutes left of the very expensive two hours of recording that Cate had paid for, and I had nothing to show for it. That's why Conor had bugged off; he knew I was blowing my chance, and who wants to watch that?

I closed my eyes. This was for Nolan's—Eamon's—big scene. I stumbled into the melody. Almost there. Maybe two notes off. *Be honest, keep going. Be honest, keep going.* I pushed myself to the edge of that cliff, but I couldn't make myself stay there. Couldn't hold my ground. All I could think about was disappointing everyone, and the song broke apart.

I dug through my bag. "Last ditch effort, coming up." I flipped through Dad's worn copy of the Elementia trilogy to the page Ryder bookmarked. Maybe if I knew what this scene was about, I could figure out how to play it.

> *The night sky was muddy and violet. Sevyn had run for hours though the white, skeletal trees of Norgatia until she came to a river that followed the base of a snow-capped mountain. She ate soft, dark berries, washing them down with icy river water. Then she collapsed in the rubbery weeds, briefly longing for the confinement of her lonely tower, for the simplicity of a world that ignored her.*

"I feel you, Sevyn," I muttered. "It's easier when no one wants anything from you."

> *Unconsciousness came quickly, leaving her limp in the heart of a strange land. In the distance, beyond the outstretched arms of the Norgatia trees, an orange halo pulsed with the remains of Maedina's still-burning tree.*

Sevyn woke hours later, retching violently. Fever berries, she thought wildly. How could she have been so foolish? She gave another violent heave and her forehead pulsed. The smell made her stomach quake, and she crawled from it, curling up along the exposed roots of a giant, white tree.

Chills and fever pounded her body until her Birth Rite responded. White flame writhed to life inside her, yet it was not her lightning. It was white fire, quavering and fearful; it had no strength, only pain. It was Evyn.

Somehow.

From a great distance, her brother was screaming through her dreams.

Goose bumps ran from the back of my neck to my arms. I glanced at the countdown clock. Nine minutes left. Where was Nolan? Had Ryder given me the wrong scene?

Sevyn held on to the ancient tree, fever dreaming a black cave. Through a whisper of light, she looked to her hands, but they were not hers; they were frail, lithe, entirely unused. Evyn's hands.

Evyn?

His head jerked. It was true then; she was inside her twin, and he could hear her. How was this possible? "Sister?"

I am here, Evyn. I can see through your eyes.

"Can you save me?" Urgency cramped his voice, but before she could respond, he added, "They come now. Save me, Sister!"

Through Evyn's eyes, a dim light grew brighter as it approached. It was not a flame, but an orb of fiery essence. Sevyn recognized it as the power Evyn had been learning to summon on Cerul before his capture at the waterfall. A dark creature held the orb, and its slinking approach filled her with dread that was magnified by Evyn's shaking. Where are you, Brother? You have to tell me!

"Thornbred," Evyn whispered, his voice rattling the darkness.

The creature swept a silencing claw across Evyn's face before pulling his head back by his hair. Sevyn's brother gave the smallest cry as the creature bit down on his neck, taking long, sucking swallows of Evyn's blood.

I cried out and threw the book at the padded wall. It's binding split and pages fell out. "You've got to be kidding me!" *Stupid goddamn book. Stupid M. E. Goddamn Thorne.* I pulled my hair over my face and yelled—anything to escape the mental image of Moss gnawing on Ryder's neck.

"It's just Julian acting with his tennis ball on a stick," I chanted several times before I remembered the flashing red light. My outburst had been professionally recorded.

And Conor was back, sitting in his booth and watching through the glass. He flipped the switch when our eyes connected. "You okay, Iris?"

I shook my head.

"Don't feel bad. You're not the first person to get in there and freeze up."

"How much was this session?" I asked. "Was it expensive?"

"You don't want to know the answer to that, girl." He gave me a small smile. "Do you want to play back what we recorded?"

I shook my head again, my hair falling in my eyes. This was bad. I'd taken money from Elementia's exhausted budget. Had this come straight out of Cate's wallet? "Conor? I want to pay for the hours." I packed Annie in her case, swept the remains of Ryder's book into my bag, and met Conor in the booth. I handed over my dad's "Only for Emergencies" Visa and didn't look at the total when I signed. Dad would be furious; he'd rip me apart for this. And Cate wouldn't have a song for Eamon's big scene.

Worst of all, I now had definitive, expensive proof.

I was not a songwriter.

Film: Elementia
Director: Cate Collins

On Location: Day 6
Killykeen Forest Park, Ireland

Filming Notes:

Magic hour shoot—NOLAN and SEVYN's first scene together.

DOWNWARD DOG AND OTHER MISERIES

I WOKE UP early the next morning, finally over my jet lag. Laundry was strewn all over the trailer, and Ryder had taped up our film sides like a record of our attendance. I fixed his copy of the Elementia trilogy and placed it beside him. He was sleeping like a baby angel, and I had to get out of there before he woke up.

Because then I'd have to tell him I'd choked.

I threw on my running clothes and went for a jog beside the lake. The sun came up with a dazzle of yellow light, the water sparkling and reminding me of Shoshanna and Eamon giggling like flirt monsters on that rowboat. I tried to listen to some raging Florence, but I wasn't feeling it. Vance Joy hit the spot instead, his moody Australian voice highlighting how much I wasn't looking forward to this day. "Fire and Flood" cut off as my phone started ringing. My dad's picture filled the screen, the image true to life: him scowling at his laptop.

I swear I could sense how mad he was on the other side of the Atlantic. The credit card. Definitely one for voice mail. I stood there for four minutes, waiting for the message notification. When my phone buzzed, dread came with it. I hit play.

"I got a call from Visa to verify a *one thousand euro* purchase at a recording studio in Dublin? You better explain fast, although I can't imagine a viable excuse. This is coming out of your allowance." There was an audible sigh-pause. "I know you're mad I'm not coming to take over with Ryder, but if you pull any more of this Jaded Iris crap, I'll cut off the card."

The message ended, and I screamed, "You probably forgot that much money in your dinner jacket, you cheap jerk!"

My voice echoed around the lake, and in the quiet aftermath, someone cleared their throat. Shoshanna was doing yoga on a mat barely a stone's throw away. I'd been seriously out of it not to notice her.

"So," she said, balanced in warrior two. "Things aren't going well for you either?"

I scowled. Did she have any idea how much her gorgeous, superior presence was trashing my feelings for Eamon? "Why are you doing yoga out in the open?" I snapped. "Aren't you worried creepers might be watching you? Anyone could walk by."

"Maybe I was hoping someone would walk by," she said. In my silence, she added, "Not you, Iris. But if you're going to stand there, you might as well join me."

I dropped into downward dog beside her, wondering if Cate had put her up to this. *Bonding exercises*, Julian had called it. I followed her sun salutation; it was different than the one I did in gym, but similar enough that I didn't seem like a total elephant doing karate.

"That was my dad," I finally said when I couldn't stand the silence. "Threatening me from a few thousand miles away. He's a—"

"Cheap jerk? I know his kind." There was something unflinching in Shoshanna that made me want to be like her. To talk the way she talked. She wasn't worried about everyone liking her all the time, and it was sort of breathtaking. We moved into warrior two, and she squinted at me. "You're a virgin, aren't you?"

"What?" I fell out of the move, twisting my knee.

"You've got no awareness in your hips. It's obvious."

"Why," I busted out, "does everyone think it's okay to pick on me?" I took back all internal compliments about Shoshanna Reyes. She was a say-anything freak. "So what if I'm a virgin? That's not illegal, is it?"

She smiled triumphantly, like she had during our very first conversation. "Oh, it's legal. And explains a lot." She kept sun-saluting, and I kept up purely out of aggravation.

"I know you get kicks out of making people squirm, but *no* virgin shaming."

"Hey, I mean no offense," she said. "This is part of how I understand people. How I handle my roles. I figure out the character's experience, sexuality range, where they are on the gender spectrum. You've been tricky, so I've been applying work tactics. Seriously, no offense."

Now I felt like I had to apologize for going slightly nuclear. "My school friends give me crap about this back at home. I'm a little hot-wired on the subject."

"What are school friends?"

While I was used to using that term, no one had ever repeated it back before. "They're my friends, but we don't hang outside of school. I have to watch Ryder."

"That's sad, Iris Thorne."

"The longer I'm in Ireland, the more I realize this," I muttered. "Don't tell Eamon I'm… I mean, don't tell anyone."

"Oh, Eamon is a virgin too. Have you seen that boy dance? I tried to get him to wiggle his lower body last night. Cement."

My face steamed in my forward fold. "You guys have fun last night?"

"I'm not hooking up with Eamon. Feel free to shove that card back in the deck." Shoshanna switched to plank, her long, thick hair tied up in an unruly braid that made mine look manageable by comparison. Also, her arm muscles were stunning. "I have zero interest in him, and I'm rarely into pork swords."

I was stuck on her statement of *I'm not hooking up with Eamon*. Did that mean I still had a shot? No way. Eamon was getting one-on-one time with Shoshanna. Even if she didn't like him, he was bound to like her. I didn't stand a chance.

Stop ranking women.

I fell out of my plank, and Shoshanna looked at me weird. "I think I just heard Cate Collin's voice in my head."

Shoshanna smirked. "She has presence, doesn't she? Although don't go all black and white on her little feminism pep talks. She's put up with some serious gender bullshit, but that's one experience, not *every* woman's experience."

"Okay…" I was in over my head. Again.

"Also, you're panting weird," she said. "It's throwing off my rhythm."

"Sorry." I glanced at Shoshanna's shoulder and noticed a bit of ink hitherto hidden by her clothes. "Is that… Do you have a tattoo of Rosie the Riveter?"

"No."

"It is!"

"You are epically bad at noticing things outside of yourself." Shoshanna twisted to show off her shoulder tattoo.

"Whoa." I put my back knee down in runner's lunge and leaned in for a closer look. "Is that Dr. Jillian Holtzmann from *Ghostbusters*?"

"Of course it is."

"What do you mean 'of course it is'? How many people

on this planet have Jillian Holtzmann tattoos?" I was trying to tease her, to connect on some basic level even if it was silly. "Oh God, you're a nerd after all! A sneaky, campy nerd."

"No, Iris. I'm queer. And that's a big fucking deal in this business. Do you know how many roles I've lost because the casting director has flat-out said, 'We don't think you can act straight enough'? And that's after getting over the bar of those who see my Filipino last name and automatically trash my résumé. I've got to get this role right. My career depends on it."

I had no clue what to say. "Sorry."

"Don't be sorry. Just know that I exist. For every mighty, whitey Cate Collins, there's someone like me, winning the intersectional bingo and all the bullshit that goes with it. Not white enough for some roles, not dark enough for others." Shoshanna's voice splintered into a long sigh. "Sorry. I shouldn't be unloading on you. There's a nightmare of a reporter going around set. She likes to push buttons. Make sure you keep your distance."

"Yeah, Julian warned me too."

We switched to downward dog. I thought Shoshanna might be ready for silence, but no.

"Did you record that song for Cate?"

Boom.

"Um, no." I'd finally said it. The truth wasn't too hard, but then, Shoshanna wasn't one of the people I was afraid to tell.

"Cate's going to be pissed."

"The poem was no good," I countered.

"You're not wrong. This fantasy crap gets so convoluted."

"Finally someone who agrees with me." The compliment strategy worked on my school friends, but Shoshanna's frown peeked under her arm, unfooled as ever.

"You're the one who insists no one gets you, Iris. I'll always be real with you. All you've got to do is see me for me, deal?"

Before I could answer, a laughing Ryder scrambled underneath my downward dog, blocking any way out of the position. "Hey, giggle hound, get out from under me!"

Eamon was there too—underneath Shoshanna's dog. He tried to tease her, but she gave him a short warning before kneeing him in the stomach and standing up.

"Ryder, move!" He crawled out from under me, but before I could come down, Eamon took his place. "Seriously? My arms are about to give out."

"So fall on me, then," he said, his blue eyes daring. *Christ.* My shoulders shook, my legs ached, and yet I was so happy to see him. We smiled at each other while a shadow fell over us.

"Don't step on his face," Shoshanna warned. "He has to act tonight."

Her shadow moved on, and Ryder ran off down the shoreline. I was still in the longest downward dog of all time. "They're going to film your scene tonight?"

"Yes, we're going to do it. *I'm* going to do it." He looked adorable when he was talking himself into something. His forehead scrunched and his lips pouted. "Iris, you're shaking and your face is all red. You should come down." He tickled my ribs, and I flattened him.

Not a graceful move about it.

He *oofe*d out all his air, and I tried not to mangle his face. And then I went from embarrassed to red hot because we were all tangled on the soft grass beside the most gorgeous green lake in Ireland, the orange sun climbing. I thought he might kiss me again, and I assessed my lips and breath. Not good. Stupid yoga dry mouth.

Instead of kissing, though, he sat up on crossed legs and pulled me close. My back was pressed to his chest, and his arms wrapped around me, which was no small part stunning. "I missed you yesterday," he said into my hair, his breath tickling my neck.

He missed me. That was a real feeling, wasn't it?

This was real.

"How did it go?" he asked.

I closed my eyes, reality popping any semblance of happiness. What I wouldn't have given to stay in his tight hold and tell him that I'd recorded the song as planned, that his faith in me hadn't been foolish. "I couldn't do it," I said slowly. "There's no song for your scene. I'm sorry."

His arms loosened. He leaned away. "These things happen."

These things happen?

I touched his hand, tried to slip my fingers in between his, but he wasn't budging. Was he *that* disappointed? "I'm sorry," I said again, flatter this time. "I'm not M. E. Thorne."

"I know that, Iris. We all know that. No one is asking you to be."

"Yeah right." My anger felt weird, held in check by our sweetheart's position before the epic scenery. All of a sudden, we felt like a joke—just like fantasy. One minute it was poetic, wild, true. The next? Plain silly. Stupid foam pointy ears and a made-up, gibberish language.

"Why didn't you record the song you were playing on the cliff?" Eamon asked.

"I couldn't remember it," I said. "That's like asking some-one to remember a poem word for word they read a few days ago. If I had a few days to figure it out, maybe I could—"

"Oh well," he said, making me grit my teeth.

"I'm not a real musician, Eamon. It was a stupid idea to begin with."

"It was my idea. Thanks, like." He let me go, and an awkward moment passed before I realized he was waiting for me to get off him. Once we were standing, he ran a hand through his wild curls. "I've got to go have my hair chopped. Say goodbye to a few inches of me."

"Goodbye," I said flatly.

He made a weird, exasperated sound and walked away.

I AM WOMAN, HEAR ME RUIN EVERYTHING

CATE COLLINS STOOD by the lake, a sliver of a person. Petite, narrow. Sharp.

She inspected a huge tree with gnarled roots that spider-climbed into the water. Henrik stood nearby, scribbling Cate's observations into his notebook.

I slowly recognized the scene I'd read yesterday in the recording studio. The great white tree that Sevyn hugged through her fever dream. Wait, the tree...the tree was supposed to *be* Nolan. Eamon. I looked over it again. Gorgeous, reaching branches, a smooth-barked trunk.

Crew members spun around Cate like satellites, close but never too close. They put down wires and set up a base for the huge camera crane on the soft shore. They were being inspected—we all were—by the same brown-haired reporter who had spooked Julian back on Inishmore. She was talking to the cinematographer, but her eyes were trained on Cate.

This was the woman who'd gotten under Shoshanna's skin. What did she want?

I approached Cate only to have Henrik shake his head at me. A warning. I started to walk away, but Cate's voice stopped me. "I already know, Iris. You didn't manage it."

I turned around. "How?"

Cate peered at the sky, one hand shielding her eyes. "Because if you had succeeded at the studio, you would have busted into my trailer last night to tell me."

Why did she have to be right about me all time?

"I'm sorry," I said, my voice gruff. "The poem was… It was too hard."

"Everything is too hard," she said. I waited for her to elaborate. Too hard for the movie? For women? What? But Cate was distracted by the reporter clearly trailing our conversation. "Her name is Grace Lee. She's freelance. A veritable spy for the producers of *Elementia*."

"Catherine," Henrik warned.

"Don't you 'Catherine' me, Henrik. I know what's going on, and they don't treat this production well enough for me to paint pretty lies for them to peddle about!" Her voice rose, her temper teetering on some cliff's edge. She growled and walked back to the water.

Henrik took a deep breath, and we both watched Cate

place a shielding hand over her eyes again. It wasn't that bright out; she was trying to hide her expression.

"What's wrong?"

"In a word? Everything." Henrik closed his notebook and played with the short brim of his floppy hat. "New budget complications, and we've been getting bad press. And Cate talked on one of Eamon's YouTube blogs about the lack of support from the studio. She's not wrong, but Jesus, she can't be honest like that without a backlash."

"Cate suffers no fools," I said. "It's what I like about her."

"She suffers, Iris. A lot." He motioned to the reporter with a nod of his head. "The powers that be over at Vantage have sent her to pronounce the film dead. The sentencing will come out through the media, and then the producers can shut us down with a shrug. It helps them save face." He looked at me. "It would have helped if you'd recorded that song. We would have been able to spin it as though your family was having a part in the production."

As if I couldn't feel worse.

Henrik looked like he might apologize, but shook his head and walked away instead. After a moment, I left, not realizing that Cate was stalking after me until I felt her hand on my shoulder.

"I'm sorry I pushed you," Cate said, surprising me so much I stopped walking.

"You don't seem like you apologize very often."

"I try not to do anything that requires an act of contrition."

I glanced back at the crew members and the most picturesque lake I'd ever seen. "What's happening? They aren't going to shut down the film, are they?"

"Maybe. We're over budget." Cate stared and I thought I'd see the fire, brimstone, and mobster side of her again—at least that's what I wanted. It was not, however, the side that was waiting. Her eyes drooped in the corners, her mouth doing something similar. "I won't give up, Iris. I'll die trying to get this right. I won't give up or back down."

Henrik reappeared and put an arm around her waist. It looked friendly, but he took most of her weight. "Cate needs to eat, Iris. And drink water. And take a goddamn break before tonight. This is the most important scene in the movie, Cate. Remember?"

She nodded, pushed Henrik's arm away, and started walking toward her trailer. I watched Grace Lee's eyes trail after her as though they were snapping paparazzi pictures.

"Cate works every minute," Henrik said, worry creeping into each word. "Sometimes she sends me off for the night, says we're done, and then I wake to find she's reworked all the dialogue and reprinted the sides." He shook his head, and I could tell how much Henrik loved Cate. Her pain left him in pain, his expression creased. "You'd think the studio would applaud her for facing the budget constraints by taking on additional crew positions herself. Instead, they send spies to document her exhaustion and say she's not strong enough."

"Would they say the same things if you were in charge?"

Henrik knew what I meant; this was—at least in large part—because Cate had matching X chromosomes. He took off his hat and rubbed a hand through his thinning, dark hair. "If I were in charge, we wouldn't be over budget, but the dailies would look cheap. She puts the art first. The story. It's what makes her and this adaptation brilliant. If we can make it to the cutting room floor, it'll all be worth it. If we can only make it..."

"What can I do to help?" I asked, the words surprising but real. *First, be honest.*

"Do you mean it?" he asked. I nodded. Henrik pointed to the reporter. "Will you talk to her? Say something optimistic. Anything. She doesn't have photographic permission, so you don't need to worry about your image being taken. I'll set it up if you're serious."

"I am, but...I can't speak on behalf of the Thorne family." I was already pulling back, already doubting my first step. "My dad will kill me."

"Why don't you speak for yourself?"

I actually laughed. When he frowned, I said, "That's, uh, not something I've been encouraged to do before."

He scrutinized my face. "That's crap, Iris. Believe it or not, people care what you think."

I sat at a picnic table at the center of the production trailers, waiting for Henrik to bring over Grace Lee. It felt like I was inching forward on my own two feet for the first time in my life… Toward what kind of cliff, I had no idea.

I texted Julian, replaying his talk about "my family's fans." I needed that to be real.

Wish you were here. Things are getting worse.

It was in the middle of the night in LA, but maybe I'd hear back. Julian was never away from his phone, but then maybe he was snuggled up with Elora. Maybe they'd sorted out their differences. I hoped so.

"When I stepped foot on this set, I was told that under no circumstances would I be allowed to talk to you or your brother. Care to discuss what's changed?"

I looked up at Grace Lee. "Excuse me?"

"Your family has refused to comment on the adaptation of *Elementia* from day one, and now you'd like to make a statement? I find I'm more curious about your change of heart than I am about your opinion."

Holy shit.

"Where's Henrik?"

"Busy. The camera crane sunk six inches into the mud and nearly toppled into the lake."

"Oh no."

Grace wrote in her small notebook before clicking on an audio recording app on her phone. "Do you mind if I record you?"

"No, that's good." *This way she couldn't claim I said something I didn't, right?*

She saw how spooked I was and smiled. She had a good smile. *Maybe she wasn't here to eat me alive.* "Let's start with a different topic. Can you describe your relationship with your grandmother, M. E. Thorne, in a few words?"

"Nonexistent," I said.

Grace squinted, and I remembered I was supposed to be helping the production.

"My father and my grandmother were not on speaking terms during my lifetime. I only met her once."

"Do you remember that?"

I shook my head, unwilling to share that snapshot of a memory with her for anything.

"How do you think she'd feel about a film adaptation of her deeply personal and effecting story? A story written about the untimely death of her own daughter?"

I gargled air. It sounded horrible, and Grace looked way too excited by such an emotional reaction.

Start with honesty, Iris, Cate Collins said, matter-of-fact and calm in my thoughts.

"My dad told me she wouldn't have been pleased about an adaptation," I admitted. "She wasn't a fan of Hollywood, although I think that's his opinion and not hers. The truth is that I came on this set with daydreams about shutting down the production. Now I'm willing to break my family's cardinal rule about talking to the press to save it."

Grace's smile deepened, and she wrote in her notebook. "Tell me what's changed."

"The people. At first I thought they were all brainwashed by the fandom, but everyone is working hard. Every time something goes wrong, everyone steps up. It's inspiring, and Cate's giving her all."

"How so?" Grace asked too fast.

"She can handle everything. She knows every detail, and she works endless hours."

"You're saying she's micromanaging the production?"

"What? No, no." I pinched my leg and pushed forward. "The actors are…great. Shoshanna Reyes and Julian Young and Eamon O'Brien. All great."

"I've been told O'Brien hasn't filmed yet."

"Yeah, but he's still great. Like as a human." *Say something other than great, Iris.* "Terrific."

Terrific?

"Do you have a comment about the rumor that Shoshanna Reyes will be pulling out of the production?"

"That's bull crap," I snapped. Grace's smirk tightened as she scribbled; I'd been played. Again. "She's committed to the film from what I've seen."

"And how do you feel about a self-identified *pansexual* girl playing the lead in your grandmother's story? Do you think your grandmother would have had a problem with that?"

I did not take the bait this time, but I felt my ears rush hot. "Shoshanna is incredibly talented." I wanted to point out what Shoshanna had told me only that morning that her life was riddled with double standards. Complications and inequality. She knew Sevyn's struggle better than anyone I could imagine, but I couldn't quite put myself behind the words. "She *is* Sevyn," I managed. "My grandmother would have loved her."

"I thought you didn't know your grandmother."

"Are all reporters this impossible to talk with?"

Now I'd gotten her. Grace closed her notebook but didn't turn off her recording app. I took advantage and kept talking. "Look, I'm not into fantasy. Not even my grandmother's story, but the people here believe in this adaptation with their whole hearts and that comes through in each take."

I was proud of myself, even prouder when I felt a hand on my shoulder and looked up to see Henrik. "Everything going all right?" he asked.

"You have had quite the sway on this young lady," Grace said. "She's a firecracker."

"Iris reminds Cate of herself as a teen. She's said so several times."

Cate thinks I am like her? For real?

"Tell me that crane broke, Henrik," Grace said, leaning forward with a slick smile.

"No, it did not." He motioned for me to leave with a hook of his thumb.

I walked away, fists tight. I thought I'd done all right, and I looked for Eamon, wanting to speak up some more. To try and explain why I'd frozen up in the recording studio. But he was nowhere in sight. I looked for Shoshanna next, planning to ask if Grace's rumor was real, but everyone was busy getting ready to film.

Even Ryder was helping Mr. Donato plan a dessert surprise for after Eamon's big scene. The best scene in the book, according to several people, although my reading in the studio yesterday had left me wondering what I was still missing when it came to M. E. Thorne's *Elementia*.

THE POINT IN THE STORY WHERE
EVERYTHING HAS GOT TO CHANGE

KILLYKEEN WAS TRANSFORMED with the sunset. The crew came together in a rush of activity that felt nearly seamless. I hoped Grace Lee was still poking around to witness the success, but she'd already left.

Ryder and I sat on twin canvas chairs in the video village—the sectioned-off area of monitors where Cate and Henrik and a few other people watched the filming. We were filming at dusk, the so-called *magic hour*, which I was surprised to learn was a film term, not a fantasy one. I watched the sun linger warmly at the horizon, while the sky ached blue and yellow.

Azure and goldenrod…

"Picture's up!" Cate hollered, making everyone snap into place. Shoshanna drew all eyes, standing farther down the shore by herself, wearing the same getup she'd worn during the burning of the tree. If I remembered my *Elementia*, Sevyn was coming here after running miles and miles from the fire she'd started. I glanced behind us. The crowd of crew members behind the cameras was larger than usual—more people were watching this than Maedina's burning tree—and the atmosphere was charged with strange emotion. High expectations, maybe? Hope?

Cate raised her hand and shushed the crowd. Even the animals of Killykeen seemed to heed her. She looked showered, refreshed, invincible again, her buzzed grey hair like steel. I remembered Henrik's talk about how much she was sacrificing for this movie. What was it like to give your all like that? Could I learn to do that with my music? If so, where did I start?

Cate called, "Action!"

Shoshanna sprang into her role, and I couldn't help looking for Eamon. Shouldn't he be here? Ready to step into the scene?

Shoshanna ran up the shore, toward us, out of breath and devastated, slipping into the water, scuffing against roots. She collapsed on the shore near the mighty tree that Cate had been inspecting earlier. Shoshanna—Sevyn—drank from the water and ate berries from the weeds.

She fell into a twisting, terrible sleep. Sevyn thrashed, burning with fever, dreaming about her brother getting gnawed upon. From the scene I'd read, I knew she could see through his eyes, feel his pain—and do nothing. I shivered.

Cate called, "Cut!"

She gave Shoshanna notes, and Shoshanna went back to her mark. They taped it again and again. In between two takes, Ryder put his foam fantasy axe on my arm and I looked down to find it was actually his hand. He was still, focused.

"Are you scared?" I asked.

"Maybe." His voice didn't sound afraid; he was deep in thought.

"Ry," I started, "does this scene make you think of Moss?"

"It makes me think about that nightmare I have. The one where you don't stop him, and he drives away with me."

I knew about his recurring dream. His therapist had marched the whole family in to talk about it without Ryder present, although my brother had never spoken to me about it before. His therapist had gotten a few details about the dream out of him, but not the whole truth, which is what had worried her. I leaned closer and brushed the side of his face where the very last of his sweet, fine baby hair was blending into dark locks. I don't know what came over me—perhaps it was the urgency of only having a few breaths between takes, but I pushed forward. "What happens in your dream after the van drives off?"

"I wake up," he said.

I sat back in my chair, taking in the way his eyes narrowed on Shoshanna, his tone mature and matter-of-fact. He was lying, keeping his pain secret.

The real Thorne legacy.

"Sevyn saves Evyn, doesn't she?" I asked, desperate to help my brother with his pain, even if only through the roles we resembled in our grandma's book. "In the end, she saves him."

"Eyeball," he whispered because they were about to start filming again. "You have to read it to find out!"

I grabbed his hand, which wasn't small anymore and yet still little-kid sticky.

"Action!" Cate called.

Shoshanna went through her routine once more. She was tired and cold at this point, and I think a few of her stumbles weren't fake. When she collapsed on the tree and shivered, her head thrown back on the gnarled roots, I believed she was witnessing something horrible in her mind. That her whole life was coming to some crucial breaking point.

I believed her because I had been there—sitting on the edge of the sandbox with Moss's blood under my nails, answering the cops' questions, my dad still missing. He'd turned off his phone to finish a chapter, and by the time he'd pulled up to the playground and listened to the police officer's message, we'd been at the hospital for more than an hour.

Shoshanna turned her face into the tree and started crying, which I'm pretty sure Cate hadn't told her to do. But it felt right.

And everything changed.

One minute, Shoshanna was shaking in her fantasy garb, the next she was Sevyn, a girl who'd never been touched by anyone. A cursed girl who'd lost the only person who had ever been there for her: her brother. And now she knew he was in pain, but she couldn't reach him.

I swear I could hear the harp solo from "Cosmic Love" and Florence singing of misery and light, and then the lights ebbed a tiny bit brighter, signaling that the CGI moon had come out, throwing silver brilliance over the whole scene.

Nolan leaned from the side of the tree as though he'd stepped from the bark—and he wasn't Eamon. He was tan skinned, his ears blended into his short hairstyle. His whole arrow-sharp body was on show but for some shorts that looked like they'd been stitched from leaves. He crouched near Sevyn, watching her violent fever with an intensity that held the light.

And then he bent down and swept her into his arms, carrying her to the lake.

I'm not sure anyone was breathing. I wasn't.

Nolan walked until he was waist deep. He lowered her into the water, and she gasped from the cool shock. From the view screen beside me, I could see the crane cam's close up on Sevyn's face…the moment she woke, finding herself wrapped in someone's arms. Her fear came naturally, wonderfully. She reached up and placed a hand on Nolan's chest. There were no bolts of lightning. No sizzles from the storm inside.

Just touch.

Sevyn's eyes closed again, not in pain this time, but in the kind of release that only comes after a lifetime of imprisonment.

"Cut," Cate whispered, and no one spoke.

Ryder sniffed beside me, and I found tears lining my eyes as well. Henrik and Cate leaned close to the monitors. She murmured, "Check the gate."

Shoshanna and Eamon trudged out of the lake in silence.

Cate's face was hidden in the playback for a minute. Another minute. The magic hour was definitely gone now, the sky black. Had we gotten the shot?

When Cate stood, everyone seemed to lean back. She walked to Eamon, clasped his face with both hands and pulled his forehead to hers. "You are a goddamn star, my boy."

A riotous bolt of excitement rattled through the set. Henrik was quick to ask Cate to shoot it again, but she shook her head. "We got it exactly the way I wanted. I won't let it get stale."

I stood up because everyone was standing, and a crew member beside me joked, "Time to take out shares in Eamon O'Brien. He's going to shoot through the roof." I knew what he meant; Eamon had been amazing. One shot and he'd nailed it, even though he'd been scared and doubting himself for weeks. I found myself torn between pride and burning jealousy.

Everyone slapped hands and hugged. Ryder danced his way to help Mr. Donato present the celebratory ice cream bar.

I grabbed Shoshanna as she tried to storm by. "You were great. Both of you. Amazing."

"Thanks." She cast a look back at where everyone had piled around Eamon, a halo of gushing fans. "All the boys have to do is show up, am I right?" Her face crashed with a wince. "I'm tired. He was great. Way better than I thought he'd be after run-through." Shoshanna shivered, crossed her arms tighter. "I've got to go warm up before I get pneumonia."

She kept her head down as she hustled to the costume trailer, and I didn't blame her. She'd worked her ass off tonight. She deserved some accolades too.

I stood there for a long, long time, waiting for my turn to talk with Eamon, wanting to tell him how I'd *felt* the scene. I really had. And I'd sort of had an epiphany about myself as well, although I wasn't sure what it meant yet.

In the end, I couldn't wait. I snagged my dad's old copy of the Elementia trilogy out of my trailer and curled up on the bench by the water. There was just enough light for reading. All around, the celebration of the crew was a hardy mix of whooping and delight. It was too bad that terrible reporter hadn't stuck around. This was the real story—the movie coming together against all odds.

I opened the book to the chapter my brother had marked—the same one that had thrown me for a whirl while

I was trying to record that song. This time I kept reading past Sevyn's fever, past the revelation of her brother's torture.

All the way to Nolan.

A veil of calm settled upon her, quieting the lightning in her heart. It was a comfort she did not deserve, and she bucked at it until her strength gave out. She needed the fire, needed it to scorch her guilt; it was all her fault that such a fate had befallen her brother. She should have saved him.

When Sevyn opened her eyes once more, the night streaked the sky with darkness. She was afloat in the cool waters of the river. Something gripped her shoulders and knees, and she reached for whatever she was stuck on, imagining a submerged tree or moss-covered rock.

Instead her fingers found skin.

Sevyn looked at the face of a boy who cradled her against the tide. His countenance was utterly wild, and yet he held her as though it were the purpose he knew best. Sevyn reached for him, telling herself that she was dreaming. Her virgin touch was charged with excitement, not lightning, as she felt the contours of his collarbone, the indent of his sternum, and the mounds of his ribs. When she reached for his face, touching his jaw and lips, she

wept. This was a dream, no doubt. Her curse did
not let her touch. This was the cruelest dream.

"You're hiding," Eamon said, slipping next to me on the bench, still all fantasy-outfitted and pointy-eared. His features were drawn out with makeup shadows and the spray stuff that had tanned every inch of him, highlighting a wide, wild smile.

"I'm reading," I said, holding up the book.

He slid closer, looked at the cover like he'd couldn't believe it, then me, then the cover again. Then he kissed my cheek. "I did it, Iris," he whispered. "I can't believe it. I was terrified."

"You were amazing!" Some inner voice whispered to be cool, but I went full fangirl instead. "It was unbelievable, and I was so…I don't know, maybe *captivated* is the right word, but I couldn't even remember what country I was in, and I had to read the original scene. Shoshanna was great too," I added.

"Iris, I know the two of us hanging out together looked bad, but she was only helping me with my role. I swear it."

"I know, and you should thank her. She was pretty exhausted after the wrap."

He nodded, his blue eyes were close, bright from the flood lamps illuminating the crew party at the picnic tables. "I'm sorry I was acting strangely this morning. I thought I was going to lose it when the cameras rolled. I was sure of it."

I should have kissed him—his lips were right there—but

my doubts rose fast, reminding me of how I'd hyperventilated in that recording booth. "How did you get yourself to do it?"

"I had to shut off the negative voices. It wasn't easy, but I couldn't let my doubts win."

"Oh."

"That's why I had to come find you. To keep that bravery going and tell you I like you." The tiniest frown formed on my face, and he read it fast. "And my feelings have nothing to do with M. E. bloody Thorne. Don't even start."

I squeezed the old copy of the Elementia trilogy. "Eamon, I figured out something while we were filming. You were right."

He sat forward. "About what? Your rascally cuteness? Your musical prowess?"

I pushed myself forward, aching to be honest with him. "You were right when you asked me if I act like the abduction happened to Ryder and not both of us. I've never thought it was something that happened to me. It always felt like I just happened to be there. It was way safer to feel like a witness. To pretend like this couldn't be my life." A tear fell, and I wiped it away fast.

He wove his fingers with mine, and I wished he'd say something, but this wasn't his problem to solve. This was all me. "It's bigger than that day on the playground. I've been trying to eject myself from my own life this whole time, but I don't want to do that anymore. I want to hit play." I looked around at the crew, at his fantasy costume, at the gorgeous dark lake. "I want to be part of this."

"Only one way to do that," he said, so solemn I held my breath. "Elementia tattoos."

I laughed and punched him in the arm, and he leaned in to kiss me.

"Iris!"

Eamon groaned, his lips nearly against mine. We turned to face my little brother.

Ryder held up a bowl of ice cream. "I'm designing sundaes for the crew. This one is special for you." I took the bowl, and he pointed out all the additions. "Dark chocolate ice cream with coconut and a few crumbled cookie bits. I crumbled the cookie myself. Mr. Donato said it shows *culinary ingenuity*." He sat on the bench, waiting intently as I took a bite.

"It's great, Ry." It really was. "Can I share this with Eamon?"

"Okay, but just a little bit. I'm going to make him a special sundae too. It'll reflect his personality and individual tastes." Ryder sprinted off, and I held out a spoonful to Eamon. He leaned forward, and I couldn't even process thoughts as his mouth sealed around my spoon.

"Mmmm," he said. "Tastes of consolation prize."

I giggled. Things were different from when we kissed on the ferry. That had been spontaneous. Now it felt like we were going to kiss again because we had to—because gravity demanded it. I took another bite of sundae, savoring the dark chocolate and Eamon's company and the potential that seemed to be everywhere all at once.

Film: Elementia
Director: Cate Collins

On Location: Day 7
Killykeen Forest, Ireland

Filming Notes:

Filming canceled.

ROAD TRIP

I KNEW SOMETHING was wrong when I woke up. Something *newly* wrong.

I peeked through the trailer window. There was no hustle to the craft services area. No disputes about lighting or power cords. Nothing. I sat up and found Ryder gone. For once, I wasn't scared. He was with Mr. Donato. I trusted that man. Or maybe the impossible had happened and I was now trusting Ryder. Either way, something was amiss—and it had nothing to do with my brother's absence.

I found our film side for the day on Ryder's bed. *Filming canceled* stood out in bold letters. I grabbed my phone and found a half dozen angry texts from Julian.

Holy shit, Iris

What the hell is going on over there?

What did I tell you about reporters?!

My hands started shaking as I replied.

What did I do?

It was the middle of the night in California. No way he'd respond…and yet his dancing ellipsis appeared instantly. I waited for what felt like five minutes, but in Julian's swift texting, it was probably fifteen seconds. He sent a URL. I clicked it.

Family of famed high fantasy author M. E. Thorne speak out about the cursed film adaptation for the beloved first novel in the trilogy.

"Elementia," which chronicles a young female heroine who must save her twin brother from demon elf-like creatures, is in production under the direction of Cate Collins ("Girls First" and "No Water This Year"). Filming on location in remote parts of Ireland, I caught up with the cast and crew for a look at a titanic adaptation on the brink of disaster.

Amidst the frustration and near-constant catastrophe, this reporter has confirmed that from the original green light, the production has suffered funding cuts and producer rollover. Iris Thorne (granddaughter of M. E. Thorne) spoke out about the attitudes on set. "They're all a bit brainwashed." She also admitted to dreaming "of having the film shut down."

Thorne continued by pointing out that the cost of this epic seems to be falling on director Cate Collins. "She's giving her all" and "works endless hours," Thorne said. An undisclosed source at Vantage Pictures revealed that the studio has had doubts about Collins shepherding this project, wondering if a production of this magnitude and cultural significance should have been placed on her unproven shoulders.

What may have once seemed like a grand idea—to adapt the feminist answer to the Tolkien legacy and to ride the popularity of Peter Jackson's "The Lord of the Rings" films—now seems post-iceberg impact but pre-sinking, even in the eyes of the famed, deceased author's surviving family who believe she "wouldn't have been pleased."

Also Read: Julian Young to co-lead in high fantasy adaptation "Elementia," alongside indie darling Shoshanna Reyes and unknown Irish actor Eamon O'Brien

I died a little, sinking into Ryder's mattress, squeezing my phone. "That was all out of context," I said to myself. Then I texted that to Julian. Twice.

He fired back:

Doesn't matter. Damage done.

There's more bad news. You should go talk to Cate.

I had a blinding urge to stay hidden in the trailer, but that was my fear talking. I could recognize it clearer and faster than ever, but that didn't make it easier to quiet. I tied my dark hair back, hurried into my comfy jeans that hung low on my hips and my favorite, softest T-shirt. Time for comfort items. If I'd brought Mr. Mellow, my favorite childhood stuffed sloth, to Ireland, I'd have him snug in my arms right now.

Outside the trailer, my first thoughts were about Eamon. He was supposed to be filming with Shoshanna today. More Nolan and Sevyn scenes. I'd been excited to see them in action again. Maybe only the day was canceled, not the entire film. That was possible, wasn't it?

At the edge of the green-and-gold lake, I found a small, grim posse made up of Eamon, Roxy, and Henrik. Eamon looked strange in street clothes, and his hair was so short it actually looked a little odd without the elf ears.

They watched me approach like I was the angel of death. Even Eamon.

My words tumbled out long before I reached them. "I said good things! She took everything out of context!"

Henrik held up a hand. "Of course you did. We all knew she had it out for us."

"Then why did you make me talk to her?" I blurted. "Why make me ruin everything?"

"You didn't ruin anything," Eamon said fast. I stood next to him, a little too aware of his hands buried in his pockets. Unreachable. "It's the damn Thornians. I think I now understand why you loathe them so much."

"What'd they do now?" I growled.

"After the article came out, they started an online boycott of the adaptation. It has thirteen thousand signatures since last night, and it's looking to go viral by noon," Henrik said, his voice as grumpy as ever, his expression basset-hound sad.

"So we keep going forward. We prove those idiots wrong." My fists went tight. I wanted to punch someone.

"It won't matter," Eamon said, deflated. He looked to Henrik, who shook his head. They looked to Roxy. She appeared almost plain today in a pair of overalls and a red flannel. She didn't even have on makeup. And why were we all looking at Roxy?

"Shoshanna quit."

I opened my mouth but nothing came out. Not even air.

"She's already gone to the airport," Eamon added. "She didn't say goodbye to any of us."

"Her talent agent thought she should get out before the really bad press hit. The boycott was the final straw though, not the article." Henrik looked at me like this might make me feel better. Well, at least now I knew who I wanted to punch: Shoshanna.

Henrik straightened up and clapped Eamon on the shoulder. "Look alive."

I turned to see Cate walking toward us. She looked a bit like Julian, dark sunglasses, leather jacket, folded shoulders. When her eyes fell on me, her steps slowed, and I wasn't imagining it. "Cate, I'm—"

She shook her head, and I stopped talking. "No offense, Iris, but I'm not in the mood."

Dead silence. Now there were five of us, standing on a glorious beach before a few million dollars' worth of production equipment wondering what the hell to do. After a long, long moment, Cate said, "I think I'm supposed to be inspiring here, but I don't fucking feel like it."

Roxy snorted a laugh. Eamon cracked a smile, and Cate rubbed her hands through her buzzed hair. "I have to call the studio and let them know," she said, more angry than sad. "I wanted to take one more stroll before my dream comes to a crashing halt."

"Don't," I said.

Everyone stared at me.

"Don't?" Cate asked.

"Don't call them yet. I'll go to the airport. I'll talk Shoshanna out of leaving."

"What are you going to say to her I haven't already tried, Iris?" Cate pulled her glasses down her nose to look at me. I'd finally surprised Cate Collins.

"I don't know," I said honestly. "But she's a nonbeliever, and I speak nonbeliever, if you guys remember."

"Fluently," Eamon said. I could tell two things in that one word. First, he was devastated. Second, he believed in me—or he wanted to. "It's not a bad idea, Cate. I'll drive her."

I looked into Cate's small, blue eyes, willing her to believe in me. "I won't back down."

For most of the ride to the airport, I was silent. Eamon was silent. Where would we begin? How do these things even work when your crush's dream role and career as an actor is at risk?

"I'm sorry this happened," I tried. "Do you blame me for the article?"

"I'd say we blame Henrik for letting a live wire like you near that reporter. I can only imagine what you actually said for her to get all those unflattering quotes." His words had a bite, but it could have been worse.

"Hey, I said great things! About Cate. About Shoshanna, Julian. You." I sighed. "I was trying to be honest. I said I hadn't wanted to be here at first, but you guys changed my mind."

He glanced at me from the corner of his eyes. "What'd
you say about me, then?"

"That you're amazing. Way out of my league." Okay, I
hadn't said that, but it's how I'd felt since I'd seen Eamon go
all actor. He looked like he was going to argue, and I beat him
to it. "You're all sure of yourselves. You're all trying so hard,
and I feel like the biggest coward. The second I stepped on
this set, I was smacked by all the ways in which I'm not brave
like my grandmother, like Cate, like you and Shoshanna.
Even Julian!"

"Iris, is this because you didn't record that song? You'll
get there."

"No, I won't. Not unless I change something huge
about myself."

Keep going, that inner Cate voice said.

I took a deep breath and pushed into the truth. Into
the lists that formed in my head all too often. "I'm afraid of
anyone hearing my music. Or that I'll read those books and
like them. I'm afraid some rabid fan is going to jump out
and grab me. Or Ryder. I'm terrified of disappointing my
dad, and petrified that I'm going to exist in this shadow of a
shadow forev—"

"Shadow of a shadow?"

"Grandma Mae is the shadow over my dad, and my dad is
the shadow over me. It's double-dark inside. I can't even play
a song in front of someone because I'm terrified they'll know

how much I care about writing music. Then they'll have this power over me."

"I know how much your music means to you, and you still trust me."

"You're different," I said. "I trust you, but I still can't play in front of you, can I?"

Eamon frowned, his palm resting on the gearshift as we rose and fell and wound around the roads. I imagined sliding my hand over his, tangling up his fingers with mine. Instead, my eyes locked on the first sign for the airport, dreading what would come next. Success or failure. Movie or no movie. "I miss your fist-fighting hair."

"Fistfight, what?"

"It looked like your curls were taking punches at one another," I said. He laughed from the base of his throat, a sound I already loved, and I used that love to tell him what was crashing through my brain. "I only have four more days, Eamon."

His eyes were fastened on the road, his voice full of nerves. "What if you went to college here? Then we'd have more time."

"What if you move to LA and become a famous actor?"

He shook his head, his cheeks pinking. "I'd say that's a bit forward to be thinking."

"I don't think so. You were brilliant. You lit up that scene, and there was something about the way it balanced out Shoshanna's anger... It was like magic."

"Like fantasy?" He winked, shuffling his hands on the wheel. "My ma has a saying. It's a life policy, really. Do something that scares you every day." He glanced at me. "I've been doing that as long as I can remember. The audition tape I made and sent to Cate? That was the scary thing I did that day. And yesterday? Well, yesterday I did two. One was to act. The second was to tell you how much I like you."

"I like you too much." My voice had come out nice and even, but my heart went nuts. I sat up and actually gasped. "Oh God, that *was* scary."

"How is that scary? I already told you I like you."

"Yes, but you could change your mind. You could have spent the whole night being like, 'Iris Thorne is too high maintenance. Terrible for my career. She wasn't even a good kisser.'"

He laughed. "Is that what it's like in your head? Is Satan in there, poking you with his pitchfork whenever you start to feel happy?"

I pictured my father in a Satan costume, sitting at his desk, typing his novels. It worked. But there was more… Something kept blocking my way.

"Story structure," I murmured.

"What was that?"

"When I was Ryder's age, my dad made me study literature. I had a tutor and everything. At the time, I thought my dad wanted me to grow up to be a professor, and I was an excellent student. Now he uses my brain to talk through his plot dilemmas. I help him a lot actually."

Those were the only times I felt truly good outside of my music—helping Dad write a book. Ryder wasn't wrong; we did have a little club. Dad would haul me into his office, and I'd kick back on the small sofa and hear what was giving him trouble, offering advice.

"Eamon, can we not follow the laws of story structure here? I mean, I know you like me and I like you. And we've got some, uh, complications, which means we should stay apart awhile longer before we get together. I don't want to do that." *Whoa.* "I'm leaving soon, and I don't want to wait until the last night of camp, so to speak, before we kiss again. It was too amazing."

Eamon rubbed the back of his neck, his cheeks vividly pink. "Well, aren't you direct."

I waited for him to say more, but he went quiet. We pulled into the airport parking lot, and I hoped I hadn't made a huge fool out of myself. I'd said how I felt and that couldn't be bad, right? *When does all this honesty pay off, Cate?*

Eamon took the keys out of the ignition. "Shoshanna," he said, bringing me back to the stakes at hand. If I couldn't somehow convince her to come back, we didn't have four days.

We had none.

DR. JILLIAN HOLTZMANN FOR THE WIN

THE DUBLIN AIRPORT was much larger than the one in Shannon. We swept every area before security without finding Shoshanna.

"She must have gone through to the gates," Eamon said, dejected.

We both glanced at the Garda. "Then we'll have to get creative," I said, leading him to the help desk and a smiling middle-aged woman. "My friend went through security but she forgot her medicine. Could you page her to come back through? Her name is Shoshanna Reyes."

"What gate?" The woman squinted. I looked at Eamon. He shrugged. "You don't know her gate? What about her destination city?"

"Los Angeles," I said, but I didn't know if that's where Shoshanna would go. "I think."

"You think?" she said, cutting so hard into the *th* it ticked. "Come back when you have more information."

We left the counter with slow steps. "Why don't we even know where she's from?" I asked, mostly to myself. "She knows everything about us."

Eamon glanced at the monitors. "There's a plane leaving for LA in forty-two minutes. It's already boarding." He sat down hard before the Aer Lingus lines and put his head in his hands. I wanted to push my hand through his abbreviated curls, settling for an awkward pat on the shoulder instead. "Thanks for trying, Iris."

His brokenhearted tone was too much. And I hadn't tried. Not really. If I had, I could make it happen. After all, I was the same person who'd marched into a music store when I was eleven with an envelope containing my life savings—and walked out with Annie despite my father's mockery and disapproval.

I felt the bulge in my pocket. There was a reason I'd doubled back to my trailer before we jumped in Eamon's car. I'd picked up my wallet and passport.

"Stay here." I jumped to the front of the Aer Lingus line. "Sorry! Emergency!" I called out to the scowling people who'd been waiting. When I reached the counter, I put on my most earnest expression. "I need to get on that flight to LA. My…" Mom? Dad? They wouldn't give me enough emotion to pull this off. "My brother was hit by a car. I have to get to him."

Honest to God tears welled in my eyes as I pictured Ryder bleeding and injured, my bleak imagination working for me for once. The woman behind the counter still appeared to doubt me, and I held up my empty arms. "I didn't even pack any bags. I came straight here when I got the call. I'm a study abroad student at Trinity."

The woman typed in her computer. "There are a few seats, but I won't promise you'll make it through security in time. That'll be three thousand, two hundred and forty-seven euro."

Shit.

I opened my wallet and stared at my dad's credit card. He'd lose his mind for sure this time. He'd try to ground me, which wouldn't work because I didn't have a life outside the house. When he realized that, he'd take away Annie.

I held out the credit card, trying not to shake. She ran it, handed me the ticket, and I sprinted toward security. Glancing back once, I saw Eamon hadn't budged from his head-in-hands position. I rushed through security and to the gate— only to nearly dash past Shoshanna at the bar. Her *Ghostbusters* tattoo was peeking out the side of her tank top while she stared at a half-drunk pint, miserable. Possibly more miserable than Eamon or Cate had been.

I tapped her shoulder, right where Dr. Jillian Holtzmann held up her proton gun the way Rosie the Riveter held up her fist.

She turned. "Oh, you. Headed to Lotus Land and your translucent yet tolerable life?"

Keep cool. I glanced at the tickets on the bar beside her. One to JFK, and the other from JFK to Providence. "You're from Rhode Island? I've never met someone from Rhode Island before."

She exhaled as though she'd been babysitting me since we met and I'd spit up one too many times. "What do you want, Iris?"

"I'm here to bring you back to set."

"Ha! The movie is done. No audience for it." Her eyes sealed on mine in a fed-up, sure-of-herself way. "You know, everything in that interview was true. The production has problems. The studio has been pulling out. And Cate is holding up the whole thing by herself."

"No, she isn't. You're holding it up too," I said.

She scoffed and took a long drink of what looked like hard cider.

"You don't think I haven't noticed you putting your all into this role? Working to the breaking point and helping Eamon in your time off? The production has problems, but every movie has problems. You know that."

"I don't want my name attached to this film anymore."

"That's bull crap."

She laughed. "Bull crap?"

"I spend all my time with an eight-year-old, who, by the

way, is going to be devastated if you kill this film by quitting. His life has been a series of disappointments and unbelievable trauma. Both of our lives have been, but we're turning it around. Starting with this movie."

It was a gamble to admit the harsh realities of being a Thorne. It softened most people with pity—unless they'd also been dragged by the hair through this world's unique trage- dies. Shoshanna didn't soften. She hardened, her back straight, her face turning into a stoic mask. I should have known she'd also suffered. After all, she had a lot more in common with Sevyn than I did.

"Shoshanna, you and I are going back even if I have to make you."

"How?" She slid off her barstool and looked down her nose at me. Shoshanna was taller, more fit, fiercer than me in every way. I'd known that from the moment I met her, and yet I'd been wrong about one thing: we were not from different planets.

"I'll haul you out of here by that voluminous hair if I have to," I said.

She chuckled and climbed back on her barstool, patting the one beside her.

I sat. "I'm serious."

"I see that. Care to explain the rather sudden change of heart?" She took a drink.

"I want to make out with Eamon."

Cue impressive spit take.

She wiped her face, laughing hard. "I just…can't. You puppies are too much."

"Why does everyone keep calling us 'puppies'?"

"Because you're adorable and clueless." She squinted. "If we could share thirty seconds of you two online, the fan concerns would evaporate. If you did that, I'd come back to the set."

I could have lied and said maybe. I could have strung her along. "I'm not letting Cate use my face for this movie. I have too much at stake."

"Fair enough. Now tell me why I should let her use mine."

"Because I saw you act last night. This is your role. And you are good. And Eamon? Eamon is on the other side of security, devastated. Think about how good he was. The scene we shot last night was amazing. This movie might actually be amazing."

The truth popped my ears. For all the things that had gone wrong or felt fantasy-nerd bizarre, there were moments when this story tugged. When Cate's settings leaped out with dramatic colors and emotion-packed landscapes. When the characters whispered real feelings…and the story actually helped me figure out my real life.

"What's going on?" Shoshanna asked, breaking my thoughts. "You look like you're about to cry or punch me. If you freak out in public, everyone will call it a lover's spat. It'll light up the media." Her voice had dropped low, a sincere warning that highlighted more than ever that I didn't understand what it was like to be Shoshanna Reyes.

Overhead, a gate attendant announced the last call for a flight to New Zealand, and I felt that familiar twist toward story logic. This was my specialty. Why hide it? Why be ashamed?

"Hobbits," I said after a rough pause. She looked at me as if I'd lost my mind. "Those books and movies are about how it doesn't matter how strong or weapon-loaded you are. In the end, two tiny hobbits save the whole world."

She blinked. "Have you been hanging out with Henrik?"

"Narnia," I said, even more certain, "where you can't escape war because war is everywhere, but you can be a king or queen even if you're a kid. Or what about Harry Potter?" Shoshanna's expression softened. Bingo. Harry Potter lived in the hearts of people our age. "No matter how bad the situation gets, all you need are a few good friends."

I paused. "I haven't read my grandmother's books, but *Elementia* is a force for good." *No matter what Dad says.* "Sevyn saves her brother. She saves the world. A girl saves the world. How often do we get to see that on the big screen?"

"You don't know what happens at the end of the third book, do you?"

I glared. "Why? What happens?"

Shoshanna shook her head. "I'm not destroying your little speech there. It was too good."

"What about Cate Collins?" I asked. "She's one of the only female directors to have been given a Hollywood blockbuster. If this movie fails, they'll blame her. They're already blaming her, even though her efforts have been heroic. But if it doesn't fail, thousands of girls are going to grow up wanting to be directors like her."

"Yeah, but…" Shoshanna grimaced. "Too little, too late. I've got to think about my career." She stood, pulling her bag strap over her shoulder—*her shoulder!*

"Dr. Jillian Holtzmann!" I yelled, making the people around us jump.

Shoshanna froze. "What about her?"

"She's a queer girl action hero. That's why you have that tattoo. She inspires you, and you're going to inspire girls. You're going to be a freakin' queer Daisy Ridley, and girls are going to get tattoos of you."

Shoshanna blushed for the first time since I'd met her. "Oh Jesus, Iris."

"I'm right!" I shouted. "All of this is important. I get that now! Okay?"

Shoshanna glanced at the audience of people enjoying my public revelation. She stepped close, almost like she was checking for sincerity in my pores. "Don't you backslide."

I nodded. And meant it.

When Shoshanna and I came back through security, Eamon actually cried, and he was much better at it than Julian. No snot. Just big, beautiful tears dropping from those crystal-blue eyes. Shoshanna told him he was embarrassing her, but gave his elbow an affectionate squeeze. I called Cate and told her the good news—that we'd be back soon and the movie could continue. She surprised all of us by demanding we take the rest of the day off and come back in the morning.

And that's how we got to see Eamon's Dublin.

He took us to Trinity College, where the historic buildings were nothing compared to the odd trees that grew strong and curved on the pristine grounds. He took us across the slow-moving Liffey River to see the old post office with its pillars riddled with bullet holes from the Easter Rising. For dinner, we ate at an eccentric upstairs restaurant called 101 Talbot, and Shoshanna drank wine and told us her story.

She'd been a child actress, movies and television—this I knew. What I didn't know was that her parents' marriage had detonated over her young career. Roles died down when she was ten, and her manager mother wanted her to do some questionable commercials abroad. Shoshanna'd left acting to live in Providence with her dad, who was battling multiple sclerosis. After he died, she broke back into Hollywood. Her first talent agent said he wouldn't represent her if she came out, claiming it would diminish the roles she'd be considered for.

"Of course that asshole was right, but I came out anyway

and got a better agent. And that's why I have Kate," she said, reaching back to touch the tattoo on her shoulder blade. "There's a spotlight for queer girls, and I'm going to be in it when we finally find the switch."

I leaned forward and nearly got soup all over my shirt. "So you've reinvented yourself a half a dozen times already?" I somehow managed to refrain from yelling, *Teach me!*

"That's a glamorous way to put it," she said. I could see why I kept thinking of her as royalty. She was weathered, tough—and yet still graceful about all she had been through.

Eamon had been quiet the whole dinner, and I turned to him when Shoshanna left for the bathroom. His forehead was doubly creased.

"You do want to be an actor," I said quietly. "Is that what you figured out today?"

He looked at the ceiling and blew out a breath. "Yes. I really do."

I knew that look. I felt that look every time the garage door opened and I had to hurry to put Annie back in her case. I wanted to tell him that we'd find a way—for both of us to pursue our dreams—but instead my brain began to list all the ways in which this movie was still falling apart. That article. The doubting producers. A damn Thornian boycott.

I wanted to promise Eamon we'd make his career a reality, but how could I when I wasn't even nudging my own dreams toward the realms of possibility?

DUBLIN'S FAIR CITY WHERE EAMON'S SO PRETTY

FOR THE GRAND finale of the evening, we went to Eamon's favorite pub, O'Sullivans. It was small and narrow, and yet packed with at least forty people, all singing along to a bald, charming guitarist at the front of the room.

Eamon had to spin some of his verbal magic to get me in since I wasn't eighteen, but he knew the doorman, and I promised—boy-scout style—that I would not drink. Shoshanna took the alternative route, heading straight for the bar, so confident that people cleared out of her way.

I hid by Eamon's elbow as he ordered a pint of something called Carlsberg. We slipped toward the back, against the side wall. Eamon leaned in close to talk over the music, pointing to the guitarist who was giving himself to U2's "All I Want Is You" with such passion that most of the bar was singing with him. "That's Brian. I wanted you to see him in action. When I think about Iris in the future, that's what I see. You singing your heart out in front of adoring fans."

"I have to find the courage to play in front of one person first. Then I'll figure out how to play to a crowd."

"You're thinking of it backwards. Playing in front someone you know? That's the tricky part. Strangers are easy. They don't judge. They're having a laugh."

I wanted to believe him. And while I was tempted to lean against the wall and enjoy the music, I wanted to keep talking even more, our faces close, my lips right next to his ear. "What should we do about Shoshanna?" I motioned to her tipsy grinning at the bartender.

"She's just on the lash," he said. "Needs to blow off some steam. Maybe we all do."

"I can't decide if she inspires or intimidates me," I said, while he said, "I kissed her."

"What?"

"It was an acting exercise," he added in a rush. "We had to get close to film that scene, and Shoshanna said it'd be the fastest way to break the ice." His neck blushed, and I swear I knew what he was thinking.

"And then she teased you for being a virgin?"

His response was to bury his face in his pint. Apparently there was a line with Eamon's great-under-pressure demeanor. And I'd tripped over it.

Brian started singing "American Pie" and the crowd responded with overwhelming glee.

"She's been on my case too," I yelled over the music. "It's okay if you're shy."

"Hey! I'm Irish." Our faces were so close it felt daring. "The Irish don't come shy."

"You're a shy Irishman!" I teased.

He slammed back his pint, a gleeful spark in his eyes, and pushed his way through the crowd until he was next to the guitarist. Brian moved over, and Eamon started singing into the microphone. At first I laughed, but then I listened, and he was... Dare I say it? A talented singer. He hit the advanced notes and brought the singing audience with him through the chorus. He didn't know the right words, but no one cared.

Shoshanna screamed his name from the bar, making me smile.

Afterward, Brian gave Eamon a side hug, and he came back to me. "Who's shy now?"

"You've proved me wrong," I said, kissing his cheek and making him blush.

Shoshanna swaggered over. "You! Hiding those pipes!" She rocked into Eamon bodily, but I wasn't jealous; I was grateful because she ended up pressing him against my side, his arm slipping around my waist. "All right, kiddos. What do we do? I'm not going back to that set if things are going to continue to be a god-awful mess."

"I've been thinking," I said. "We need Julian to do more on his social media. It's too bad he's not here right now."

"Are you kidding? If he were here, we'd be mobbed. And everyone would see your pretty, redacted face." Shoshanna pinched my nose.

"Hey! I'm not a five-year-old," I said, squeezing her nose right back.

A brown-haired girl came over, her eyes glued to Eamon. "Can I have your autograph?" She held out a pen and bar coaster. Eamon turned a brand-new shade of fire, but he took the pen, signed, and handed it back. She thanked him and left. Shoshanna and I looked at each other.

"First time?" Shoshanna asked.

"Yeah," he squeaked.

"You're all grown up now, son. Next time I see you, you'll be in a bar in LA with three girls on each arm." She patted his shoulder and returned to the bar.

Eamon leaned toward my ear. "I'm not that kind of guy."

I almost said, *I know. That's why I like you.* But I chickened out. "I can't believe you sang in front of all these people!"

He pressed his cheek against mine, and I felt slight stubble. "You say you're not brave, but you're always helping, which is amazing considering how much you're not into fantasy."

But I *had* been into it. I still hadn't worked up the courage to tell him. And I might have been helping out when Cate asked, but I'd still wanted the film to be canceled.

Coward.

It wasn't my dad's or Cate's voice this time. It was mine.

I pulled away from Eamon and pushed through the crowd. My heart slammed at my ribs, but I made it to the front. Brian was playing "Knocking on Heaven's Door" on the electric guitar—the acoustic one he'd been wailing on earlier sitting in its stand.

I reached for it. He smiled and moved over like he had for Eamon. I looped the strap over my head. Felt my chest about to burst. His chords pulled away as the song ended, and I leaned into his ear. "Coldplay? 'Yellow'?" My voice was terrified. My fingers were terrified. But I knew this song; it was pretty and easy. If I couldn't play this, I couldn't play anything.

Brian grinned like a maniac and held out his hand for me to start. I stepped toward the mic, but then immediately stepped back. I couldn't look in Shoshanna and Eamon's direction, so I stared at the crowd. They were ready, waiting. Hooting with anticipation. It made me smile to think of them as owls, and I fell into the opening chords.

Just like that.

It took me a full progression to adjust to the dislocation of the amp and a new guitar, but then Brian came in with the electric guitar part, and I felt like I was a better guitarist simply by standing with him. I realized—with a minor coronary— that one of us needed to start singing soon. Brian looked to me, one eyebrow lifted high, and I closed my eyes. Leaned into the mic.

And I sang.

The words came out in that way I adored. Like I was speaking unfathomable truths or casting a spell or pulling poetry up from some deep well. This was why I loved music, why lyrics lit me up. At one point, I opened my eyes, and the crowd was singing with me so loudly it didn't matter if I was a good. I sang louder. I played more strongly. Brian kept the whole melody alive with the electric accent, and when I got to that "bleed yourself dry" line, we both let the guitars fall away and only our voices rose up.

~

Shoshanna dragged me out of the pub and into the stunning quiet of the street.

"Look at you, Iris Thorne! Look at you!" She danced on the sidewalk and hugged me. We sort of jumped in a circle.

"I did it!" I said.

"You fucking did!" Shoshanna crowed.

"Language, young lady," the doorman said, but he was smiling. "Nicely done."

It took me a whole series of beats to realize he was giving me a compliment.

"Thank you."

Eamon came out of the pub, and my nerves spun out of

control all over again. I couldn't look at him, and Shoshanna didn't wait for me to. She hooked both of us by the elbows and skipped up the red brick of Grafton Street, pulling us along, whooping in triumph.

The sky was full of stars, which was strange for a city. No light pollution, but then, there weren't towering sky-scrapers here. I snuck a look at Eamon and caught him look-ing at me.

Shoshanna was lit up as well, delighted with everything in her tipsy way. "You know, I feel like singing an Irish tune," she yelled. "'Oh Danny b—'"

"No, no." Eamon clapped a hand over her mouth. "You're in the republic, Shoshanna. That's the Northern Ireland anthem, girl."

Shoshanna licked her lips and grimaced. "Salty. Why are boys' palms so salty? Do you guys ever wash your hands? You know who has great hands? Roxy."

"Roxanne?" I blurted. "The makeup artist?"

"The one and only. You guys don't think twenty-five is out of my age range, do you? Wait, don't answer. She's out of my league. She's probably in the same dating pool as Ellen Page. And then there's queer, little me."

"There's nothing little about you, Shoshanna," I said.

"Especially your interest in girls," Eamon finished.

Shoshanna roared with laughter. I didn't know a person could actually do that. "Do you know what we need?" she asked. "We need to bring our fourth wheel into this little triumph." She got out her phone and made a FaceTime call.

Julian picked up right away, his face looking all weird in the camera's intense close up.

"Shosh! You better still be in Ireland!"

"I am!" she said. "And you know what happened? This girl"—she shoved the phone in my face—"played guitar and sang for a whole crowd of people! She nailed it."

Julian got closer, frowning. "Iris? What's going on over there?"

"Shoshanna's drunk," I said. "We're going to bring her back to set." I was so happy to see him it took a moment to realize, the last time we'd texted, he'd been pissed. "She was going to quit, but Eamon and I talked her out of it."

"I never should have left you three."

"You had business, you heartthrob," Shoshanna said.

Julian looked off camera and said something.

"Hey! Let us see her! Elora, come to the phone! We want to see if you're real!" Shoshanna yelled.

Someone laughed off camera, and Julian held his arm out farther, showing off the prettiest, most petite girl I've ever seen. She had her knees up to her chin and a smile that seemed…well, peaceful. "Hi," Elora said. "I'm real!"

"Oh, Jules. She is the cutest. You were not kidding. *Wow.*"

I snatched the phone from Shoshanna, worried for Elora who might not have enough context to appreciate our drunk heroine. "We're going to get Shoshanna in a bed. You guys have a nice night!"

"Iris?" Julian held the camera close again. "Things are… all right over there?"

"They're getting better," I said. "And we're going to come up with a plan to turn things around." I pressed end, and Shoshanna skipped ahead of us, singing an improvised song about the beauty of Elora, or was it Roxy?

I turned to Eamon for the first time since I'd charged onto that stage.

He stood, hands in his pockets, his expression mightily shy. "You were amazing, Iris."

"I think I'll die if we talk about it."

"Just so you know."

I spun around to face the gorgeous night. "What should be our plan to save the movie?"

"Step one, get Shoshanna off the streets. Step two, figure out a step two."

"Good. I like a two-pronged approach. Where are we going?" I asked.

"To my flat," he said. "It's a short walk that way."

"Tell me you've got an awesome bachelor pad with three flat mates, a few lava lamps, and nothing but a brick of cheese in the fridge!" Shoshanna yelled.

He rubbed the back of his neck. "Ah, not quite."

Twenty minutes later, we were walking along a row

of old stone houses with brilliantly colored doors. Eamon stopped before a vibrant-blue door with a lion's head knob. He tried to turn his key quietly, but his mom yanked open the apartment door. I would have known she was Eamon's mom out of a casting call of a hundred Irish moms. Mainly because she had the same crystal eyes and curly hair that was likely part of an underground fight club.

"What are you doing in town?" She wrapped him in a huge hug that was no small part wrestling maneuver. Shoshanna took this as her cue to join the hug. Eamon's mom let go of her son and took a good look at her. "Well, come in. I'd say this one is in need of some Digestives."

We entered the house, and I couldn't believe I was meeting Eamon's mom smelling like a pub, wearing a stretched out T-shirt, and accompanying a drunk Shoshanna. "You could have warned me," I muttered at Eamon as we filed into the kitchen. Eamon's mom wasted no time in giving Shoshanna a sleeve of chocolate biscuits.

"Don't worry," he murmured before turning to his mom. "Mam, this is Shoshanna Reyes, our Sevyn. Shoshanna, this is Gráinne. If you call her Mrs. anything, she'll make you pay for it."

"*Mrs. O'Brien* is my mother-in-law. How would you like to be called by your mother-in-law's name?" Gráinne took Shoshanna's chin, giving her a hard stare. "So this is Sevyn, is she? Yes, I see it. Leave no pints behind. That's definitely the girl I read in those stories."

Shoshanna smirked and crunched into a biscuit.

Eamon touched my shoulder and time jerked to a halt as I waited for my inevitable title of *M. E. Thorne's granddaughter*.

"This is Iris, my girlfriend," he said.

"What?" I blurted.

He cocked his head. "This morning you said we should skip to a better part in the story, right?"

"But I was talking about..." *Making out.* "I didn't... I wasn't trying to force you into titles," I said, painfully aware of our audience. "Can we talk about this later?"

"If you want to shift some more, I want to be your boyfriend." He crossed his arms.

Was this actually happening? In front of his mom? Out of the corner of my eye, Shoshanna offered the sleeve of biscuits to Eamon's mom. She took one. Now they were both snacking while they watched us like we were some romantic comedy.

"Do you not want to be my girlfriend?" Eamon asked, hurt slipping in his tone.

"No, but you can't say someone is your girlfriend without asking her first."

Eamon's eyes were a tad fiercer than usual, and I sort of liked it. "Oh Jesus, will you be my girlfriend, Iris?" Eamon's mom cleared her throat, and he added, "Please?"

"Yeah," I said.

We stared at each other. Shoshanna started a slow clap.

Gráinne reached for another biscuit. "I should have read more Jane Austen to him when he was a boy," she said. "He's not a great romantic, is he?"

"They're just puppies," Shoshanna said, and Eamon and I grumbled.

"Excellent performance, but it's late, and you'll all be too knackered to make movies if you don't get some sleep." Gráinne filled a glass with water and handed it to Shoshanna. "You're going to sleep in Eamon's sister's room. Last door on the right." She turned to me. "You get Eamon's room. Lucky you. Have fun poking in your boyfriend's things." She winked, and I now I knew where Eamon got his sass.

Lastly, she put an arm around Eamon. "You, dearest son, get the sofa."

"I could sleep on the floor in my room," he said. "I'll leave Iris be."

His mom squeezed his shoulders and kissed the side of his head. "Beautiful try. Gorgeous. Winning. *Sofa*."

BOY BEDROOMS AND OTHER
UNSOLVED MYSTERIES

GRÁINNE WASN'T WRONG. I used the moonlight stream-
ing through the window to investigate Eamon's room. It
wasn't like American boys' rooms. He had a lot of books, a
neat closet, and a pile of soccer paraphernalia that looked long
neglected. His ancient brass bed was tiny, and his furniture
was wooden and timeless, like maybe it had belonged to his
great-grandmother.

The bookshelf seemed like it had been loved the most,
and I ran my fingers down the spines. Mostly fantasy, but
some literature in there too. He didn't have *Jane Eyre*; I'd have
to get him a copy. When I reached a paperback, cracked-
spine copy of *Elementia*, I pulled it out.

I wasn't used to seeing the first book in the trilogy on its
own. It wasn't terribly long, only an inch thick, and I'd never

seen this UK cover before; it was way more interesting than the elf-crazy covers of the North American editions. There were no blurbs, no ridiculous taglines. Only a stark lightning bolt splitting an elemental compass. The title and author's name were stamped in black letters with silver embossing. It felt ominous and alluring all at once.

What had Shoshanna meant when she said I didn't know what happens at the end of the trilogy? Could it be so surprising? Maybe she meant the end of the first book, when Evyn kills the king, his own father. That was fairly common knowledge; my dad made a lot of jokes about it.

I'd never heard a joke about the end of the trilogy.

I placed the book on Eamon's bed and let it fall open to wherever the binding was most worn through. I wasn't terribly surprised to find the scene by the river—Cate's favorite moment. I skimmed to the morning after Nolan saved Sevyn from her fever and read on.

Sevyn awoke to a small fire crackling next to her. The dampness of her clothes brought back memories of the river and her fever. Her mouth tasted foul.

Before her, a boy leaned against the great, white tree she had surrendered to in despair. His arms were folded across his bare chest, and he watched her with narrowed eyes. At first, Sevyn could only remember the feel of his skin over his ribs. His lips parting when she touched them.

Sevyn bolstered herself on her elbows. "Who are you?"

"Be still." His voice held the wind. Her father's voice had done that when he spoke lovingly with her brother. Sevyn bristled and examined him. He was slim yet strong. He wore only thin trousers that fell below the knee and appeared to be woven of fallen leaves. His features were angled as if the wind had sculpted him over a millennia of seasons from the finest stone imaginable. His ears fell into a slender slant, ending in dramatic points.

Sevyn balanced on her trembling arms, determined to force her savior to answer. "Who are you, elf?"

"You need not know who I am. Be satisfied you have recognized my true image." His tone hinted at caution.

"You should not have touched me." Sevyn's unexpected emotion choked. The fire swelled in her eyes, blurred bright orange by her tears.

I paused to look around the room. I could picture this story now. Eamon was Nolan. But Sevyn? She wasn't Shoshanna. She was me. Sick. Afraid. Desperate for anything that felt like hope.

The elf's demeanor eased. He sat beside her, his age indecipherable, his maturity fluctuating with the shift of his eyes. He was close enough that she could have reached out, but she didn't trust it. Her earlier ability to touch him had something to do with that veil of calm. It had quieted the lightning, but how she'd achieved such serenity eluded her. Instead she reached out with an even rustier tool of her character: a soft voice.

"My name is Sevyn. Daughter of…" Her words drifted as she decided against sharing her royal birth. "Daughter of Cerul. It's an island kingdom not far from the coast. Do you know it?"

The elf gave a small nod.

"May I know your name? I have never met an elf before. There are rumors your kind no longer exist."

"A name is not trivial," he said, his deliberation etched across his face. "I am Nolandriav. You may know me as Nolan. Please do not use it against me."

"Iris?" Eamon crept through the door and shut it behind him.

I closed the book. "Your mom will kill you if she catches you in here with me."

"Worth the risk." He sat on the edge of the bed, folding

his legs beneath him in a way that made him seem fourteen instead of eighteen. "You know"—he picked up the book— "this is the second time I've caught you reading *Elementia*. What would your father say?" He was teasing, but his words filled my chest with lead.

I crossed to the bookshelf and put the book back. "He'd say, 'I raised you to be on my team. What's wrong with you, Iris?'"

Eamon frowned. "Say, I know that pressure. My da went all the way to the final tryouts for the Green Army when he was my age." He pointed to the abandoned soccer gear. "Irish national football team. He didn't make the cut and tried to rectify the situation with a football star of a son. When I didn't have the talent, he lost interest in me."

I leaned against the bookshelf, weary. "Why do people think they can mold their kids into whatever they want? Don't they realize how stupid that is?"

"I got used to feeling disappointed a long time ago." Eamon smiled sadly. "But I got over it. My da's the sort of guy who swims the English Channel but forgets to call his kids at Christmas. I don't need his approval, but I wish he didn't mess my mam around. He hasn't lived here in years, but they're still married. Every so often they try again, but he always gives up."

My jealousy was heavy because I *did* need my dad's approval. Or maybe I wanted it. I was still leaning against the bookshelf, holding the wood behind my back with two tight hands. "I want to tell you something. Something I've never told anyone. When I was Ryder's age, my dad hired this special tutor to teach me literary theory, which sounds ridiculous, but it was okay. I liked Mr. Sams. He gave me *Jane Eyre*, which is my favorite, by the way."

"Noted," Eamon said, exactly as he should.

"I read dozens of classics from my dad's list of preapproved titles. I got into it, and my dad loved bragging about his eight-year-old reading *Moby Dick* and *Great Expectations*." I took a deep breath and said it fast. "But then Mr. Sams started giving me secret books. Barrie, Lewis, Tolkien, Rowling." I turned to the shelf and plucked one of the titles, presenting it. "Pullman."

Eamon's mouth hung open. "You read *His Dark Materials*? And you still hate fantasy?"

"No." A tear slipped out, and I reshelved the book. "I loved those stories. All of them. And one day Mr. Sams gave me *Elementia*. And that was the same day my dad caught me reading it. He freaked out. He screamed that I was filling my head with garbage. He fired Mr. Sams. Took all the books away."

Eamon stood, making the old bed squeak, and crossed the room. I wasn't ready to be held, though. I had to keep going. Let it all out. "But don't think I've been lying about not liking fantasy. I did start to hate it, especially the fans. Especially after

Moss. And I didn't want to come here or get to know any of you—except Julian—and I wanted the movie to get shut down so my life didn't get trampled even more by Elementia."

I'd run out of breath. Eamon still looked like he was about to hug me, and I turned back to the bookshelf, touching the spine of *Elementia*. "This past week I've realized he probably freaked out because Grandma Mae had just died, not because of anything I did."

I sat on the window ledge. Eamon sat beside me, a few inches between us. "I don't think I ever put that together before. I'd never disappointed him, and I thought that's what happens when you do something wrong. His freak out felt like it was all my fault. I've been trying to do everything right since then. It's impossible."

I closed my eyes. "I still have nightmares about the way he screamed at me, but then I feel terrible because my dad's temper is nothing compared to what happened to Ryder."

"It's not a competition, Iris," Eamon said quietly. "Those events can be brutal in their own ways. And in the spirit of honesty, I'm having a hard time not hating your da."

"Welcome to the club." I kissed his cheek, and he pulled me into a hug I never wanted to leave, and I started crying because I had to leave. Soon. Back to the incessant sun of LA, my hollow school friendships, babysitting Ryder twenty-four seven and writing secret songs. Songs about having so much emotion inside that is not welcome to come out.

And now there was a new special torture: there'd be no Eamon.

"You have to come to LA and be an actor."

"Maybe. But that's far from now. And far from my home."

"Then why do you want me to be your girlfriend?" I asked. "Is this only until I leave?"

He looked a little scared. "I don't want to figure that out yet. I mean, I don't know if I could. Would you rather we didn't?"

"Hell no. I'm glad you said all that."

"Coulda fooled me." He smiled.

"I'm new at this stuff. I've gone on a few dates but never had an official anyone." The moment skewed embarrassing, but Eamon fixed it.

"Me neither. Too busy reading fantasy novels in secondary school to talk to real girls." He shrugged adorably. I wanted to kiss him, but Eamon pulled out his video camera. "I'm going to show you something, but you have to promise not to strike me dead right here."

"You taped my song, didn't you?"

He opened the screen and held it out. "Watch yourself. You'll be dazzled."

He pressed play, and my hands curled into tight, tight fists. The first couple of chords stumbled—followed by the moment when Brian and I got in sync. I could barely hear myself over the singing crowd, but it sounded…good. I felt the buzz of the music all over again. The high of performing. The moment when the song bled like its lyrics.

If only Dad could see this...

The song ended, and Eamon closed the camera. I touched his jaw and felt his fingers trail the neckline of my shirt, stopping on the spot where my shoulder had popped out from the wide neckline. "I like this shirt," he said, his voice so low it sounded new.

"It's my comfy shirt. I've had it for ages." I paused. "I never wear it out of the house though. Dad hates it when I dress 'like a teenager.'"

"What a goat." He pressed a kiss to my shoulder that left me speechless. I touched his hair, finding nothing harsh about his curls. They were thick and wild. Soft.

He leaned toward my lips, and I laughed. "Sorry," I squeaked. "It's just, you make me happy. That's a weird feeling for me."

He laughed too. "We need to figure this out. If I don't get to kiss you soon, I'm going to burn down like the Blackened Wastes of Thornbred."

I grabbed him by the front of the shirt. "No fantasy references whilst kissing."

I lifted my mouth to his without pause. His lips were full and soft, and the kiss started off as slow and sweet as the one on the ferry...but it changed. I took his face with both hands, leaning us into something deeper. He slipped his arms around my waist and held me as close as possible. Chest to chest.

We kissed until it felt like we were fizzling out of reality, out of his room, out of Ireland, to some sunny, warmly lit place reserved for Iris and Eamon where nothing else mattered.

When we parted to catch our breaths, his eyes were happy. "Iris. I think we found a portal."

I couldn't hold back a laugh. "I know what you mean."

We kissed again, wound in each other until my lips ached and my hands had left clench marks on his shirt. I rested my head on his shoulder, and his fingers slipped through my hair.

The moonlight streamed through the window, turning everything silver. "This light is crazy." I held out my hand in the beams. "What would its fantasy word be?"

"I thought you said no fantasy?" I scowled up at him, and he added, "Argent?"

"Hoary?"

We giggled. This close, nose to nose, Eamon looked like a brand-new person. My person.

"Shiny?" I whispered, my lips brushing his.

"Shiny," he agreed. "Wait, have you ever seen *Firefly*?"

I squeezed my eyes. "Okay, I might've had mono last year, and I might've spent a lot of time on Netflix, and... how in the blazes did that show only run for half a season?" I caught my breath. "Please don't tell anyone. I'll sound like a space cowboy nerd."

I opened my eyes and found him staring at me like he was in love.

"But, Iris, you'd make a breathtaking nerd."

Film: Elementia
Director: Cate Collins

On Location Shooting: Day 8
Killykeen Forest, Ireland

Filming Notes:

P.M.: SEVYN & NOLAN's morning after

Etc. Notes:

Studio heads will be visiting on set for the
next two days.

BACK TO ~~REALITY~~ FANTASY

THE NEXT MORNING, we were off early to get back to Killykeen. I sat in the passenger seat and Eamon reached for my hand whenever he didn't have to shift, and then at some point, he started changing gears while still holding my hand.

"I think I know why you call it shifting now," I whispered, not wanting to clue Shoshanna in to what we'd done last night. Eamon eyed me from the side and bit his bottom lip in a way that was unfair because my teeth wanted to do the same thing to that lip.

"So." Shoshanna sat forward from the back seat, all too chipper. "How do we get Iris to play her music for the movie? She can wail, and we've seen it. She's got no excuse."

"That was a one-time-only event," I said, hoping with

every piece of me it wasn't. "Besides, playing for strangers is one thing, but playing on a major motion picture soundtrack is out of my league."

"I'm going to get Julian involved," Shoshanna said. "He'll talk you into it."

I leaned around the seat to look at her. "Aren't you supposed to be hungover?"

"I'm nineteen, Iris. My liver is in its prime." She leaned forward to whisper. "A virgin and inexperienced with alcohol—what am I going to do with you?"

"You're doing nothing with her. She's mine," Eamon said.

I grinned. "I'm his."

"Cate would not approve of this language," Shoshanna pointed out. "I don't either."

"So you're saying you wouldn't be Roxy's if she wanted you to be?" I asked.

Shoshanna opened her mouth and then closed it. "What did I say last night?"

"Quite a bit about Roxy's beautiful hands…and something about Ellen Page's dating league that I didn't follow," I said.

"*Heteros*," Shoshanna muttered. "You two will be cool, right? No embarrassing me with Roxy."

"Maybe. If you behave. Although I don't think I'll be satisfied until you're *hers*." I saw what Shoshanna meant by the problem with the language. People can belong to other people but only if it's mutual, right? I glanced at Eamon. "You're mine too?"

"Sold. You can tattoo your name on me, Iris... What's your middle name?"

Dead silence.

"Gertrude!" Shoshanna crowed. "Hermia! Francis! Oh, wait...is it something fantasy? Tell me it's Galadriel."

"It's two names actually. Mae Ellen." I waited for them to lose their collective mind.

Eamon wasn't fazed. "Then you can tattoo your name on me, Iris Mae Ellen Thorne."

"So your name is Iris *M. E. Thorne*?" Shoshanna frowned. "That's not fair. Who wants to be named after a famous dead person?" She leaned back in her seat and crossed her arms, and I had to admit I appreciated both of their reactions.

"She wasn't dead when I was named after her. Besides, that's not the weird part." I didn't say anything else, and Shoshanna had to poke me to keep talking. "Well, my dad hates her. Or hated her. He named me after someone he hated. That's messed up, isn't it?"

"Yes," Shoshanna said, while at the same time Eamon added, "Sounds complicated."

The road turned toward the forest park of Killykeen, and Shoshanna said, "If I were you, I'd grill him. It's your name after all. Your family. You get to know these things."

Her words didn't settle well, and I couldn't tell if it was

because we were heading back into the Elementian lion's den or because I wanted to do exactly what she said.

Also, I still had to deal with the flight I put on my dad's credit card…

I glanced at my phone. It had died sometime last night, and I couldn't believe how much of a relief it had been to be out of contact for a little while. Then again, what if something had happened to Ryder while I was gone?

My anxiety came on strong. Eamon glanced at me. "You all right, then?"

"I have a bad feeling."

Eamon pulled up beside the line of trailers. The crew mingled about, eating breakfast at the picnic tables in the center. "Everything looks normal to me," he said. Strange that this—wires and lights and boxes of equipment everywhere—was normal.

"Those're new," Shoshanna said, pointing to a trio of big, black SUVs across the parking area. "We have company. Maybe Julian's back and needed three cars for his wardrobe."

Eamon snickered, but I froze, searching for Ryder. I found him behind the picnic tables, standing beside a familiar, strained face who was talking to Cate Collins.

"Oh Christ. My dad."

"What?" Eamon startled.

I pointed.

"That does not look good," Shoshanna said from the

back seat. She was right. Cate was gesturing while she spoke to my dad, as though they heartily disagreed about something. "What if we drive off?"

My dad's eyes swept the scene until they found me, sitting in Eamon's car.

"Too late," I said.

"We go together," Shoshanna tried. "There's no way he'll lay into you if we're all there."

Oh, Shoshanna. I almost felt bad for her. "You have no idea how unpredictable Michael Edward Thorne's temper can be. Yeah, that's right. He's got her initials too."

~

I approached my dad with Eamon on my left and Shoshanna on my right. It was a fool's errand to think their presence could keep him from blowing up, but it meant a lot that they wanted to try.

"It's an odd business to have kids," my dad said when I was in earshot. He was speaking for my benefit even though he wouldn't look at me, holding my brother's elbow at an awkward angle—to prove how displeased he was with both of us, no doubt. "You're petrified when you lose track of them, and then you find them and the relief is pure, relentless anger."

Ryder squirmed. Cate had enough decency to look surprised by his threatening tone.

I knew better. This was all for show. My dad was a

dramatic, artistic nightmare. He'd never lay a hand on us; his fury came via freeze-out neglect. "I'm fine, Dad. My phone died while we were getting Shoshanna from the airport."

"I believe that was yesterday," he said, turning his dark eyes from Cate to me. "And today is not yesterday, is it, Iris?"

"Oh, well spotted," Shoshanna snarked.

"I gave them the night off," Cate said, stepping in front of Shoshanna's sass. "They've been working hard. They slept at Eamon's family home, right?"

All three of us nodded in sync. Even from my perspective it looked suspicious.

Cate beckoned to my friends. "Makeup. You have a scene to shoot. And the studio execs have decided to grace us with their presence." She bit into that last sentence as though it were pure gristle.

Shoshanna left with Cate while Eamon moved in front of me. He touched my shoulder. "Let me know if you need anything. Promise?"

I nodded, and while he was being sweet, I couldn't help thinking, *Run! Run before my father makes a scene!*

Eamon put his backpack in my hand. "Show him," he whispered.

Eamon, Cate, and Shoshanna walked away, and I pointed to my trailer. "We can go in there and talk, Dad."

"I have to go help Mr. Donato," Ryder whined. "He needs me."

"Absolutely not. You're staying with me until we leave." My dad sort of pushed Ryder toward the trailer, and I could see my brother's feelings expand and spin. His face was red and sweaty, his breath coming through his mouth in harsh pants as he twisted in my dad's hold. I knew those feelings well—only where Ryder exploded, I had long since learned to quietly, painfully implode.

"Ryder," I said, trying to get him to look at me. He wouldn't. I turned to my dad. "Let him go," I said through gritted teeth. "You and I should talk. Alone."

"I already said no, Iris." My dad tried to drag my brother, and Ryder let his legs go, dangling by the elbow. *Oh no…*

"Ryder's doing great here." I crouched down to face him. "Aren't you, Ry? Tell Dad how helpful you've been to the crafty crew. How much responsibility you've had. He'll be proud of you."

"I want to help Mr. Donato!" Ryder cried out. "I want Mr. Donato!"

"Did you not hear me?" my dad snapped. "You're not leaving my side until we get back to LA tonight!"

Ryder's lungs exploded, his screams paralyzing everyone in earshot. His fists beat first against my dad and then against me as I tried to get him to stop. I took a pop to the jaw that made my head bump, and then my dad was yelling at me to get him under control. I could feel the crew switch from pretending not to watch, to debating about stepping in—particularly when Ryder knocked both my dad and me over.

Mr. Donato appeared, scooping Ryder in a bear hug that held down both of his arms. He sat on the picnic table and talked right into Ryder's ear. I'm not sure what he said, but Ryder switched from anger to sobbing tears.

My dad got back on his feet and moved forward like he was going to grab Ryder from Mr. Donato, and I decided that now—right now—was going to be the moment I spoke up.

"Leave him alone!" I shouted. My dad spun at me, and I kept yelling. "Follow me. Now!"

I walked to the trailer, my pulse on fire. I was terrified but also spilling over with words. I shut the door behind my dad. His lip was bleeding from where Ryder had popped him. He opened his mouth, but I beat him to it. "I take it you haven't finished your draft."

"Of course not," he spat. "I was on the second-to-last chapter when I got a call from Visa about an international flight booked on my credit card. I thought you'd lost your mind and were flying back without Ryder. I drove to LAX and waited for you. Surprise, surprise when the flight arrived and you weren't on it. I was so angry that I jumped on a plane, and here I am in my own personal Elementian hell! Jesus Christ, Iris. There is a woman walking around this set that is a carbon copy of my mother!"

His eyes were bloodshot. His fists were shaking.

We were on new ground. I'd never truly felt sorry for my dad before. He always seemed too angry to be pitied, but I could see the way he hated—or feared—Elementia as though it was personally attacking him. Like I'd felt only a week ago.

"I would never have taken off without Ryder," I said, sitting on the bed, attempting to calm the situation. "You know I wouldn't."

"I'm sorry," he said sarcastically. "Did you or did you not just pull up from a Dublin bender with your new actor friends?"

"That was because…"

He sat on Ryder's bed and crossed his arms. "I'm listening, Iris. This is going to be a brilliant work of fiction. I can already tell."

I glared at him. My dad looked like me. A lot. Or I think I'm supposed to say I looked like him. Either way, we both looked like M. E. Thorne. Dark hair. Dark eyes. Sharp features that belonged in fantasy illustrations. People said my dad looked manic in an attractive way. I had yet to grow into such a description.

"I'm waiting."

"I had to help Eamon bring Shoshanna back to the set. I…I was the reason she left, sort of. I spoke with this reporter to help out, but I'm apparently terrible at talking to report—"

"Yes, I've read your little interview," he said. "You know better than to talk to the press."

"Yeah, well, I screwed up, but not as much as you think! And I went to get Shoshanna back because this movie needs her to stay alive!"

My dad's eyes flared. "You've got to be kidding me. One week and you're falling in love with this fantasy crap all over again?"

In love? Yes, I was, but not with Elementia. I pictured Eamon in his Nolan costume. Shoshanna's frank banter. Julian's best acting face melting into that fragile sincerity that proved he was actually a huge-hearted guy. Ryder flipping pancakes with Mr. Donato, and Cate grilling me as though she gave a sincere damn about my life.

Be honest and don't back down.

My chest grew tight as I pulled Eamon's camera out of his backpack. "I'm in love with something, but it's not Elementia. Let me show you."

I opened the screen and pressed play. My pulse drummed. Would he get it? He wouldn't.

What if he did?

My dad watched for about twenty seconds before he closed the flip screen and set the camera on Ryder's bed. "Coldplay, Iris? Seriously?"

"What?" I felt dazed. Tricked.

"Coldplay is so…maudlin."

"But you made me listen to that album, remember?"

His tone iced. "Playing someone else's song is the

literary equivalent of going to a poetry slam and reading Emily Dickinson."

"What?" The word barely escaped my lips. I'd been sure he'd be impressed. Or at least surprised. "But I got up there. I played in front of everyone. You said I should—"

"I knew you lied."

"What?" The word kept tumbling out. "*What?*"

"You weren't rescuing some actor from the airport. You were at a bar, drinking heavily by the sound of this. And that's why you didn't come back until this morning. You were out drinking while your little brother was here, in a foreign land, in the hands of strangers."

"They're not strangers! The crew loves Ryder. Ask anyone."

"I'm disappointed. You're not half as mature or responsible as I thought you were."

"Not mature?"

"You heard me, young lady."

I'm raising your kid! The words were like a bubble coming up through the black mud of my feelings. I could feel them rising, rising, rising…until I burst.

"I'm raising your kid, you self-centered egomaniac!"

"Iris!" He threw his hands in the air. "First of all, your insult is completely redundant. Secondly—"

"Why don't you go finish your draft so you can be a human again!"

That hit a nerve. His stare drilled into the ground as he mentally reloaded, but I fired first.

"Ryder has been brilliant since we got here. He's been listening and helping. He's been confident and trying new things. And then you show up and he lost his mind. Whose fault do you think that is, Dad? Your demands freak him out just like they've always freaked me out. And I might have learned way too early that the only way to make you happy was to do exactly what you wanted, but that doesn't mean I'm okay either. We're both messed up, and from what I've figured out since I arrived here, apparently screwing up your kids is the real Thorne family legacy!"

His pale cheeks stormed red.

I couldn't breathe. I couldn't see. I stomped out of the trailer and past people who had most definitely heard every single word of our fight. I jumped in the rowboat that Shoshanna and Eamon had commandeered when we first arrived in Killykeen and rowed out to the tiny island with its crumbling tower.

I stayed there until the sun went down. Alone with Eamon's backpack—where I found his copy of *Elementia*, the same one I'd been leafing through on his brass bed the night before.

And I read it. Every word.

AS IT TURNS OUT, CALLING DOWN THE LIGHTNING IS EXHAUSTING

EAMON SWAM OUT to my little island when the sky was on the edge of dark. The lake was too cold for such ridiculously romantic behavior, and he was a shivering mess when he crawled up the weedy, muddy shore. "I'm here. I made it." He was breathing hard but otherwise in good shape.

I wrapped him in my jacket, and we sat with our backs to the crumbling tower. "I'm shocked you did that."

"My da swam the Channel. That was nothing." He coughed and grinned. "I am fit."

"You are," I said, remembering how he'd deadlifted Shoshanna. "Despite being skinny."

"Hey, I'm wiry. As in strong like wire." I laughed and leaned my head on his wet shoulder. The sun crept down into a red sliver and the floodlights around the trailers and picnic area turned on with a *pop*. "We didn't shoot the scene," he said, rubbing a hand through his hair. "We're going to try again tomorrow. Cate is held up with the studio execs. They're not happy. How'd it go with your da?"

Thoughts streamed through my mind. I ran away again. *My dad hated my playing. I told him off. I love you. I can't believe you swam across the lake. You're absolutely ridiculous. I read* Elementia. *I didn't get it.*

"Your lips are blue," I finally said.

He got up and did some jumping jacks, his teeth chattering. When he sat back down, I crawled on his wet lap and pulled my jacket around both of us. "Your da left, by the way."

"He did?" I sat up fast. "Did he take Ryder?"

"He left Ryder with Mr. Donato."

"Oh, good." I couldn't contain a huge sigh of relief. "It's not surprising. My dad taught me this whole *run from hard stuff* policy."

"Did you tell him the truth? How'd it go?"

"Good enough for me to maroon myself," I joked. Eamon half smiled, and I kissed him. It was a sad kiss. "We should go back before it's too dark and you get hypothermia."

In the middle of the lake—Eamon rowing in a way that showed off his arm muscles—I reached in his bag and held up his book. "I read it. All of it."

He frowned. "And now you're wondering what the big deal is?"

"Well…yeah. It was good, but I didn't have an epiphany like everyone else. Cate discovered her driving force. Ryder forgave Moss. Julian fell in love with Nolan."

Eamon paused rowing. "He what?"

"He thinks Nolan's the best romantic role since Heath Ledger in *10 Things I Hate About You*."

"Ah, okay." He kept rowing. "Let the story sink in a bit, Iris. Also, you've got to read the whole trilogy before you make any firm judgments."

"Okay," I said, but I flat-out doubted him. The book had been good, but it had felt like a story I already knew all the way through. Wasn't it supposed to be groundbreaking? A feminist legend for the ages?

I think Eamon could read my mind. "You should talk to Cate."

"What did you like when you first read it?" I asked.

"Well, I was eleven, so I thought it was exciting and strange and much better than this world. I also had a huge crush on Sevyn. I told Mam the girl I married would be like her, and she said good luck finding a girl like Sevyn who wants to be tied down to a silly boy." He rowed, the wind ruffling his hair until it looked more like when I'd first met him. "Took a bit, but I found you."

"I'm like Sevyn to you? Why? Because I electrocute people who get too close? Or I cause great grief for my family?"

"No. You're headstrong and motivated. You're clever

and kind." He saw me rolling my eyes and added, "Plus you're so damn positive. My own personal ray of sunshine."

"Ha! I'm a black cloud."

"The kind that shoots out lightning?"

I pointed at him. "Watch it, elf."

"Certainly, mistress." He smiled, kept rowing. "You do remember you're also the person who charged onstage in a foreign country and tore into a song like Chris Martin himself."

"That was unusual."

"So you didn't verbally tackle that reporter for doubting the people working on this film?"

"That was a terrible idea."

"How about when you singlehandedly saved the teaser trailer?"

"How about when I choked in the recording studio?"

"How about when you saved your brother's life from a man in the middle of a psychotic break?" He stopped rowing. "Don't discount your bravery just because it doesn't always pay off, Iris."

I folded my arms, wanting to believe him. "So wise, Eamon O'Brien."

"Not wise. *Irish*. Genetically endowed with cleverness and freckles."

I turned to the copy of *Elementia*. "You know the weirdest part? My dad kept me from reading this like he was guarding a wicked family secret, but I can't tell what he's so afraid of."

"I think you have to ask him, then."

"Yeah. That would go over awesome." I rubbed my face, braided back my hair. The shore was close, and my brother's dim-lit silhouette grew closer. The bottom of the rowboat slid against the silt and Eamon jumped out to haul us the rest of the way. I stepped out, and Ryder was hugging my waist before both of my feet were on the shore.

"I'm sorry, Ry," I said. "I was mad. Had to take off for a few hours." I ruffled his hair. When he didn't let go, I knelt down to look in his face. Well, not quite, because he wasn't six anymore. When I knelt, his head was a solid foot above mine.

He looked down at me. "I'm sorry I hit you. I'm sorry I got upset."

"Dad wouldn't listen. That was his fault."

"He's horrible and I don't ever want to go home."

"Oh God, Ry." I snuggled him into a hug. "We can't go down that road. We can't." I pulled back and stared into his eyes. "Think about Sevyn and Evyn's dad. He wasn't great, but he was important to the story." I held up Eamon's copy of *Elementia*.

"You read it?" His voice quivered. "You understand now?"

"Some," I admitted. "The rest you can explain to me." He hugged me all over again, and we walked back to the center of the action. "I have to talk to Cate, Ry. I don't know what's going on with Dad, but I'm sure he set something in motion before he left."

Eamon put a light hand on my back. "Love, I've got to find a hot shower."

"Uh, yeah, you should do that," I managed.

He grinned like he knew I was picturing him naked. Good Lord. "I'll come to your trailer later." He kissed me and walked off, and when I looked down, Ryder was squinting.

"You've been kissing Nolan."

"He's Eamon to me, Ry."

"No, he's Nolan. That makes you Sevyn."

"Ha!" Apparently there was a conspiracy, but you know what? I knew this reference now, and if I was going to live up to it, I'd have to find some more lightning.

~

I knocked on Cate's door, and she hollered, "Come in, Iris!"

Cate sat in the back, surrounded by script pages and computers.

"How do you always know when it's me?" I asked, climbing the steps.

"Well, usually I've sent for you. But this time I was waiting for you to come to your senses and leave your sulking island." She paused. "Literally."

"I wasn't sulking. I was reading." I dropped Eamon's book beside her laptop. She pushed her screen away and picked it up.

"Look at this. I'm telling you, the UK knows how to

make a cover. The American cover's all about grabbing attention, but look at this." She turned it toward me. "This is a cover to fall in love with and treasure for the rest of your life."

"It's Eamon's."

"I'm not surprised. I've been informed by Shoshanna that you two are embarking on puppy love together." Her mouth quirked with amusement.

"I am about one puppy joke away from barking at people."

"All right then." Her words were light, but I could feel the current underneath them.

"How's the…boycott?"

"Thirty thousand signatures. If it hits fifty, we're done."

I stalked around Cate's trailer, too angry to be still. "Those idiot Thornians with their tattoos and their cats named after all the characters! They could actually help this fantasy become reality, and yet they're doing the opposite. Why don't they want this movie? You'd think they'd die for it."

"They're afraid, Iris. Books are endlessly interpretable. Movies are set. The odds that this movie is not what the book means to each one of them is high. Very high." She sounded like a professor who'd given this class too many times. "That is the vast gamble of movie adaptation."

I studied the woman I'd grown to respect against my will. "Help me understand?"

She grinned ever so slightly. "Say that the book is a

sculpture. You can walk around the story. You can touch it. You can view it up close or far away. That is why people love books. The stories interact with your memories, your experiences. They're personalized. Movies? Movies are a picture of that same statue. The parameters are set. The characters have defined faces. The scenes artistically rendered to one person's vision."

"But your vision for this book is good! So what if some people have to see the book differently? Who cares? It's a movie! A gateway to my grandmother's story."

"Iris." Cate stood and took my shoulders in both hands. Her face was lined with the kind of exhaustion that kills people, and yet her eyes still held that spark. "We're moving forward. Hoping for the best. If nothing else goes wrong, we may yet pull off this impossible dream."

I wanted her to be right, but there was still an ugly fly in the ointment. "My dad—"

"Is an absolute nightmare. I didn't fully understand your attitude before I talked with him today, and now I understand too well."

"Did he say anything before he left?"

"Only that he was going to stay in Dublin for the remainder of the shoot. I am to contact him if you guys put one toe out of line. As if I would rat you out to that tyrant."

"He wants to finish his draft," I said coolly. "Typical."

"I don't think he wants to leave you and your brother,

but he sure as hell doesn't want to stay here either. He's going to ping around our lights like a moth, I fear."

Cate really did get my dad; I was impressed.

"You know everything," I said, but that wasn't it. "You *say* everything."

"Be as sharp as you are, Iris. It's a lot more fun than acting like you're catching up. Lead. Be opinionated. Don't say you're sorry unless you did something wrong." She touched the streak of lightning on the *Elementia* cover in my hands. "That's what your grandmother's story gave me. That's what I hope it gives to its audience. To you. Be your own power source."

"My dad would love that," I tried to joke.

"He won't understand because men don't have this problem. They grow up learning to think outward. Act on their impulses. Women are taught to think inward, act rarely. Women who don't stay underground? Well, they have about as easy a time as I've had."

Henrik knocked and opened the door. "Cate, I—" His eyes narrowed on me, and I waited for a *Done having a tantrum on your island?* remark. "Iris, your dad is an asshat."

Cate clapped and pointed at Henrik. "See, Iris? Case in point. He never doubted for a second that he should say that." I laughed so hard that Cate laughed too.

Henrik stood in the doorway with a confused expression until Cate beckoned him in. "Bad news," he grumbled as though he didn't want me to hear. "They're going to stay around for the Cashel filming. They've decided to make the move with us tomorrow."

"They're spooking my actors!" She glanced at me before adding, "The studio execs."

Henrik scowled. "The boycott was the last straw. What if they shelve the sequels?"

"They already have."

"What?"

That was me and Henrik. *Jinx.*

Cate sat down, straightening the pages around her. "They've shelved them. I'm sure the news will leak tomorrow or the next day. I'm not letting that shake us. I'm *not.*" The trailer filled with the sound of Cate's shuffled papers. "They want us to lose steam. Then they can pull the plug and say it happened naturally. I'm not giving that to them."

I hated the way Cate's expression fought itself, determination wrestling back despair. "If the movie is good, they'll revive the sequels, so we just need to make the movie really good," I said.

Cate snapped her fingers and pointed at me without taking her eyes of Henrik. "She gets it, Henrik. Tell me you're with me."

He touched her shoulder, and she grabbed his hand firmly. I couldn't tell if they were more than film partners in a *wink, wink, nudge, nudge* kind of way or if they were truly, deeply friends. The latter seemed more likely, and for what-ever reason, also much more powerful.

"I'm with you, Cay," Henrik said. "But how do we recover from all this bad press?"

"You put M. E. Thorne's grandkids in the movie."

Their heads turned toward me in unison.

"There's no way your dad will give us permission," Henrik said.

I shrugged. "I'll email my mom. I can have it for you by morning."

"You're serious?" Henrik asked.

"My dad won't stop us. He's in the dog house—particularly with Ryder. He hates being hated."

Cate's blue eyes were alight, and I wanted to memorize her fearlessness. "Call our friends at the Wrap, Henrik. Tell them to meet us in Cashel. We're going to need coverage of M. E. Thorne's grandchildren filming their big-screen debut."

⌒

"This is like a sleepover!" Ryder whisper-yelled through the dark trailer.

"Sure, buddy. A sleepover. So go to sleep!" I said. Eamon giggled from beside me in the bed. He rolled on his side, and I snuggled into his chest as casually as possible. All the while my brain screamed, *We're in a bed together! Oh my god, we're in a bed!*

"Is he ever going to fall asleep?" Eamon whispered.

"Since we want him to, not likely." A nearby light slipped through the blinds, revealing Eamon's open eyes only a few inches from mine. "He's too excited."

"What's my costume going to look like?" Ryder asked. "Will I get elf ears?"

"Definitely," Eamon said at the same time that I yelled, "No!"

"I don't want to be a human, Iris!"

"I don't know any more than I told you. Go to sleep!" Ryder moaned and flopped around. "I'm actually excited," I whispered to Eamon. "What roles are even available for the scene at Cashel?"

"I think you'll be ghosts," Eamon said. "When Sevyn enters the ruins of the castle and encounters the elves and men who died there centuries earlier."

I pictured the scene I'd read earlier. After meeting Nolan, Sevyn wanders south to where she believes the Knye are holding Evyn. She passes a dead, falling-down castle town full of memories and pain. She gets caught up in it and doesn't come to her senses until Nolan reappears and leads her away. Then she goes to the caves beneath the Blackened Wastes of Thornbred…

"They'll be shooting all the Thornbred, kidnapping, blood-drinking stuff in LA, right?"

"Yeah. That'll be the majority of Julian's scenes," he said.

"Good. I don't want to see that, although I do miss Julian. He's too funny."

"He makes me mad jealous." Eamon pulled me closer. "You do go faintish around him sometimes. And you have his face on your pants."

"Those were a gag gift from friends who, in hindsight, aren't good friends." Eamon scowled, and I added, "I had a minor crush on him, but that was before I knew him. Now he makes me laugh. Besides, only one of us has kissed Julian Young, and it wasn't me, Charles."

Eamon turned his head into the pillow and groaned. "I'm never going to live that down."

"Guys! You better go to sleep!" Ryder called out.

"Iris," Eamon whispered. "You sure your da is going to go for this?"

"Doesn't matter. Mom already signed the permission form and sent it back. I always have her sign stuff for school because she doesn't care."

"You don't talk about your mam much."

"When we've been dating three months, I'll tell you about her."

"I accept that challenge," he said, leaning over to kiss my neck.

I curled closer to Eamon, my nerves lighting up every place we touched. "I've never slept in a bed with a boy before."

"First for me too," he said. "So what do we do?"

"Think you can sleep?"

"No."

"Me neither. So let's stare at each other all night." I was joking, but we did stare. I held my hand up in the muted light, and we tangled fingers over and over. It was part examination, part exploration, and it left me wanting to memorize him freckle by freckle.

"We have to make it a success," I whispered long after Ryder's breath proved he'd fallen asleep. "If my family is attached, it has to be great. The story has to have a chance to reach people. I won't be embarrassed if that happens. I'll be—*oh*."

Earlier that day, I couldn't figure out what *Elementia* was supposed to mean to me. Now I knew what had changed irrevocably when I read it.

"Wow," I murmured.

"Have you had an epiphany? Do you know how we can boost support?"

"I'm proud that my grandma wrote it. It's honest and sad, yet hopeful. I'm *proud*. And it's like my grandma feels like a real person all of the sudden."

Eamon pulled me closer, which shouldn't have been possible, but somehow we managed. "Of course she was real."

"But she's never felt real. My dad talks about her like she was a famous, obnoxious stranger, and I only met her that one time." I pictured that sepia-colored memory, walking in the park with a woman with long, black hair. She'd made me nervous. I remembered that now. She'd corrected me when I said something simple…that the sky was a pretty blue.

It's azure.

She'd said something else as well. I could remember the tip of it. Sort of. I reached deeper into the memory. It felt like digging with my fingers.

"I'm glad he let me meet you."

"What?" Eamon asked through the dark.

"That's what Grandma Mae said to me. 'I'm glad he let me meet you.'"

Film: Elementia

Director: Cate Collins

On Location: Day 9

Killykeen Forest, Ireland A.M.

Cashel, Ireland P.M.

Filming Notes:

A.M.: SEVYN & NOLAN's scene around the fire

P.M.: Evening shot at the Rock of Cashel.
SEVYN, NOLAN, 24 human and elf extras. Cameos
by IRIS & RYDER THORNE.

Etc. Notes:

Moving lock, stock, and barrel to the Rock of
Cashel by one o'clock.

Mandatory tour of the ruin for all cast and
crew at two with specific instructions to
respect the property.

UNTANGLING THE TIMELINE

THE VIDEO VILLAGE was farther back from the action today because they were shooting dialogue. I sat in the canvas chair like I had the night of Eamon's first scene, only now I wore headphones and peered into the monitor, watching like it was a movie. A *real* movie.

They weren't even Shoshanna and Eamon anymore. They were Sevyn and Nolan, up all night together beside the lake, Sevyn fighting a fever. Nolan caring for this strange, cursed human who had woken him from a thousand years of slumber in his great, white-barked tree.

A small, real fire crackled between them, and I watched the wind catch the smoke and throw it at camera one. Cate yelled, "Cut!" and the grumbling from behind made me peer over my right shoulder at the Vantage studio execs. They weren't watching; they were judging. Coolly, confidently. Their nearly matching suit coats and dark jeans made me feel like they'd come for a *Matrix* movie and were quite disgruntled to find themselves in Elementia.

Henrik spoke quietly to Cate. "We could douse it. Put the flames in later with CGI."

"No," she said.

More grumbling from behind. I checked the desire to give them my best stink eye.

Cate moved forward and spoke to her actors. Then she returned to her seat and called, "Action." I fell back into the scene, holding my headphones tight over my ears.

Sevyn sat up from where she rested by the fire and eyed Nolan. "Who are you?"

"Be still." Nolan moved closer, but she pulled away. "You cannot hurt me."

"I can hurt everyone," she snapped. "Who are you, elf?" When he didn't respond but stared with curiosity bordering on passion, she turned, tears bright in her eyes. "You should not have helped me. You should not have touched me."

Nolan's whole body eased as he sat beside her. She glanced at him a few times before taking a deep breath. They stared at each other for so long I became aware of Eamon again beneath the makeup and the prosthetic ears. He looked at me that way. That was his love look. The scene continued, but I could barely pay attention. My mind flitted through my memories of us tangled up in the small trailer bed. I'd woken up this morning with my head on his shoulder and fought back tears.

Three more days in Ireland.

I focused on the scene as Sevyn stood in a rush. "My brother is hurt! Dying! I have to get to him!" She blacked out, collapsing into Nolan's arms, and I marveled at how close she'd let herself fall toward the actual fire. From my reading, I knew Nolan was using his elven affinity with the elements to calm Sevyn's lightning. He would help her learn to control it. To use it. To find that it was never truly a curse.

I didn't even hear Cate call "cut," and all of a sudden the crew was breaking down the set in a hurry. Henrik took over running things while Cate spoke heatedly with the Vantage execs. I swear her lax Irish accent returned to full strength.

Glancing around at Killykeen, I felt even worse about leaving this place than I had about watching Inishmore disappear behind the whir of the ferry engines. I took out my phone and started taking pictures of everything. Of Shoshanna and Eamon talking in their costumes. Of Ryder stuffing brown bag lunches into each crew member's hand. Of the lake's lonely island with its sulking tower where I'd first read my grandmother's story.

I even snuck a photo of Shoshanna getting a makeup inspection from Roxy. True to form, Roxy looked like she stepped out of her own movie. The half of her head that wasn't shaved had beautiful curls that cascaded over one shoulder, and she was wearing a flannel hoodie and about five men's ties braided into a belt around her waist. Roxy started laughing at something Shoshanna said, and I snapped a couple more pictures of the two girls smiling at each other.

Shoshanna saw me with my phone, glared hard, and then whisper-hissed, "Text that to me immediately."

I sent all my pictures to Julian as well, and I felt so damn in love with everything that I wanted more. More truth. More friends. More happiness. I couldn't stop thinking about what I'd remembered last night. *I'm glad he let me meet you.* Had my dad kept Grandma Mae away when I was little? That's not the story he told. He said she was too busy writing to care about us.

I touched the app for my Gmail, wanting to be the one to reach out first after our fight. I tapped his email and left the subject line blank. Only one sentence in the body.

Why did you keep Grandma Mae out of my life?

I hit send.

Would he respond? Would he even try to answer?

Eamon and Shoshanna headed toward me, and I pushed past the hard thoughts. Back to Ireland, where life felt good. I snagged Ryder. "All right, guys. Game faces." I hauled us all together and took a selfie. When Ryder realized what was happening, his smile turned as huge as a Muppet's. Eamon kissed my cheek, which brilliantly showed off his elf ears, and Shoshanna posed with some sort of *I kill people with my eyes* expression.

We laughed as we reviewed the masterpiece.

"Getting sentimental?" Shoshanna teased.

Henrik looked over my shoulder. "I'll give you a thousand dollars to post it. Scrub that, I'll give you the spare room in my apartment. Free rent in LA for a year. Think about it, Iris."

"That would be a stretch way too far for my dad. Letting us be on the sidelines of a shot in full elf makeup is one thing. Selfie faces on the internet is entirely different."

I squinted, realizing I hadn't cited the Thornians or our safety as the reason why I couldn't put my face online. This policy—like everything else I hated—was about appeasing my dad, wasn't it?

"Wait for me in my car?" Eamon asked, handing over the keys. "We'll head to Cashel together. I've got to get out of my hottie leaf pants for the drive."

"Hashtag hottie leaf pants." Shoshanna held up a triumphant fist.

They walked away and my phone vibrated. I found myself staring at a reply from my dad.

None of your business.

My fingers flew over the tiny cubed alphabet as I fired back my response.

> Really? Because I thought she was my grandma.
> Or is it a fluke that her name is in the middle
> of mine?

I hit send, and this time I felt uneasy about what I was doing. There was a reason I never poked my dad about Grandma Mae. I didn't know that reason, but you didn't have to be a wizened wizard to figure out the backstory was tragic.

I found Ryder learning how to properly coil an electrical cord.

"Look what the juicer taught me to do with this stinger!"

I laughed. My brother was getting into set lingo. "Very nice, buddy. Come on. We've got to get ready to go south."

We went to our trailer and grabbed a few things for the drive. One of the things he grabbed was his broken-spine copy of the Elementia trilogy. My dad's old copy.

"Can I borrow this?" I asked.

He nodded with a huge grin. "You want to read it again? I wanted to read it again the second Dad finished reading it to me. Only the words were too big."

We stepped outside and a mild breeze came off the lake, lifting, almost singing. "What was he like when he read it to you?" I asked.

"Unhappy," Ryder said simply.

"Do you know why?"

"He never told me, but he told my therapist the book would make him go UPS and—"

"PTSD?"

"That's it. He told me to sit in the waiting room." I thought that might be the extent of Ryder's knowledge, but then my brother leaned in conspiratorially. "It's because of Samantha. His twin sister. The one who died when she was a kid."

"He talked to you about her?" I couldn't keep the incredulity out of my voice. The one time I'd asked about my deceased aunt, he'd spazzed like it was so long ago I was asking him to remember his own birth.

Ryder stroked the cover, fingers trailing over the raised letters of the title. "Sometimes he'd stop reading in the middle of a sentence. Slam the book and turn off my light. He wouldn't even say good night." Ryder's face fell. "The more I liked the book, the meaner he got, so I pretended I wasn't listening."

There were a lot of things I wanted to say to him. *This isn't right. He's got more baggage than both of us. I'm sorry I didn't understand sooner.*

I put my arm around him. "It sucks being a Thorne, doesn't it?" He shrugged, and we approached the craft services van. "Do you want to drive with Mr. Donato?" I asked.

"I'm going with Eamon."

"You don't want to come with me?" he asked.

"Let your sister have time with her boyfriend," Mr. Donato said with a wink. He pulled the van door open, and Ryder climbed in. "Get in a mild amount of trouble, young lady. You've earned it." He slammed the door, and I touched his arm.

"Thank you for yesterday. For helping Ryder when our dad got all…"

Mr. Donato—who still reminded me of Stanley Tucci too much—waved a hand to stop me. "Dads aren't perfect. In fact, I've never met one who's come even close. I've been telling Ryder all about it." He patted my shoulder. "I forgot one of my kid's birthdays last week. Blame the filming stress or the time difference. Worst part is, I couldn't even tell which daughter it was from the crying voice mail."

"That's terrible."

He shrugged. "Give your dad a break. He'll probably give you one right back."

I turned to leave but spun back for a question. "When Ryder was screaming, you said something in his ear and he starting crying instead of fighting. What did you say?"

Mr. Donato smiled sadly. "I reminded him that he loves his dad. No matter what."

⌒

In Eamon's car, I leafed through the worn copy of the Elementia trilogy that had my dad's handwriting in it, looking for answers. I scanned the marginalia, but nothing jumped out.

Next I flipped to Grandma Mae's bio. Born in 1945. Okay, my dad was born in 1965, so Grandma Mae was young when she had him and his twin sister, Samantha. I'd only heard her name a few times before, and just thinking it now made my aunt feel more real all of a sudden. Where was she buried? What did she look like? What did I even know about my own family?

Samantha died when she was thirteen. I knew that much because my dad had robotically told my pediatrician once in front of me. I also knew that Grandma Mae published the stories in the 1980s, after Samantha's death. But this copy wasn't that old. I flipped to the front and checked the printing year. It was a newer edition, published in 2001. The year I was born. So around the time I entered this world, my dad bought a copy of his estranged mother's book and read it, leaving scribbles in the margins. What happened after that?

I pulled out my phone, Mr. Donato's words in my head, and wrote a new message. This time I appealed to my dad's writer senses.

> Dad—I don't get the timeline. You named me after her, but then you didn't let me meet her until...

I paused. This next piece was a guess.

> ...until she found out she had cancer. Eight
> years later.

I hit send as Eamon slid into the driver's seat. "Everything all right?" he asked.

"I don't know." I took in his adorableness. He'd changed into a T-shirt and jeans, but his makeup was still on and so were those darn ears. They were, however, starting to grow on me.

"Eamon, what happens at the end of the trilogy?" I held up the book. "At the airport, Shoshanna made some comment about it being sad."

Eamon pumped the clutch and started the car. "Ah, I think you should read it."

"Yeah, but what happens? Is it as bad as the end of *The Amber Spyglass*?"

He shook his head. "Worse. Iris, keep reading."

"One of them dies," I guessed. "One of the twins because..."

That's what happened in real life.

Which left the question, which child did Grandma Mae kill off? Her daughter?

Or her son?

CASTLE ON THE ROCK AND OTHER BIBLICALLY CHALLENGING IDEAS

I'D BEEN READING for an hour, a third of the way through the sequel to *Elementia*, and already the characters were getting older and more complicated. And the love story? *Hot.* I kept backing up entire pages to reread—although I had to stop picturing Eamon and Shoshanna as Nolan and Sevyn because they were, um, kissing too much.

"Ready?" Roxy turned the chair around to face the mirror, and I looked up and screamed.

The sea of extras mingling around the makeup trailer jumped, including Eamon, who had been reviewing his script in the corner. I clapped my hands over my mouth and tried not to die.

"What? Is something wrong?" Roxy asked. "Are you having an allergic reaction?"

I shook my head back and forth. "I'm an elf. I can't believe…I'm a freakin' elf."

Ryder—who had gotten his ears first—shot up the steps and started giggling so hard he fell over Eamon's legs. Eamon started to laugh too. I tugged on one of the pointy ears lightly. "Don't laugh! This is my own personal hell, and it's glued to me!"

"It *was*," Ryder corrected between giggles. "Now you love us."

I glanced at the pile of my brother and my boyfriend and couldn't disagree. Then I looked down at my rather spiffy elf outfit, complete with leather bodice and leggings, and felt out of place all over again.

Henrik stuck his head in the trailer. "Ten minutes and I want everyone up on the hill for the scene set up. Got it?" He glanced at me and snorted a laugh into the back of his hand.

"Okay, okay!" I got out of the seat and tried to act in charge. I did look pretty darn amazing in my warrior elf outfit; I just had to own it. "Let's go. March."

We left the trailer, joining the stream of people making their way up the hill toward a massive, old castle atop a two-hundred-foot-high limestone outcropping. I'd learned a few interesting details from the tour we'd taken earlier. For exam-ple, it wasn't a castle but a series of towers and cathedrals, even a bishop's palace, amalgamated over many hundreds of years. There had been real freakin' kings crowned there. One of them was even named Cormac MacCartaigh, to which I joked, "He was high king? When did he find the time to write *The Road*?"

No one laughed, so I texted it to Julian. He'd ROFled; he might not know literature, but the guy knows his Viggo Mortensen. One more day and Julian would be back. I couldn't wait to find out how it'd went with Elora and tell him all about Eamon and me.

There was a laundry list of even more history attached to the Rock of Cashel, including Saint Patrick and, everyone's favorite, Satan. But mostly I could feel Cate's genius in the setting—how ripe this place was for fantasy filming. The great, green mound of the rock beneath the structure was called the Fairy Ridge, and the rolling planes to the north were known as the Golden Veil.

The *Elementia* crew and all our trailers were camped out to the west, out of the way of the town, and half in the middle of some poor pasture. We were close to a neglected old stone abbey that, in my opinion, was cooler than the Rock of Cashel, but then, I'd always been a fan of underdogs.

Eamon was back in his Nolan gear, and he seemed tense. "The Vantage execs thanked me for my time before they left, like they were trying to make themselves feel better. They were supposed to stay around until the end of the day, but I guess they've seen all they need to see."

"Hope they're gone for good," I said.

We reached the top and filed through the gate. There were many extras; I wasn't used to that, and neither was Eamon. We found an empty spot by a huge stone cross and waited for Cate and Shoshanna to reappear. They'd been filming for hours, and the only time I'd seen Cate, she'd been wearing those black sunglasses again.

Ryder was pretending to battle foes, wearing the little leather elf outfit that made him look like he won a cosplay contest at Comic-Con. I sat in the grass beside Eamon, running my fingers over the lines on his palm while he looked over his script.

Shoshanna appeared like magic, sitting beside us with a deep scowl. "That's it. I'm joining this puppy-love party. Let's all cuddle and howl."

I barked, and she fell over backward on the grass.

Eamon laughed, and I pointed a finger at Shoshanna. "One more puppy comment, and we're going to stop everything and make out every time we see you."

"You wouldn't dare because you two are *puppies.*"

I grabbed Eamon and kissed him like the sky was breaking. When we pulled apart, he was the shade of a red associated with vine-ripe tomatoes, but I wasn't done. "Oh no, I smudged his makeup. Let's find Roxy, shall we? Does anyone know if she's single? I bet Julian knows." I took my phone out of my cleavage—because that was the only place I could hide it in this getup—and texted while reading my message aloud. "Julian, is Roxy single?"

"He doesn't know," Shoshanna growled. "And he's got the biggest mouth in LA, Iris!"

"Of course he knows. He's Julian." I held out the screen to show Julian's insta-response.

Single. Why?

"Should I tell him how cute you two are together—or will you chill out?"

Shoshanna opened her mouth and then shut it. "Nice one," she huffed. "So nice that I think you two have graduated to high school sweethearts. When is the prom?"

Eamon held out his hands between us. "I call truce, ladies. Truce!"

Shoshanna didn't agree. "So what are you two love birds—"

"Oh, wonderful. We're birds now," I muttered.

Shoshanna continued, "—going to do in two days when we finish filming and head back to LA? Eamon's not coming with. His scenes are done when we finish here. *Long distance relationship* takes on a whole new meaning when you've got the Atlantic Ocean and the length of the United States between you."

Eamon looked paler than usual beneath his tanned-skin makeup. Did he want to break up when I left? My chest twisted and then bloomed with embarrassment. Of course we were going to break up. How could we stay together?

Time lock, my dad's voice slipped in. *Always makes books more interesting.*

Two more days.

I put my hands over my ears, finding them rubbery and foreign. "Shut up, shut up!"

"Hey." Eamon wove his fingers with mine. "Don't let Shoshanna get to you. She's a fiend. A troublemaker. Look at her, she's the cat who got the cream."

"It's not her."

He gave me a questioning look.

"It's leaving you. I can't stand it."

His expression was as stunned as I felt for saying the words, but he nodded like he felt the same way. The throbbing inside calmed a little. I would miss Eamon beyond belief, and that was...good? It was good to care that much, wasn't it?

"I know what'll cheer you two up," Shoshanna said, leaning in between us and popping our bittersweet moment. "Listen to my bloody awesome Irish accent. How's the *craic*, fellas?"

Eamon's eyebrows smashed together as though they'd been in a vehicular accident. "Is it funny to do that? Is it? You, Shoshanna Reyes, sound like a chipmunk when you play Irish. I don't know what you're thinking, but in Ireland we talk at a normal vocal range."

Shoshanna scowled. Then she repeated the same line and didn't go crazy high with it.

"See?" Eamon said. "Now you sound like an Irish *human*."

"It is much better," I agreed. "Let's hear your American accent, Eamon."

Eamon gave me an overconfident look that had nothing

to do with his personality. When he opened his mouth, a movie stereotype fell out, albeit without a hint of Irish accent. "Surf's up, dude. Hang ten. Did you catch the new Bruce Willis flick, man?"

"No!" Shoshanna and I yelled together to make it stop.

"I can do John Wayne too," Eamon said. "Howdy, partner. Let's fire up the iron horse and ride into the Wild West." I had to admit, his drawl had comedic preciseness.

Shoshanna began to roll with laughter, and she didn't stop for minutes. "That's the worst impression I've ever heard," she managed. "That should be on YouTube, oh wait—you are!" She was still laughing, and I mean I was too, when Eamon leaned a little closer to me.

"You're not impressed? Not even a little?" he said in a perfect, smooth American accent.

"What?" My voice actually shook.

Shoshanna quit laughing and leaned closer.

He smiled, but not like Eamon. Like an American boy with that irrefutable sense of confidence glazed in laziness. "I asked if you were impressed. I can't be that bad, can I?"

I blinked at him. He was pulling this off far too well, and it was like seeing someone barefoot when they'd always worn boots. I stared at his face as though I'd realized his toes were wicked hairy.

"Keep going," Shoshanna murmured.

He glanced at her. "You should stop doubting me."

"Turn it off!" I yelled. "I hate it!"

He grabbed my hand and kissed my knuckles. "Sorry, sorry."

"There you are." I breathed an actual sigh of relief.

"Wow," Shoshanna said after a minute of silence. "I did not think you had it in you. Shit, kid. You're going to win an Oscar someday."

⌒

Filming mode kicked in and we took our assigned places. All around, the impressive landscape was crowned by an epic smear of clouds against a vivid, azure sky. I spent most of the next few hours staring up into it, learning pretty fast that being a film actor meant a lot of waiting.

Ryder and I had lucked out in that we didn't have to wear wigs, but our hair had been coifed and cemented with hairspray around our prosthetic ears in a way that became less and less tolerable with each passing hour. We were stationed in a crowd of two dozen extras in similar costumes, all local Irish actors. The ghosts of Castletown. At the bottom of the hill, Shoshanna stood in her Sevyn getup, getting instructions from Cate.

"Keep still," I warned Ryder. He was fiddling with his leather boots and had somehow convinced Henrik to give him a bow, even though the rest of us didn't have weapons.

Cate had looked a little green when she put us all in our places earlier, which had me worried. If something had shaken her, I'm not sure any of us could withstand it. She was the rock this whole production was built upon, and I kept having the weirdest daydream of Grandma Mae being proud of Cate Collins.

After reading *Elementia*, I felt like I did know my grandmother a little, and when I thought back on our one time together, it no longer felt like a walk in the park between two strangers. She had been trying to shove a lifetime of knowing me into one afternoon.

I pressed my leather elf boot against the vivid grass and thought about earthquakes. Plate tectonics and fault lines— Mae Ellen Thorne and her son, Michael Edward. What the hell happened between the two of them after Samantha died? My dad hadn't responded to my messages. Had I gone too far? Probably. Did I regret it? No.

This was my family too.

Cate called action, and I held my brother's hand while we all stared forlornly at Shoshanna as she climbed the pathway through the castle, encountering a host of extras who moaned and wept without seeing her. The camera moved along the track beside her, sweeping by us with a slight pause.

When they'd cut and were resetting, I turned to my brother. "Ryder?" He was pretending to fire his bow while we waited for the next action call. "Do you remember when I said we should find lessons for you that make Dad and you happy?"

"Yeah."

"That's bull crap. Let's get you cooking lessons. You can become a real chef."

He actually dropped his bow. "You mean it?"

"I do. Dad won't be happy, but he's never happy unless he's in control. This is your life, Ry. I'll help you make it happen."

"And I'll help you with your music!" His grin was big. I didn't have the heart to ask how he would do that, but he continued, "I'll get him out of the house so you can practice more."

"Thanks, Ry." I hugged him. "But you know it'll be hard, and he won't be nice."

"If you can do it, I can too."

I was struck by what I'd realized two years ago after the cosmos dropped Felix Moss in our lives. My brother was resilient. He had to be; he hadn't had a single break his whole short, overactive life. Well, except for being invited onto this movie set. "You know how I know Dad's not so bad?" I asked. "He made sure I brought you here. And he didn't come with us like a giant wet blanket. He could have said no way, and he wanted to, but he gave us this trip."

"That's a weird way to think of it, Eyeball. We all tricked him. I even got my therapist to push him into it."

"That was you?" I asked. He grinned. "Nicely played, Brother."

Ryder bounced on his toes and peered down the hill. "Cate's about to call action again. Assume the position."

THE TRUTH ABOUT SCAPEGIRLS,
I MEAN, SCAPEGOATS

THEY CALLED WRAP for the day.

Henrik dismissed the extras, asking Shoshanna, Eamon, Ryder, and me to meet him by the old cross, where we'd been sitting and joking only a few hours ago. I could tell something was wrong by the way the assistant director's hat was tugged low, and my brain started rifling through lists of what it could be.

Eamon met me at the cross, all mischief. "Is it wrong to think you're a mighty attractive elf?"

"Yes, I think it most definitely is," I said pulling at my ears. "I feel like I'm late to some *Shannara Chronicles* fan party."

"You make fun of that show a little too often to not have seen it, methinks."

"I got the flu. There was a marathon on MTV. There was nothing else to watch, I swear."

"So you get sick and secretly watch fantasy TV shows. Tell me more about the classified files of Iris Thorne." He pulled me in for a kiss. Granted it wasn't a thing for me to make out dressed as elves, but being in costume did mean that Eamon was practically naked, and I was, uh, rather fond of getting my hands on so much of his chest and hip lines.

Ryder made gagging sounds, and we broke apart. My joy died as Shoshanna approached in her Sevyn getup, her shoulders drooping and her hair falling in her face. I could tell she wasn't duped by Henrik's call for a meeting either. She gave me a look that was no small part impending misery.

"Do you know why Henrik wants to talk?" Eamon asked, still entirely too buoyant.

"I have an idea. I just hope I'm wrong," I said.

Henrik appeared as Eamon started to catch on to my tone. His face fell, and Shoshanna snapped, "Where's Cate?"

"In her trailer. She's taking the news hard, although she admits she's being a coward."

"Cowards don't admit to being cowards," I said quietly. Everyone looked at me, and I said it: "They've canceled the filming. Those assholes shook all of our hands and left smiling, and then they axed the movie."

Ryder yelled, "No!" He punched me in the arm. Hard.

Henrik took off his hat and rubbed his head. "Of course

they're not saying that exactly. Their official position is that they're canceling the rest of this location and the next one. We're to make do with the shots we have, although we don't have the end."

"So they'll shrug and say, 'Too bad,'" I snapped. "Is that it?"

Ryder looked like he was going to hit me again, and I grabbed his hand. "Are you going to have a tantrum?" I'd never flat-out asked him before. The question seemed to shock him, and he shook his head. "Go see Mr. Donato. I'll come talk to you when I have answers."

He ran off, and when I looked back, Henrik's expression was so taut I could have smashed it with a tack hammer. "Flights are being arranged. We'll all be out of here by tomorrow. The studio believes it would be better to shut the filming down quietly. Maybe in a season or two when the negative energy from the boycott dies down, we'll be able to film the remaining scenes. Maybe."

"That's bullshit!" Shoshanna yelled. "They never put things back in motion after they've been shut down like this! They'll sell the establishing shots and call it a loss!"

I looked to Eamon. His head was turned away, his bare chest collapsed. I tried to take his hand, but his fingers slipped away. He left, and Henrik said, "Leave him be, Iris. His dreams just flatlined."

Shoshanna continued to berate Henrik. She even called Julian and the two of them launched into the AD over speakerphone like he was the reason this was happening. Moving in a sort of daze, I went to the costume trailer and put my real clothes back on. Then I went to makeup and had Roxy remove my ears. The extras were talking about the scene; no one knew we had been shut down yet.

"You all right?" Roxy asked, peeling one of my elf ears free. "You were awfully combative when I put these things on you. Now you're still as a rock."

"You should talk to Shoshanna. There's been some… news."

"Oh." Roxy caught on immediately. Her hands dropped to her sides. Today her pants were being held up by braided rainbow twine, and the side of her hair that wasn't shaved was knotted via a pair of chopsticks. "That bad?" she whispered.

"You should talk to Shoshanna," I said again, even though it was probably weird.

"I bet she wants to be alone."

"Nope. She wants to be with you. A lot." Part of me worried I was crossing a line, part of me didn't care. Roxy went to work on my remaining elf ear, and I could see the faintest hint of a smile in the mirror. At least there was some silver lining in all this mud. But then, I didn't want to jinx it with hope. That's what always happened. I wanted something, and then the second I started to hope for it? *Gone.*

Hope was the kiss of death.

After I'd been de-elfed, I knocked on Cate's door and

wondered if this would be the first time she didn't see me coming.

"Come in, Iris," she called out.

I stepped inside and found her still wearing her sunglasses. There was a stillness to her posture that felt rather dangerous. "Can I help, Cate?"

"We're beyond that, girl. Unless you know where we can find a few hundred thousand dollars and a fan base that promises to buy tickets to this movie and the special edition DVD, instead of signing a petition to do precisely the opposite."

"They're out there," I muttered. "Maybe we can find a new way to reach them?"

"It's too late."

"What if I appealed to the Thornians?" I tried. "I'll go on Eamon's YouTube show. I'll call each and every one of them on the phone! You can raffle off a date with me. Anything!"

"It's too late, Iris."

"I'll give you the money. I have a trust fund," I said, ignoring the fact that I couldn't access it without my dad's say-so. "Henrik said it'd be like an investment. When the movie is a huge hit, I'll make it back threefold in book sales and merchandise."

"Iris! It's too late." Her shoulders folded in on her tiny frame. "Once we leave this location, the pieces of this production will fall apart fast. This time next week, no one will remember the production was filming. It isn't personal, Iris. It happens all the time in Hollywood. At least we have valid reasons for shutting down. Some films don't even get that much."

"What will happen to you?"

She wouldn't look at me. "I'm staying here in Ireland. I've been marked a failure. The blame falls on me"—she took a deep breath—"so I bear it. This was my adaptation from the start."

"So it *is* personal! The studio kept slashing your budget and hoping the movie would go away, and when you persisted, they said *you* were the problem." She didn't have to confirm my suspicions. The undercurrent had been clear from the moment that reporter had stepped foot on the set, which reminded me of her terrible *Titanic* metaphor. "You're not going down with the ship, Cate. Movies need women like you. Girls everywhere need you. Look at me: I didn't have a single adult to look up to before you." Tears filled my eyes, and I scrubbed at them.

Cate got up and hugged me. I held on tighter than I'd ever hugged my own mom. She couldn't disappear now. She couldn't be beaten down to nothing.

"Great. Your life's work is on fire, and you're consoling me," I said between sniffs.

"Same continent, Iris Thorne. Same pain."

"Hollywood is full of goddamn miracles," I whispered. "I hear about them all the time."

"The miracle is you," she said. "And if we have to stay

married to Grace Lee's unoriginal *Titanic* metaphor, you are
the unsinkable Molly Brown. You're the one who comes out
of this stronger."

Angry tears tumbled out. "Don't be proud of me. That
means it really is over."

Henrik entered, looking mightily disheveled. "Can you
go comfort your boyfriend and brother, Iris? They're taking
the news hard."

"Shoshanna?" Cate asked.

"Hulking out. I wouldn't be surprised if she knocked the
castle off the rock."

Somehow we all laughed the tiniest laugh. Everything
seemed impossible. Everything felt doomed. But isn't that the
exact moment when fantasies get real?

~

When I left Cate's trailer, I couldn't find anyone. Not Ryder.
Not Eamon. Not Shoshanna. I still had no response from my
dad, and only one unread text from Julian:

This blows. I was finally starting to dig my role.

The news must have spread while I was talking with Cate,
and almost everyone had gone into town to drown their disappointment in a pint. I went for Annie, grabbed her out of
the case, and swung her strap across my chest. Guitar on my
back like a rock star, I walked to the top of the rock, passing
Irish crosses and headstones so old they'd been worn down

to nubs. I thought about playing in the cemetery, but somewhere else caught my eye.

Below the rock and behind our circle of production trailers, that cool, old stone abbey stood in the middle of a cow pasture. I hiked down to it, wondering if someone would appear and shout at me. They didn't; I was alone.

Inside the ruin, the lack of a roof meant my view of the sky was framed by ancient stonework. I turned in circles to take it all in, pulling Annie under my shoulder and securing my left hand to the frets.

No notes came.

I sat on the stone window seat and waited, holding myself right there. Right at the edge of this wretched moment.

"What would you have done, Grandma Mae?" I asked.

She didn't respond. She wasn't in my head like my dad. Like my doubts.

"This blows," I said, echoing Julian. That feeling was definitely a minor chord. D minor. The one that sounds as sour as if it's bitten its own tongue. I struck it, and the reverberation off the stone walls caused a magpie to take flight with an angry squawk. "You better run!" I yelled.

The next chords came easier. They started out agitated with a swift rhythm and then slammed into a looping progression. Suddenly I was all over the neck, not caring if it sounded good or not. I let my fingers spread into bar chords while my right hand did its best impression of a furious Ani DiFranco.

The anger shot out like Sevyn's lightning. Why had I been against this movie for so long? If I hadn't been an idiot, I could have been flirting with Eamon from the first day. I could have given an awesome interview instead of that stilted one, then maybe the boycott wouldn't have started and the studio execs would have stayed in Lotus Land where they belonged.

Flying home tomorrow was a sudden, sharp grief, and my chords turned pretty. Sadness, after all, was rather beautiful. Especially when Grandma Mae wrote it. The pain swelled into mountains like two continental plates shoved together, reaching for the sky with desperate peaks. Everyone else got to read *Elementia* and discover something about the world or themselves. Not me. I'd read her story and began drowning in a loss I'd never known was mine.

My grandmother was a brilliant author—and I'd never read her books because of my dad.

My grandmother was a great woman—and I'd never get to know her.

Tears fell on my hands and strings. None of this was fair. Not to me. To Cate. To Ryder, Eamon, Shoshanna. None of it to anyone.

Fair is fantasy, Cate's voice slipped in.

Then what's real? I asked—but I knew the answer. Reality came with a bite, a pinch, a kiss. Longing, loss, resentment, and the most impossible of all, *passion*. Passion was real. It wasn't an obsession with the thing you couldn't get better at,

like my dad had coldly told me long ago. It was the only thing
you could get better at.

Without passion, there could be no growth.

I threw my head back while the stone abbey wrapped my
song around me, surrendering to all the ragged notes inside
that wanted to turn into one strong melody. Maybe that's
what Elementia was for Grandma Mae—an abandoned, dying
continent she created to house her grief for her daughter, an
entire fictional world to make sense of her broken one.

The words came in a rush. I took out my notebook and
scribbled. I gave each feeling a bittersweet chord, each line
its own heartache, and I let the rhythm build like sadness,
reaching a whole mountain range of empty hands toward the
untouchable sky.

I played forever, the sunset turning the roofless place into
a spread of orange. My eyes mostly closed, my heart as wide
open as a well-loved book.

When I finished writing the last verse, I looked up to find
Shoshanna sitting on the stone altar. I had no idea how long
she'd been watching.

"There were feelings in that," she said. "Strong ones."

I nodded, wanting to put away my notebook and guitar in
a rush, but she stopped me.

"You feel naked?"

I glanced around. "Yeah."

"I always feel like someone stole my clothes when I give

myself to a scene." She jumped down and stepped closer. "You'll get used to feeling like you're on display. Somewhat."

"I don't think I want to get used to it." I was shaking hard enough to prove my point.

She shrugged. "That's what it means to be an artist. You've got to be courageous to snag the high of creation, but if you want to make this world a little more decent, you've got to turn around and give it away. That's where the bravery comes in. And the nudity."

I stared at my notebook, the words I'd blindly written. "This is about my grandmother."

"I picked up on that."

"But I never knew her. How can you miss someone you never even knew? How can I want to be like her when I can't even know her?"

"You read her book, Iris," Eamon said from the crumbling doorway, startling me.

"How long have you been there?" I asked. Shoshanna was not lying about that naked business. I had the sudden urge to cover myself.

"We heard you playing from all the way up at the trailers," Shoshanna volunteered. "Your boyfriend was afraid if you saw him you'd stop, so he hid."

"He's right," I admitted.

His smile only lifted one side of his face. "That song had lightning in it, Iris."

"Maybe." I stood, resting Annie against the wall. The sadness inside that had shifted into sharp mountains was suddenly less like stone, more like water—and I wanted to pour it out. "You guys are saying you…liked that song."

"Yes," Eamon said, while Shoshanna added an eloquent, "Duh."

"What if we recorded it?" I faced Eamon. "Do you have your camera?"

He reached into his pocket and pulled it out.

"What are you thinking?" Shoshanna's expression had gone fiery. "You saying you'd let the world have that? The Thornians would lose their minds. It's got all that *Elementia* crap in it."

I held Eamon's eyes. Did he know how terrifying this was? How truly horrible it felt to have to trust that the world could take something I'd made without tearing it—and therefore me—apart. Each pound of my heart was hard, threatening, but I kept going.

"Will you sing it with me, Eamon?"

HOPE IS FANTASY, OR MAYBE IT'S THE OTHER WAY AROUND

I SUPPOSE IF you have to record a song in the ruins of a roofless Cistercian monastery at dusk, it's best to do it with two actors who are used to reshooting. Again and again.

My fingers grew thick and slow on the chords. Teaching Eamon the words felt like having sex with him—at least I think so, having little experience on the subject. It was awkward and wonderful, and our harmonizing was in all the wrong places at all the wrong moments. Until it wasn't. Until we'd figured out how to sing together without stepping on each other's voices.

On the last take, the one that reached the very limit of my fretting strength, I ended the last chord hard and had to suck on my fingers.

Eamon took my hand and kissed each of my throbbing, swollen fingertips.

"Cut." Shoshanna looked over the camera with the widest eyes. "If that doesn't make you two sweethearts internet sensations, then I'll never trust the world of prying eyes again."

"We can't put that mushy stuff with the song!" I said.

"Why not? You two are a real couple, aren't you? It's not propaganda. Don't make me get Julian on the phone to confirm the media value here." Shoshanna packed up her stuff. We'd lost the twilight glow some time ago and filmed by the light of iPhone flashlights. How would it look in the old stone abbey? Dumb? Magical?

We hiked to the trailers; Shoshanna was trekking fast. "We're going to get this online ASAP. Eamon, how many followers do you have on your YouTube channel?"

"Only about thirty thousand," he said. "I lost a fair few during the boycott."

She frowned. "That'll have to do."

When we got to my trailer, Ryder sat up in bed, looking like he'd cried himself to sleep. He rubbed his eyes. "What's going on?"

"We're scheming." I plunked on the edge of his bed, pulling an arm around him.

"Good schemes?"

"Great ones," Shoshanna said, pulling out Eamon's laptop. She wasted no time in plugging the camera into the computer. "What's the name of this song, Iris?"

"'The Height of the Fall,'" I said. "Or is that too cheesy?"

Eamon sat on my bed. "It's a touch fantasy, but that is what we're going for."

Ryder was trying to worm his way over to Shoshanna to see what was happening. I let him go and slid next to Eamon. He put an arm around my waist and I buried my face in his neck. I thought Shoshanna was opening the file, but when I looked at the screen, she was already uploading it. "Wait! We have to watch it first."

"No way. You'll chicken out," she said. "And...done."

I shot up and started pacing. "Oh crap. Take it down. Oh my God, my dad might see it!"

Eamon grabbed my hand and pulled me to him. "It's grand, Iris. Watch."

Shoshanna played the video, and I watched it as though I were seeing a movie. It was intriguing. Shoshanna would make a decent director, and the stone walls helped the music sound full. Eamon's voice was what killed me though, *so* sweet, and the moment he kissed my fingers...

"Should we write the lyrics in the information box?" Shoshanna asked.

"No, out of context, lyrics always look awkward," I said. "Like poetry that's too proud of itself."

"Look." Eamon pointed at the screen. "Sixty views already. That's good."

I yanked out my phone and dialed. "If we're going to do this, we're going to do this huge." I tapped speakerphone.

"Hey, Ire..." Julian paused. "Iss. Your name doesn't shorten, does it?"

"Neither does mine!" Shoshanna hollered.

"Julian, we need you to repost something. Maybe send it to your famous friends too."

⌒

When I woke up, curled against Eamon in the tiny trailer bed, I was smiling. We'd stayed up until we were delirious, cracking jokes and watching the view count on our video crawl up past one thousand and then five thousand.

My face was pressed to Eamon's shoulder, breathing his warm, unique smell, while I dreamt about staying together. After all, our feelings were too big. Too important. I might be leaving, but we weren't going to vanish from each other's lives. "We're going to make it work," he'd murmured sleepily into my hair when we were the last to drift off.

I felt good, and I even dared to hope something could change with the movie. Perhaps I'd find our side stuck on the door like usual. I slipped out from under the covers, passing Ryder with his baby snores, and Shoshanna asleep on the couch, her curly hair like a nest for her face. I grabbed my jacket and stepped outside. After I'd closed the door, I counted to three, calling all the good energy to this place, and turned around.

No side.

I glanced at the other trailers. No sides on any of them. No lights either. I slumped on the nearest picnic table, closed my eyes, and sunk my head into my hands.

A door opened and closed, followed by Eamon's arms wrapping around me. "You're not regretting what we did last night, are you?" he asked in a quiet, careful voice.

"Doesn't matter. It didn't work. The Thornians probably hated the video."

How could I think they'd like it? Of course they wouldn't want me standing in for my grandma with my simple melody, asking them to support this movie. I pictured all the thumbs-downs and ugly comments, matching what they wrote on my dad's Goodreads page. *Hack. Amateur. Heartless. Guess the apple fell pretty far from the Thorne tree.*

"Whatever you're thinking right now is abuse."

My eyes popped open, and I stared at Eamon's rather serious face. "What?"

"When you do that—go all inner demon—I can feel it. Whatever you're saying in your mind is not right. You're abusing yourself."

He was earnest. Like there was some other way to be.

"But I don't…" A tear trickled out of one eye, and I squashed it with my palm. "I don't mean to. The voices in my head are vicious."

"The voices in your head are you. Tell them what to do."

I almost laughed; it could not be that simple. "Tell myself I'm wrong?"

"Yes," he said. "And say something nice while you're at it."

"Out loud?"

"If you want. Or just think something that doesn't make your whole body collapse with despair. Something hopeful."

I tried not to roll my eyes. "But isn't hope 'the exhausted remains of dreams'?"

His arms pulled me tight, his body still as warm as our bed. "As much as I appreciate you quoting *Elementia*, I think your grandmother was wrong about that one. Hope isn't desperate."

Could he be right?

"I'm serious, Iris Mae Ellen. Say something nice and hopeful."

I put my head on his shoulder. "Maybe…we can still make a difference. Maybe it's not over," I whispered into his neck. I closed my eyes and dared the rest in a rush. "Maybe the Thornians liked my song, and they're rallying, and we get to finish this movie. How's that?"

He kissed my hair. "Do that more often."

"No way. I've completely jinxed it. It won't happen now because I said it. And now I'm going to have to leave. Today." I started to shake, my thoughts as blinding as if lightning were taking over my brain. "I have to say goodbye to you and I can't even…"

I pressed my hands to his chest and felt the spot where his heart pounded. I flooded with a range of hopes all at once, some so surprising they felt brand-new. *I hope we stay together. I hope he moves to LA and becomes an actor. I hope I can tell my dad how I really feel. I hope my songs are part of something bigger. I hope I become a music supervisor for films, like Cate said.*

"Iris." Eamon touched my face, making my eyes open. I hadn't realized I'd shut them. "I have something good to show you. Wait here." He ran across the circle to his trailer, coming back a few seconds later with Grandma Mae's biography.

"I don't think I can read that yet, Eamon."

He opened to the picture of her standing on the very edge of Dun Aengus. "Remember how I said I wanted to know who she was looking at like she was in love?" He pointed at the caption. PHOTO BY JOHN WARREN. "The answer was right here all along."

"That could be a publicist photographer," I said. He shook his head and flipped through all the other photos of her in Ireland. All by John Warren. "So, this guy was her... late-in-life boyfriend?"

"Husband," Eamon corrected. "I finally finished reading a few days ago. I had no idea she'd moved here for a fella. Seems like the Thorne ladies have a thing for the Irish." Eamon smirked as he flipped to the last picture in the book. He held it out and leaned back.

The picture was sad; there was no way around it. Grandma

Mae's long, dark hair was gone, replaced by a scarf to cover her chemo-inspired baldness. She was sickly thin and so tired looking, and yet she seemed content, snuggled up next to a kind-faced man. He reminded me of an old Eamon.

"Iris," Eamon said. "He was her Nolan."

"Wonder if he's still alive," I said, a bit dazed.

Eamon took a napkin with a phone number out of the book. "He lives in Kerry. I spoke to him the other day." My mouth fell open, and Eamon rushed his words. "I wasn't trying to be sneaky. I didn't know if he was the right guy, and well, he was, but then I wanted to make sure he wasn't awful. He's not awful, Iris. He still loves your grandmother *a lot*, and he wants to talk to you and your brother."

I buried my face in my hands, flushing hot all over.

Eamon clearly thought I'd take the news better. "Sorry, sorry. I'm an arse."

"No, no. It's just...I hoped we could bring the movie back and instead you give me a grandfather? That's an odd trade. And now all I can think about is that my dad hid this from me."

"Maybe he had reasons," Eamon said, kissing my elbow, my shoulder, my neck. "I shouldn't have told you."

"No, thank you. There's someone alive who knew her and remembers her and won't mind talking to me. That's got to be a good sign."

"There's my hopeful girl." He pulled me close for the

kind of kiss that makes the sun rise. I pulled him tight around the waist and even slipped my hands under his shirt. His back was smooth and warm. A tiny groan slipped out of his mouth and that made me kiss him even deeper.

Cate's trailer sprung open, interrupting our kiss, and out stomped Cate and Henrik. "Skip them for today. We have bigger fish to fry," Cate said in a loud, commanding voice. "I want everyone in motion by nine. Skip the Castletown extras. We'll add them in digitally if need be. And about the—"

Cate stopped short at the sight of us tangled in each other's arms. Henrik placed a hand over his grin. Cate's eye's narrowed. "Where is the rest of your little coup?"

I pointed to my trailer, and she stormed inside. What was happening? Were we in trouble? Eamon and I filed in behind Henrik.

"Wake up, Ryder. Shoshanna." Cate stood with her hands on her tiny hips, Henrik beside her. Shoshanna and Ryder woke up, glancing around.

"What's going on?" Ryder asked.

"There's been some collusion." Cate's Irish accent went to work on that word, turning it downright poetic. She trained a hard eye on all of us, her energy back. Brilliantly so. "Was no one going to tell me about your royal plan to infect the internet with this *Elementia*-inspired love story?" She pointed at Eamon and me, arms still entwined.

"Did it go viral?" Shoshanna asked.

"Four million views and counting," Henrik said. "All the secret Elementia fans are crawling out of the woodwork. Everyone from Taylor Swift to Benedict Cumberbatch have been lighting up their social media."

"Benedict!" Shoshanna and I shouted in stereo.

"Truly?" Eamon asked.

"I'm only human," I muttered. I turned to Cate's tight smirk. Was she pleased? Mad?

"You two." She pointed to Eamon and Shoshanna. "Makeup and wardrobe. We've got until one o'clock to shoot here and then we need to hightail it to Dingle. Julian is already on a flight so we can shoot the last on-location scene tomorrow."

"The filming is back on?" I asked, a buzz in my head that yelled, *This isn't possible!*

"We are experiencing a brief stay of execution. Two days to film five days' worth of shots," she said. Everyone's faces fell a little. "But I'll take it. Won't you?"

Ryder, still in his pajamas, rushed out to help Mr. Donato. Eamon, Shoshanna, and I ended up in a group hug of sorts. Eamon even kissed me in front of Cate and whispered, "Admit it, Iris, hope works. Admit it!"

"Maybe," I said. He winked and flew out the door. I found myself alone with Cate.

"Your grandmother would have been proud of that song, Iris."

My cheeks were hot, and I couldn't look her in the eye. "I think you have to say that."

"I never say anything socially compulsory. I say what I mean." I could feel her stare, and I finally looked up. "Call your dad, Iris. No doubt he's seen it. No doubt the two of you need to talk. Break some *new* ground this time."

"I'll try," I said, pausing. "Does this mean things might work out for the film?"

She sat on Ryder's bed. "The odds aren't good. Too many financial complications. Perhaps this will turn into a TV miniseries. I think the Syfy channel might buy it. They had some success with *The Magicians*. This is a similar audience."

I shook my head. "This has got to be a major motion picture."

Cate went flinty eyed. "Your reasons?"

"Because my grandmother's story is important. It'll empower girls, like you said."

Cate didn't budge. "And?"

"Because Shoshanna was made for this role! And people respond to this story and your vision. And my dad is wrong. And a hundred other reasons. And because Eamon has to be a big damn star so he can move to LA and stay my boyfriend!"

She erupted in laughter, and I worried I was about to get a lecture. Instead, she stood and touched my chin. "Look what happens when you take charge, Iris. You're a force of nature. Remember that when you talk to your dad."

I was tempted to email. That was safe. Distant. But I didn't want to be safe anymore. I wanted to stand in front of my dad and ask him what the hell went wrong between him and his mother. Then maybe I could start to understand what the hell went wrong between us.

"Dad."

"Hello, Iris. How are you and your brother doing?" His phone voice was so courteous; he might has well have been talking to his publisher.

"We're fine. We're on our way to Dingle later today. They've had to…rush the last bit of filming. This is all going to wrap up by the end of the day tomorrow."

"Is it now?"

I held the phone away from my ear and counted to five. He was being civil because he knew it'd drive me into an emotional response from which he would always win. "We'd like you to join us for the last day on set."

"You would?" he said, genuine surprise in his voice.

"Yes. Well, if you've finished your draft. We don't want to interrupt."

His tone cracked with aggravation. "No, I haven't finished. I haven't been able to write since your little blow up. I do care about being your father. I do care about my children. I know I've been painted the villain since I was late to pick you up at the playground that day. I know I'll never live that down." My dad had never brought up the abduction before. How often did it weigh on his mind? If the heaviness of his tone was any indicator, it was *a lot*. "But, Iris, I'm honestly just trying to have a career as well as a family. This is Human Motivation 101."

"I understand that."

"Do you? I spent an entire red-eye flight sick thinking something happened to you and Ryder. When I arrived and found you two were fine—that you were off having fun, no less—I was angry. And I wasn't wrong to be angry."

I winced at his tone, but I also remembered how I'd unleashed on Ryder after he'd gotten lost on Inishmore. I'd been sick with worry, and yet when I found him, the relief came through as pure anger. "We know you care about us," I tried.

"Please stop speaking for your brother."

"Fine. *I* know you care. I also know you're self-obsessed and have serious mom issues, and I don't want to be in the dark anymore about our family. And I don't want to be your pet."

"My *pet*?"

"Your 'literary-fiction girl.'"

Dead silence. The kind of silence that follows a guillotine's swish.

"Have you seen my song yet?" I asked.

"Is this about Coldplay again?"

"No. I posted a song online. A song I wrote. You should watch it. And then you should come to Dingle. We'll be waiting for you." I hung up.

Film: Elementia

Director: Cate Collins

On Location: Day 11

Last Day

Dingle Peninsula, Ireland

Filming Notes:

A.M.: SEVYN enters Thornbred scene

P.M.: SEVYN & EVYN escape Thornbred, aided by NOLAN & MAEDINA.

Etc. Notes:

Wrap dinner at John Benny's Pub

MICHAEL EDWARD THORNE, THE EDMUND/ GOLLUM/SEVERUS SNAPE OF THIS PRODUCTION

THE DINGLE PENINSULA was gorgeous. Rolling green pastures in all directions, dotted by a picturesque, colorful town on a tiny, sweet harbor. And then? Dashing cliffs, giving way to a glittering ocean and the silhouettes of skeletal islands.

The filming took over everyone's attention for the entire day, leaving me with *Elementia*. My grandmother's language reached into my head, painting the world with better colors, sharper outlines, deeper meanings. I sat at the picnic table by the trailers for perhaps the last time, reading the scene we were currently filming.

> *The sun cast brilliance, and the twins tumbled out*
> *of the cold, black caves into its powerful, warm*
> *beams. The rays shone on the mystery of Evyn's*

new power. He was still thin and small—smaller than she'd ever known him to be—but he was no longer weak. His chest bloomed as red as fire, and something dark pulsed beneath his fair skin.

"Are you all right?" Sevyn held out her hand and wondered if her brother would be too afraid to take it. He looked over her fingers. "I can control the lightning now. An elf named Nolan taught me."

"It's dangerous to name names," Evyn said in a voice she barely knew.

Screeches and howls echoed toward them.

The Knye were coming. They banged through the black caves below, their snarling voices charging ahead of them.

"Come on!" she called, still holding out her hand to him.

"Why bother?" Evyn said. "They will catch us, and they will make you into their own power as well."

Sevyn shivered. "What's happened to you?"

The Knye had nearly reached the cave's entrance, and she couldn't wait for an answer. She grabbed his hand, sending him a small shock for good measure. They ran together, hand in hand, across the Blackened Wastes of Thornbred. Tree stumps stood like charcoal graves, marking the fire

*that had turned a peaceful nation of elves into the
charred-hearted Knye.*

*Sevyn thought this place might be damned—
except green grass had begun to grow through the
black ash, as thick as carpet. Perhaps life was
returning to Elementia after all.*

Peering into the distance, I watched the small figures of
Sevyn and Evyn run hand in hand across a green hill, having
escaped the black caves of Thornbred. A crane camera zoomed
after them, while Eamon and Nell Waterson were in costume
off to one side. They were waiting to sweep in and help defeat
the Knye—a host of stunt doubles in all-green spandex suits—
chasing them.

After this, the cast and crew would pack up and head
back to LA to film the scenes in the island kingdom of Cerul
where the twins are welcomed home, and Sevyn gets hailed
as a hero. Right before Evyn murders the king, sets fire to the
entire island, and disappears. Sevyn is left to save her people
by taking them to the only land available—Elementia. *Bam.*
End of Book One.

Nice one, Grandma Mae.

It was too bad that the sequels had been canceled because,
the story twisted deeper, darker, and more passionate as the
characters grew older. *Maybe the movie will do so well that the
fans will demand it*, I hoped. I still didn't know what happened

at the end of the third book, but I was mostly through the second, and falling in love with all of it—which made me want to look up Mr. Sams and drop him a line.

Which then made me think about the challenge I'd issued my dad yesterday, and the phone number for John Warren in my pocket.

Time was doing that screwy thing: moving too fast. I wanted our last day to be years long, so each minute felt like an hour. I pulled out my notebook, scribbling lyrics before I caught sight of a narrow figure in a black casual suit. His nose was in the air; he was trying to seem composed, even though he looked downright scared.

I could see it in every inch of him. My dad was as terrified as I'd been ten days ago.

I closed my notebook and approached him. "Walk down to the harbor with me?"

He squinted, surprised, but I'd said the right thing. Getting away from the filming would help him relax. We headed down the road toward the town and the blinding-white rays reflecting off the water. We were halfway there before he spoke.

"I thought your song showed promise," he said. I nearly sprained my neck looking at him. "Don't seem so surprised. I have good taste, don't I?"

About ten answers yammered through my brain, but I didn't speak.

"Iris, I'm not going to pretend I want you to be an artist. I'd love for you to become a doctor or professor. Some career that doesn't suck the marrow out of your bones for a paycheck the size of an insult which is then taxed at forty percent." He sighed. "But if it's in you, you have to let it out."

"Is that what Grandma Mae said when you told her you wanted to be a writer?"

"You're going to keep asking until I answer, is that it?" he snapped.

"Yes." I paused, eyeing the water. "Maybe it's not fair to make you remember, but it's not fair to keep me in the dark."

"Sam…" His voice was rough with old pain, his temples full of gray. Guess time was sneaking up on him too. "None of this is about your grandmother, Iris. It's about my sister. She died. We were thirteen."

I didn't tell him I'd figured out that much. "That's horribly sad."

"You can't imagine," he said roughly, but then he sighed. "It had been the three of us. My father was more neglectful than yours, if you can imagine." He cast a glance at me that I didn't respond to. "So when Sam was gone, it was the two of us. I was angry. My mother was depressed. She started writing. She disappeared into her pages. I could have gotten addicted to heroin and she wouldn't have noticed. She published that first book the same year I graduated from high school and I refused to read it. She moved to Ireland, fell in love, and made a new life without me. I hadn't spoken to her in ten years when you were born."

The road beneath our feet connected to the shore, and the bright squawk of seagulls filled the air, a salty tang on the wind. "Then why name me after her?" I asked.

"You came out looking just like her, like Sam. I called Mom from the hospital, and we had a nice talk. She was happy, and it was rather impulsive, but I wanted my mom back, so I gave you her name. I thought you could help us heal," he said quietly.

"Sorry I failed." My voice came out serrated.

"Of course *you* didn't fail. Don't be melodramatic." His steps picked up as we crossed the harbor. We sat on a bench before a dolphin statue. "The fallout was all my doing. I decided to finally read her books." He glared at the copy of the Elementia trilogy in my hand.

"And you hated them?"

"*Hate* is a lazy word." He took the book and flipped through it. "I don't hate this. I *lived* it. My mother is in all these characters. And I am too. And there's so much Sam, I can't even…" He handed the book back. "Sam was a firestorm, Iris. Like Sevyn. I swear she died yelling at her doctors. Even when she couldn't breathe, she'd yell. There was no peace about it."

No peace.

That's what I'd always felt rushing through the bones of my family: a startling lack of peace. It made songs rush through me and good moments feel like tricks of the light. My imagination shrunk my dad to a thirteen-year-old who'd lost his twin and mother in one swift blow. Furious and powerless, he'd been older than Ryder, younger than me.

"She put our family's grief in a blender and hit puree, Iris. Sam's pain, my pain, her pain… Then she gave it to the world dressed in elves and foolishness. For that, I will never forgive her."

He sighed and touched his forehead, tapping a spot. "Although I wouldn't have seen her again before she died if it weren't for you, that's true enough. She showed up on my doorstep, demanding to meet you. To this day, I don't know why I said yes. Do you remember?"

"She took me to the park." I squinted into my thoughts, into my tenuous grasp on the memory. "She told me the sky wasn't blue."

"What'd she say? Cobalt?"

"Azure."

"You might've only had one afternoon, but you got the real Mae Ellen Thorne experience." He looked at me, and I'd never realized how much sadness had carved his features and left him frozen in his pain. "I'm not going to talk to you about her, Iris. I'm sorry. But there is someone who will. Your grandmother's husband. I've never met him, but I can put you in touch." I burst into tears and hugged him all at once. He patted my back rigidly. "Why are you crying?"

"Because I thought you wouldn't tell me about him. I thought you'd be a real asshole."

He let out a surprised laugh, which made me hug him harder. "You already know him?"

"Sort of." I sat up, pushing back tears. When I spoke again, my voice was flooded with feelings. "Dad, I know your sister died and you lost your mom to all this fantasy stuff, but remember that I know what it's like not to have a mom around too." My dad winced. "And I can't be Ryder's single parent anymore."

He slid his elbows to his knees, pressing his face into his hands. "Iris…"

"I'm going to college next year to study music. It's going to be you and Ryder."

"Oh? And what will you be studying to become?" he challenged, but I was ready.

"I want to be a music supervisor."

He frowned. "You mean work for Hollywood?"

"I've been researching. I need to study music, business, fine arts, and multimedia platforms, but if I work hard and get my foot in the door, I could make a decent career out of it."

"Sounds tricky."

"Maybe, but I'm up for the challenge." I turned to face him. "When I leave, Ryder is going to need more from you. You can't get lost in your pages like she did." He took the lecture with a slight nod, and I actually felt less like a parent, more like his daughter. Was that seriously all it took to shift some of the load? Honesty and persistence?

Wow, Cate.

"Ryder's doing well here," I continued. "He wants to be a chef."

"No," my dad said fast. "I don't want—"

"This isn't about what you want. This is Ryder's life, and we are going to trust him. He deserves that much. He's smart and has been through more than both of us." I swear the shadow of Felix Moss crossed my dad's features. "And I know you think we're never going to forgive you for what happened, but that's not true. We'll forgive you if you let us live our lives. It's your job to help support us with our choices, not make them for us."

My dad leaned back, appraised me. "And what is it you'd like to choose, Iris?"

I didn't hesitate.

"Remember my purpose money?"

SLÁINTE

RYDER, MY DAD, and I were the first to arrive at John Benny's for the wrap dinner. We waited for more than a half hour for the others to arrive, and I started to worry that something had gone wrong with the last shot.

Ryder told Dad about his cooking lessons, and my dad—without faking enthusiasm—agreed to set them up if Ryder was serious. My wild, elf-loving little brother swore he'd given it a lot of thought and even offered explanations as to how his high-energy personality would help him stay on his feet in a kitchen environment. I'm not sure if Mr. Donato told him about that, but I made a mental note to thank that man.

I was about to text Eamon to make sure he was okay,

when Julian busted in, followed by the entire cast and crew. They filled the small, charming pub in a hurry, causing the handful of regulars to grumble and move out of the way.

Eamon walked by with Shoshanna's arm slung over his shoulder and winked.

I hooked a finger at him, and he glanced at my dad warily before stepping forward.

"Dad, this is my boyfriend, Eamon O'Brien. Eamon, this is my dad, Mr. Thorne. Or do you want to be called Michael?"

My dad appraised Eamon. "I'm not sure. This is new ground. Michael will do, I suppose." They shook hands and I breathed out with such a gust that Ryder giggled. First boyfriend meets Dad? Check. I honestly hoped it'd be the first *and* last, but that's probably so romantic it's ridiculous.

When everyone had filed in and found chairs, I spotted Julian and his fiancée, Elora, at the bar. Elora had flown in with Julian, surprising all of us. She was built like a ballerina, with flawless brown skin. Only a week ago, I would have taken one look at her and put a bag over my own head, but I wasn't doing that anymore. What's more, they were nearly spooning while they ordered drinks, so I guessed they were ready to come out to the world.

Julian gave me a side hug. "I leave for a week and you hop in bed with a handsome elf named Charles?"

My cheeks burned with happiness—something I didn't know could happen. "We just cuddle," I muttered. He raised

a gorgeously sculpted Julian eyebrow at me. "What? It's Grade
A, First Class, Cosmic Love cuddling."

Eamon appeared, hanging on to me the way Julian held
Elora. "What's this about?"

"I was bragging about how good our cuddling sessions
are."

"Top notch," he said, his cheeks pinking.

"We should double date," Julian said. "Right? When we're
all back in Cali?"

"I'll check my schedule." I wiggled my phone at him.
"I've got your number."

"Hey, are you playing it cool with me? I'm a movie star,
Iris Thorne."

Elora laughed, and I held on to Eamon even tighter, not
wanting to point out to Julian that we couldn't double because
I didn't know when Eamon would even be in the States.

After this night, our love story was up in the air.

"Hold on a sec," I said. "I need to make an important introduction." I stepped away from the bar and ran straight into Roxy.

She grabbed my arm. "Iris, I want to chat with you about
something."

"Sure." I couldn't stop myself from looking at Shoshanna
at the other end of the bar, watching us completely indis-
creetly. "What's up?"

"You made a not-so-veiled comment about Shoshanna
being interested in me."

"I did?" I feigned.

Roxy gave me an exasperated look that was adorable. "Were you playing matchmaker or do you think she might actually be into me?"

"Massively," I said. "Sings about you when she's drinking." I patted her shoulder and let gravity take over from there.

I grabbed my dad from a conversation with Mr. Donato, bringing him over to where Cate sat at a table with Henrik, both of whom looked exhausted and yet pleased. She sat up when she saw my father's gloomy mug, and I smiled, hoping she knew I wasn't bringing a storm cloud to her parade. I motioned for my dad to sit.

Then I sat.

"I'm going to reintroduce you two," I said. "All other interactions have been stricken from the record. We're starting anew." I sat up a little taller, trying not to smile at how amused Henrik looked. My dad and Cate were both still on edge. "Dad, this is Cate Collins. The director of seventeen feature-length motion pictures, my role model, and a major fan of your mother's fictional world. Cate, this is my dad, Michael Edward Thorne. Author of fifteen crime mysteries and my other role model."

He eyed me for sarcasm, and when he didn't find it, he shook Cate's hand wearily.

"Now, Dad, tell Cate the good news."

"You're investing!" Henrik nearly shouted, making Cate and my dad jump.

"Yes," I said, holding my dad's eye and daring him to disagree. "We are."

Cate leaned forward, staring at my dad in a way that made him tilt back. "I will not accept your money with no strings attached, and I will not accept your money with strings attached that I dislike. Is that understood?"

Mobster Cate Collins. God, I loved her.

"It's not my money," my dad said. "It's Iris's."

Cate looked at me as tears lined her cool-blue eyes. "Iris."

"It's an investment. I can't think of a better way to use my grandmother's financial legacy." For a long moment, Cate and I stared at each other, and I hoped she knew I wanted to be part of her continent. Her struggles were my struggles, but that also meant we shared victories, right? "We're in this together."

She gave a fierce, certain nod that I would practice in the mirror when I got home.

"Thorne producers!" Henrik crowed, making us all laugh. I glanced at his empty glass. Had the grumpy AD finally let loose? "Cate, we're going to get more investors with their name attached. Guys, I swear I just felt our IMDb rating jump a thousand percent!"

Although the train was slow to start, Cate and my dad started talking to one another like fellow intelligent, hardworking humans. They were, after all, rather similar. Headstrong, passionate—artists to a fault. I faded into the background, following Henrik to the bar where Julian, Elora, Shoshanna, Roxy, and Eamon were hanging out. Eamon looped an arm around my waist and kissed one shoulder.

"Eamon, you're Catholic, right?"

"Of course."

"And how does one become Catholic?"

He squinted at me for a long moment before his face dawned. "Iris Thorne, you're not losing your religion for me. Are you, girl?"

"Nope. Don't have a religion to lose."

"I love you too," he murmured into my neck. I pressed my chest to his, sealing our mouths in a kiss that swiftly turned into my hands in his hair and his hands twisted into my shirt at my lower back.

"*Iris!*" my dad roared from the corner, and we broke apart laughing.

Our friends were laughing as well, and I shrugged. "Worth it."

Eamon winked, his cheeks all red.

Julian looked mournfully into his empty pint glass. "I just got back in this country and its already time to leave. We have to do something wild before we go. Make the news."

"We'll be filming for a few more weeks back in LA," Shoshanna said. "It's not over."

"It is for Eamon," Roxy pointed out. "His scenes are done."

I pulled his arms a little tighter. "Should we skinny dip in the harbor?"

"Hell no. There's a famous dolphin in that water. *Fungie*," Eamon said. He shuddered. "Imagine running into him out there with all your bits out."

"*The Lord of the Rings* cast got tattoos together," Henrik supplied. Everyone stared at him. "What? They did."

"Nerds and their tattoos," I snarked.

"I'd do it," Shoshanna said. Roxy agreed as well. And Eamon and Julian. "But what would we get? It's too bad J. K. Rowling claimed the lightning bolt. That would have been cool."

"Rowling drew quite a bit from Tolkien too," Henrik said.

"No more Tolkien, Henrik," Shoshanna said. "We're Thornians. You're one of us, whether you like it or not."

"*I ambar na-changed.*" Henrik lifted a shot glass to his lips. "That's Sindarin, *one* of the elf languages Tolkien created."

Shoshanna stole his shot and drank it. "What's the elvish translation for, 'Thorne elves are better than Tolkien elves'?"

"Come to the dark side, Henrik," Roxy said, smiling at Shoshanna. "We've got girls."

"And some color," Shoshanna said, high-fiving Julian.

"Look," Henrik launched into a well-prepared speech, "we all have problematic favorites—"

"How about this for a tattoo?" I asked, pulling Eamon's copy of *Elementia* out of his backpack. Everyone leaned in to look at the stylized elemental compass with a lightning bolt splitting it.

"Perfect," Shoshanna said. "And edgy. I'll put it on the other side of Kate."

My grin faltered. "You guys should do it, but I can't. I'm not eighteen until next December, and I just convinced my dad to give away my trust fund, so no way he'll let me ink myself."

Julian smiled. "Like hell would we do it without you, Iris."

Eamon swung me around to face him. "You did *what*?"

"Tell you later," I said. "For now, we can say I saved the day. Maybe."

Cate whistled loud enough to grab everyone's attention. She stood up on a chair, and I flashed back to seeing her like that on Inishmore. I waited for her speech, wondering what wisdom she would impart. She raised her glass high and seemed to make eye contact with everyone in the room before she spoke. Her gaze fell on me at the last.

"*Sláinte.*"

COMIC-CON
PRESS RELEASE!
FILM PREMIERE COMIC-CON
SAN DIEGO, CA

JOIN THE CAST AND CREW OF
ELEMENTIA AT COMIC-CON AND WIN
A CHANCE TO SEE THE SNEAK PREVIEW
OF THE FILM WITH THE CAST!

SURPRISE! YOU GET AN EPILOGUE

STORIES END IN a rush.

One minute, Will and Lyra are in love on their bench. The next, they're in separate worlds. One minute, the Pevensie kids are kings and queens. The next, they're back through the wardrobe. One minute, the One Ring is lava-dissolving in Gollum's hand, the next...well, that example doesn't work. *The Return of the King* has like seven ending scenes, but for good reason.

When a story is that vast, it takes time to bring all the pieces back together.

Either way, I blinked in the pub on Dingle with my friends, and suddenly it was a year later—and I was signing autographs at the *Elementia* booth at the San Diego Comic-Con, a.k.a. Nerd Mecca.

I'd just spoken to my fourth Nolan cosplayer—which was pretty cruel considering Eamon wasn't even on this continent until tomorrow. I checked the countdown on my watch. Twenty-three hours and twenty-two minutes until his plane landed.

The current fan standing before me was dressed in a remarkable Wonder Woman costume. "Are they giving Julian Young a tattoo up there?" she asked, peering behind me.

"Yep," I said, scribbling my signature on an *Elementia* soundtrack CD for her. "All day you can come by and see us getting inked. Help us spread the word?"

Her mouth drooped as she watched a shirtless Julian lie back on a chair, getting a hip tattoo. What a show-off. He totally chose that spot so he could sit on the stage of our booth with his six-pack out—which was actually brilliant. He might even win the current pool about which one of us could run the most outrageous marketing ploy. We'd had to get creative over the past year, but it was working. For one thing, the boycott had vanished. The entire website disappeared one night as though it had never happened.

"Are you getting a tattoo as well?" Wonder Woman asked. I flashed my forearm where a white bandage covered my new ink.

"It must be nonstop fun to make movies," she said.

"You've got the nonstop part right. The fun is…surprising." I handed her CD back. "Make sure you get in line for the movie early. They're only letting in the first five hundred people."

"Thanks!" Wonder Woman moved down the line toward Shoshanna and then Cate. I took the twenty-second break between fans to stretch. We'd been at this for over an hour— and tonight we'd all be watching *Elementia* on a stage in front of the most hardcore Thornians.

I hope it goes well.

Shoshanna leaned over and talked behind her hand. She hated the publicity part of this job more than me. "I told Roxy she couldn't come because then I'd be even more nervous, but now I don't know what I was thinking. She should be here. Especially for the viewing tonight."

"She should be here," I agreed. "And look at you being cool about your girlfriend, as if it didn't take you six months to ask her out." Getting those two girls together had been like pushing a boulder uphill—Shoshanna being the boulder— although it had been fun.

"Yes, you're wise, my long-distance-relationship guru," she said. "Speaking of taking your time, what are you going to do with Eamon when you see him tomorrow?"

"None of your business." I tweaked her nose, but my thoughts raced with ideas. Naked ideas. A whole trilogy of them.

Shoshanna looked back at Julian and then over the crowds on the main floor. "Iris, what if the preview is crap? What if they don't like it and it has to be recut?"

"It won't be crap. It's perfect."

"Wait." She spun me around. "You've seen it, haven't you?"

"Thorne family privilege." I grinned. "We're producers."

"But I'm the star! I should get to see it first."

"Guess I know things you don't." I was enjoying this too much because: Shoshanna.

"Wouldn't you like to know what I know…" she said teasingly, patting down the bandage on her shoulder where she'd gotten her Elementia tattoo.

"What do you know?" I asked fast.

She didn't have time to answer because the people in line pushed forward. I took a worn copy of the Elementia trilogy from the next person, without breaking eye contact with Shoshanna. I hoped whatever she was scheming had something to do with Eamon. I missed him in a way that made me feel starved.

I flipped to the title page to sign. This whole autographing thing had gotten old hat rather fast, but I was trying not to be too jaded about it. Pun intended.

"I like your new aesthetic. Sort of cute punk."

I looked up. "Huh?"

He smirked, and I didn't recognize him right away. "Remember me?"

"I do now," I said. My ex-in-flight romance. Mr. Nerd Torso Tattoo.

"I came here to see you." He leaned on the table making

it creak. "So we can set up that date we talked about all those months ago."

"I have a boyfriend," I said. "And he's definitely not you." He leaned back, and I tried not to smile too wide as I inscribed a message.

To the guy from the Shannon Airport ~
Don't be a creep to underage girls.

Cheers & orbs,
I. M. E. Thorne.

I signed my name, matching up my middle initials with my grandmother's printed ones, and felt a little closer to her than I had a minute before—like we were sharing an inside joke.

"Five minutes!" a stagehand called out.

I peeked around the curtain at the auditorium of people in full cosplay, *Star Trek* shirts, and Harry Potter house ties. They'd been waiting in line for hours, and the staff had finally let them in a few minutes ago. The ones closest to the front were decked out in *Elementia* gear and elf ears, and the excitement on their faces was infectious—and nerve-wracking.

I tried to relax, enjoying the atmosphere and a rare day off from the internship Cate had secured for me at Vantage Pictures. I worked mostly in dark editing booths with eccentric coffee-enhanced film editors, but I wasn't complaining. Movies were magic, after all, and making them felt like reaching elbow deep into fantasy of my own choosing.

Cate, Julian, and Shoshanna were getting microphones attached to their shirts. Eamon's absence was a black hole, but he was in the UK, filming a *Downton Abbey*–styled miniseries. I hadn't seen him since he'd come to record voice-overs two months ago.

"Hey!" Shoshanna yelled, drawing my attention. "Quit it."

Julian was pulling her arms over her head in some sort of relaxation stretch. "This will help your nerves, Shosh." She threw him in a headlock, and he cried out about his hair.

The Comic-Con crew rolled plush chairs onstage and the moderator walked out next, the audience cheering. You could barely hear him as he called out Julian's, Cate's, and Shoshanna's names. They filed out and sat down. I moved to the corner to see them better. Julian's expression was all fan love. Cate was trying to hold down a smirk. Shoshanna had on her game face.

Ryder watched from the other side of the stage, peeking out like me. He gave me a thumbs-up, and I gave him one back. He was doing great, attending junior chef academy afterschool, which was as cute as it sounds, with the little white coats and toques. My dad went with him once a week, and between the two of them, the food in my house had gotten edible.

As far as I was concerned, my dad was still my dad. After our talk in Dingle, we hadn't bonded or developed a new-found respect for one another. Instead, we learned to give each other breathing room. Ryder's therapist—who was now also my therapist—said we were developing healthy bound-aries. My dad even surprised me with a solo trip to Ireland for my birthday, where I got to see Eamon and meet John Warren—a man who'd wasted no time in telling me every detail about my grandmother while plying me with potent black tea and albums full of photographs.

I glanced out on stage. The audience was taking a long time to quiet down, and I noticed something strange. "One too many chairs?" Henrik asked, appearing near my shoulder.

"Are they waiting on someone else?"

Oh God, Eamon. Eamon was here, and he was going to surprise the audience—and me!

The moderator pointed to the empty chair. "Looks like we have one more spot. Iris Thorne, will you join us?"

Wait—what?

Henrik gave me a small shove onstage. The cheers made my face burn, and I sat down on the extra chair, looking any-where but at the crowd. A crew member snuck out to attach a microphone to my shirt.

Cate spoke first, beaming. "We couldn't talk about the movie without you, Iris."

"It was Shoshanna's idea," Julian volunteered.

"That I believe." Everyone laughed, which—*Jesus*—felt pretty good.

"Do I win the pool?" Shoshanna asked, but Cate shushed her.

The moderator sat on a stool, shuffling cards. "We're going to run a small interview before the preview, and afterward, we'll take questions from the audience. Let's jump in."

I started to fuzz out. My heart wouldn't stop storming as Cate talked about what the story meant to her. Shoshanna discussed having to harness her anger to play Sevyn. Julian said cutesy things that made the audience coo. Seriously, only Julian Young could make five hundred people turn pigeon.

Finally, the moderator turned to me. I assumed he'd ask what my grandmother would have thought of the adaptation, but he didn't. "Iris, can you tell us about your song? The one you wrote and performed with Eamon O'Brien during the filming."

The audience *awww*ed and called out sweet things.

"Well…I'm not going to play it for you, if that's what you're asking. That'd be way too cheesy, but—" I glanced at Cate, and she gave a go-ahead nod. "The *Elementia* soundtrack is on sale in our booth, and my song is on there. Lucky track thirteen."

"How come Eamon O'Brien isn't with us today? There are rumors he's taking on the lead role in the next Wes Anderson film."

"Yeah, he's signed on, but I don't think I'm supposed to say anything else." I played with a tiny loose string on the arm of the chair. "He'll make it here tomorrow for the final day of the con." *I hope.* People whooped. Some girl screamed. "Hey, that's my boyfriend," I said and the audience rolled with laughter.

"Do you miss him?" the moderator asked.

I was going to say something mature, but instead I nodded. Life without Eamon was life without dessert. The audience clapped. Then they began to cheer. Riotously.

Psychotically.

I glanced at Julian and Shoshanna, and they were smirking like they had a secret. I turned to the other side of the stage, and Eamon was walking toward me. Eamon with the freckles and the crystal eyes and that gorgeous, brawling hair.

I jumped up. I jumped *on* him.

He held me fast, and then I remembered we were onstage and had to crawl down him. We slipped into the plush chair together, hip to hip, his arm around my waist.

"We're shameless," Shoshanna said over the cheers. "But they're so cute."

"Everyone loves a love story," Julian concluded. I barely heard them. I couldn't believe Eamon was here. *Right here.* I stared at him like I'd never seen him before.

"Sorry I'm late. Couldn't fly fast enough," he whispered, although I was wearing a microphone, and everyone got to enjoy his sweetness.

I laced my fingers with his. "I think this means you win the marketing pool."

His crystal-blue eyes fell on my bandaged arm. "Iris! You got your tattoo without me?"

I pulled off the bandage to show my untouched skin. "I waited for you, although I kind of had to fake it."

He kissed me, and the audience screamed. At first all I could hear was their cheering, but then I remembered how much I loved his lips. His breath. His cheek against my cheek.

"What do you say we watch the preview?" the moderator yelled to the riled audience. The crowd screamed as the theater darkened and a projector lit up a screen above our heads. "Your mics are off," the moderator whispered at us. "Feel free to talk."

"What if it sucks?" Shoshanna squeaked.

"It won't suck!" Julian snapped.

Henrik came onstage, sitting on the armrest beside Cate. I beckoned for Ryder to come out too, and he sat at my feet. The opening credits filled the screen with Grandma Mae's name, accompanied by the skin-prickling music I'd helped pick out.

"I suppose this is a good time to let you know the first

sequel will be back in production by the end of the week," Cate whispered.

"Seriously?" Ryder yelled. I squeezed his shoulder, and he looked back at me. "Iris, does this mean we get to do it all over again?"

"Of course!"

Eamon grinned wildly, and I kissed him.

"Cate," Julian said. "I've been thinking. What if we wrote in a love interest for Evyn?"

"Quiet, Julian," Shoshanna barked. "I'm watching my breakthrough performance."

The movie began in earnest, and I rested my head on Eamon's shoulder, breathing deeply. We were all taking off in new directions.

Into the azure sky of this so-called fantasy.

IRIS'S SOUNDTRACK FOR
NOW A MAJOR MOTION PICTURE

1. Landing in Ireland: **"Free Life"** by Dan Wilson
2. Filming fantasy: **"Manifest Destiny"** by Guster
3. Maedina's Tree: **"Into the Fire"** by Thirteen Senses
4. It's Not a Tantrum: **"Navy Taxi"** by Kate Nash
5. Ferry Kissing: **"Love Like the Movies"** by the Avett Brothers
6. Recording Studio: **"Blinded By Rainbows"** by the Rolling Stones
7. Yoga Bonding: **"As Cool As I Am"** by Dar Williams
8. Giving an Interview: **"Flaws"** by Bastille
9. Eamon's Big Scene: **"Cosmic Love"** by Florence + The Machine
10. Dublin Bender: **"Then OK"** by Julia Nunes
11. The Thorne Family Legacy: **"Mess Is Mine"** by Vance Joy
12. Filming Canceled: **"Pompeii"** by Jasmine Thompson (Bastille cover)
13. Going Viral: **"Speak Plainly, Diana"** by Joe Pug
14. Dad: **"Wisemen"** by James Blunt
15. Goodbye Ireland: **"Haunted"** by Shane MacGowan & the Popes
16. Comic-Con/Theme Song: **"Do It Anyway"** by Ben Folds Five

GLOSSARY
FILM, FANTASY, AND IRISH

BLACKENED WASTES OF THORNBRED: (fantasy) The remains of Thornbred Forest, burned to the ground by the survivors of Manifest, following the earthquake that dropped their city into the Kryeng Sea. Home of the Knye.

BYERS: (fantasy) Half-Knye elf, survivor of the Blackened Wastes of Thornbred and Evyn's abductor and eventual savior.

CERUL: (fantasy) The island kingdom off the coast of Elementia, which is burned to the ground by Evyn at the end of the first book in the Elementia trilogy.

CRAFTY: (film) Nickname for craft services, the food people.

CRAIC: (Irish) Fun.

DAILIES: (film) The raw, unedited footage collected at the end of the shooting day.

DINGLE PENINSULA: (Irish) The northernmost major peninsula in County Kerry, Ireland, containing the town of Dingle at Dunmore Head. *Corca Dhuibhne* in Irish.

DRAEMON: (fantasy) Monastic community of element-worshipping women, just north of the Island Kingdom of Cerul, off the western coast of Elementia.

DUN AENGUS: (Irish) Anglicized name of the Bronze Age prehistoric fort on Inishmore. *Dún Aonghasa* in Irish.

ELEMENTIA: (fantasy) A dead continent cursed by humans and elves, which is saved by a lightning-cursed heroine.

EVYN: (fantasy) Antagonist of the Elementia trilogy, cursed by fire, twin to Sevyn.

GOAT: (Irish) An idiot.

JUICER: (film) Nickname for the production's electrician.

KILLYKEEN: (Irish) Forest park in County Cavan, Ireland, straddling Lough Oughter, a lake that contains a small island with the ruins of the circular Cloughoughter Castle.

KNACKERED: (Irish) To be severely tired—usually from staying up drinking.

KNYE: (fantasy) Elves who were scorched during the burning of the Thornbred Forest, turned black-hearted. Blood drinkers.

INISHMORE: (Irish) Anglicized name of the largest of the Aran Islands off the coast of Galway, Republic of Ireland. *Inís Mor* in Irish.

LAST LOOKS: (film) A call for any last-minute makeup touch-ups before filming resumes.

MAGIC HOUR: (film) The perfect light to shoot at twilight.

MAEDINA: (fantasy) Half-elf Draemon apprentice who accidentally curses Sevyn with lightning at birth.

MANIFEST: (fantasy) The prehistoric great city of humans on Elementia, lost to the sea following a massive earthquake.

NOLAN: (fantasy) Elven prince of Norgatia, Sevyn's mate.

NORGATIA: (fantasy) The coastal northern woods of Manifest marked by white bone trees, containing Maedina's mother tree and Nolan's tree.

ON THE LASH: (Irish) The intention of getting fully drunk.

PANTS: (Irish) Underwear.

ROCK OF CASHEL: (Irish) A collection of ruins situated atop a limestone outcropping in County Tipperary, Ireland. Also known as Cashel of the Kings and Patrick's Rock. *Carraig Phádraig* in Irish.

SEVYN: (fantasy) The heroine of the Elementia trilogy, cursed by lightning, twin to Evyn.

SIDE: (film) Shooting script pages and notes distributed daily for the cast and crew.

SHIFT: (Irish) Kiss.

SHINY: (fantasy) Seriously? You don't know shiny? To Netflix with you. Watch *Firefly*. This is not a drill.

SLAG: (Irish) Tease.

STINGER: (film) Electrical cord.

VIDEO VILLAGE: (film) Reserved area for the production crew during filming.

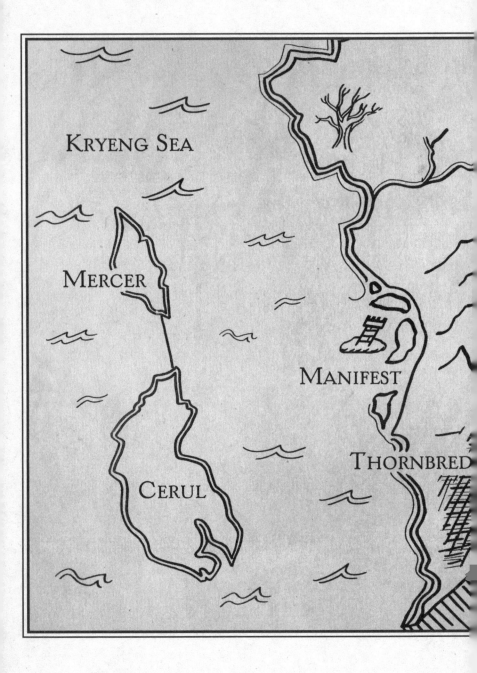

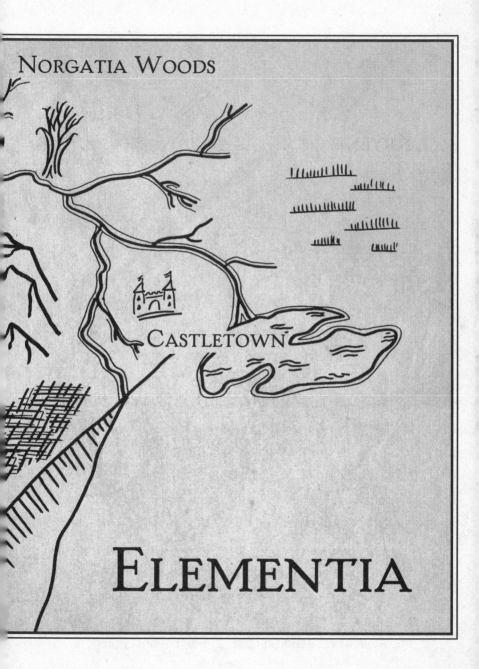

NORGATIA WOODS

CASTLETOWN

ELEMENTIA

ACKNOWLEDGMENTS

I dedicated this book to a bunch of straight, white dudes. That doesn't exactly sit well with me, but here's why I did it (beyond my killer quote game). When I was growing up, these guys were my role models. Now I have new role models to put on the list. First, the female powerhouses of *The Lord of the Rings* movies, Fran Walsh and Philippa Boyens. Secondly, Edith Tolkien who deserves all the romance credit, in my opinion. Additionally, and in no particular order, Kate McKinnon, Ani DiFranco, Ellen DeGeneres, Cate Blanchett, Ellen Page, Florence Welch, Julia Nunes, and so many others who help us queer ladies hold our heads high. And while Cate Collins is a figment of my imagination, I have to thank Patty Jenkins, director of *Wonder Woman*, for helping me believe that Hollywood is indeed turning an important corner.

The Lord of the Rings sat at the very heart of my child-hood, and I thank my dad for reading it to my brothers and me when we were small enough to perch on him like birds. Next, I thank those same brothers for repeated LOTR view-ings, Tolkien tattoos, and for nicknaming one of my exes "Nazgul." Super classy, guys.

An additional thank-you to all the friends I made while living in Ireland. Specifically, Margaret, Marla, Conor, John, Damien, Gabrielle, and Brian. If you're in Dublin, don't miss seeing Brian Brody play at Peader Kearneys.

I'm so thankful for my detail-oriented beta readers. Specifically, Joan McCarthy, Robin Reul, Polly Nolan, and Lily Anderson. I'd also like to thank my film agent, Jason Dravis, as well as my friends in Hollywood, Eric and Liz, for meeting up in LA and making me feel so shiny. Another thank-you to my local Panera, who kept me coffeed, and for the SAGA writers who cheered me on while I wrote.

A very special thank-you to my three wonder editors: Annette and Kate, who guided this book along its nerdy, wind-ing way, and Aubrey, who started the fire for this story—with Dr. Jillian Holtzmann's blowtorch. Another special thank you to Alex for being there for me through all my Sourcebooks titles, and Sarah Davies, my agent and rock.

Okay, confession time. Like Iris, I grew up rolling my eyes at feminism. As I started to wake up to gender inequality—in the world and in my own family—I felt like Iris does at the beginning of the story: like feminism was a job I hadn't signed up for. Now I am not only aware of my own journey, but also of the massively important intersectionality of the feminist movement. I invite you to head over to CoriMcCarthy.com for a list of my favorite titles that illuminate the powerful diversity inherent in global feminism, as well as information on how you can support the diversity and gender equality movement in Hollywood.

Elementia is a high-fantasy trilogy I wrote throughout college and grad school, my feminist answer to Tolkien's legacy. You can read the shooting script for *Elementia* and find out more about Sevyn and Nolan at CoriMcCarthy.com.

Saving the best for last, I thank Maverick, my sword-wielding, inspirational mini-hero, and Amy Rose, who is the wondrous love of my fantasy life…and my real one too.

ABOUT THE AUTHOR

When she was twenty, Cori McCarthy moved to Ireland with little more than her black guitar named Annie. Over the next year, she wandered the countryside, wrote hundreds of poems and songs, and went to the theater dozens of times to watch Peter Jackson's *The Lord of the Rings* films. Now, Cori is an author, editor, and teacher, and lives in New England with her family. You can find out more at CoriMcCarthy.com or tweet your favorite fandom GIF @CoriMcCarthy.

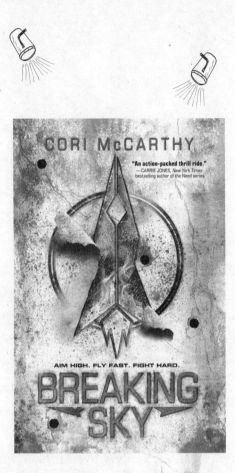

CORI McCARTHY

"An action-packed thrill ride."
—CARRIE JONES, New York Times
bestselling author of the Need series

AIM HIGH. FLY FAST. FIGHT HARD.

BREAKING SKY

To save her country, Chase may just have to put her life in the hands of the competition in this high-flying, adrenaline-fueled thriller.

★ "Smart, exciting, confident—and quite possibly the next Big Thing." —*Kirkus Reviews*

Grief turned Jaycee into a daredevil, but can she dare to deal with her past?

An emotionally taut page-turner perfect for fans of E. Lockhart, Jennifer Niven, and Jandy Nelson

"A beautiful coming-of-age story, this book will leave readers thinking about it long after they close it." —*VOYA*